M000114221

THE UNDEAD AVENGER

BROTHER BONES

BY RON FORTIER

AIRSHIP 27 PRODUCTIONS

Brother Bones
An Airship 27 Production
www.airship27.com

ISBN-13: 978-0615725536
ISBN-10: 0615725538

Printed in the United States of America

Third Edition

10 9 8 7 6 5 4 3 2 1

Airship 27 Productions Presents

BROTHER BONES

Contents

THE BONE BROTHERS

By Ron Fortier

Life and death are absolutes. You get born, live and then you die. The end. Period. That is, if you live anywhere else in the world except Cape Noire. You see, in Cape Noire there are no absolutes. There is only hell and it just goes on. And on. And on.

Not so long ago, when things were a little quieter, there were two major crime lords in the city. Big Swede Jorgenson controlled everything from the 8th Street Bridge down to the docks of Old Town.

The other half of the city from midtown to the ritzy northern boroughs of Marlowe Heights was under the thumb of Boss Topper Wyld. Wyld was a man of reckless appetites. And as much as he loved women, food and the life, he loved power even more and saw himself as some sort of old world Ceasar.

Which is why he detested the delicate balance of authority that existed in the underworld between himself and his hated rival, Big Swede. It bothered him daily, no matter what he was about. Whether it was doing business or entertaining the high mucky-mucks of Cape Noire's social elite with a lavish dinner. The fact that he only controlled one half of Cape Noire wore away at Wyld like an itch he could never scratch.

This arrangement had lasted for ten years, much to everyone's acceptance and no one really believed Boss Wyld would have the balls to upset the apple cart. Thing is, no one knew just how crazy he really was.

The fact that he employed the Bone Brothers should have been a serious clue. But then again, this is the underworld we are discussing and not high society.

Jack and Tommy were identical twins born seconds apart to a hooker on Locust Ave. Jack was the older by three seconds. Story had it he was born with Tommy holding onto his heels. Their mother sold them for drug money when they were a year old and the rest of their legend is lost

5

on the streets of the past. All you need to know is that by the time the boys were in their teens, they were two of most sadistic, cruel souls ever dumped on the mean streets. Somehow, the Bonello brothers, that was their mother's name, survived. No one ever knew who sired them, as if it mattered. Lots of folks think it was the devil himself and they could have been right considering the carnage they caused.

Dark haired, piercing black eyes and ruggedly handsome to a fault, the boys were exact copies of each other. This was the cause of constant sibling rivalry and what prompted them, at age thirteen to have tattoos etched on the back of their right hands. Jack had a Black Ace and Tommy's was of a red skull. Instinctively the boys knew their future careers would be mapped with blood and guts.

Bottom line is they liked causing pain. They were tough and they were brutal. It was the law of the streets and both brothers took to it with a savage delight. Depending solely on themselves, they grew and prospered as petty thugs until one day when they were summoned to the presence of Boss Wyld. The crime-boss had heard stories about the brothers and their exploits and he saw in them tremendous potential, with the right training of course. The kind only he could provide.

He offered them wealth, luxury and more mayhem than they could ever have imagined. The brothers accepted immediately and under the tutelage of Wyld's lieutenant, Harry Beest, they were soon transformed into cold-blooded killers. Of course there were several other soldiers in the gang who had held those positions prior to the brothers' arrival. Once Jack and Tommy came aboard, some of them mysteriously disappeared, one by one. Both Beest and Wyld approved. It was enough of an abject lesson that word spread throughout Cape Noire like a wildfire. You did not mess with the Bone Brothers.

So back to our narrative of Boss Wyld's annoyance at only controlling one half of the city. For ten years, he contained his lust for power with Herculean resolve. But it was only a matter of time. Obsessions have a way of swelling in the soul until nothing else remains but a single desire that has to be met. Thus Fat Jacob, Wyld's strategist, after months of careful planning, set forth a bold scheme that would ultimately lead to his total dominance of Cape Noire.

The first step in this devious strategy was to make Big Swede look like the instigator. On the lower east side of the once fashionable Whittington Park, Wyld owned a popular and highly profitable bordello operated by one Sadie Levine. It was said that half of her clientele were made up of members of the City Council and the Police Department. Wyld ordered the Bone Brothers to fall upon the establishment like a Biblical plague, and exterminate everyone within the house, leaving no living witness behind. Then they were to leave clues behind that would point a finger at Big Swede. After all, who would believe that Wyld would destroy one of his own establishments?

Once people thought Big Swede had broken the truce, the uproar would be great on both sides of the political track. It would then be simple for Wyld to fuel this spark and from it build a fire that would devour his nemesis.

Naturally Jack and Tommy were only too eager to carry out their contract. Arming themselves with half a dozen pistols and wielding two Thompson submachine guns, the brothers descended upon the old, sleepy brownstone in the dead of night, long after midnight when things were quiet as a tomb. Most of the house's inhabitants had long succumbed to slumber from either too much booze or sex.

Having themselves been customers on several occasions, they were familiar with the building's layout. They entered via a kitchen door facing the back alley. Using silencers, they took out the kitchen staff and then like ghosts, made their way into the parlor.

Henry the piano player, and several of the girls who were not asleep, were lounging about, smoking dope and drinking cheap bourbon. Only a single table lamp lit the huge, overly furnished main room. When the brothers emerged from the back door, the girls and the black musician were hardly aware of their presence until Jack raised the machine gun and opened fire.

The bullets cut across the room like lead encased bees and tore their victims apart. Blood and flesh spewed up everywhere and what screams arose were easily drowned away by the gunfire.

"Let's go!" Jack snapped, rushing towards the stairs. Now that they had virtually wakened the dead, they had to work fast to make sure no one got away.

At the top of the stairs, they ran into the Madame of house, Sadie Levine. She was coming out of her private room fumbling with a handgun. At the sight of the brothers she gasped and dropped her pistol. Laughing, Tommy grabbed her by the neck, pulled her to the railing and threw her over. Sadie screamed once and then her body crashed into the hardwood floor below, snapping her neck.

"Nice move," Jack said.

"Mmm," Tommy replied. "Guess fat cows can't fly."

It was the end of their witty repartee as by now scores of doors were popping open and dozens of whores and their dates rushed out to see what had shattered their dreams.

For the next twenty minutes the brothers were busy dispensing their lead greetings to one and all in that ill fated house of pleasure. Twenty short minutes to snuff out the lives of twenty men and women, not counting the six in the parlor and the three in the kitchen. Twenty-nine dead. It was a new record for the brothers and clearly one they were quite happy with.

As they were walking down the circular flight of stairs, having made sure no one was left breathing behind them, the brothers laughed and joked. As they were crossing the parlor, they heard a soft groan and both of them reacted like skittish cats, instantly alert, guns ready.

Tommy was closest to the sound and looking down beside an overturned chair, found the source. A young, painted girl, her face half hidden in the shadows, was staring up at him from a pool of her own blood. How she had stayed alive after taking so many hits was nothing short of miraculous. Tommy was impressed and he leaned over to see if the bitch would say anything.

She did. She gasped and said, "Thank you."

Tommy Bonello blinked. "Huh?"

But the skinny girl was dead and there was no taking back the gesture.

"What she say?" Jack asked, having been too far away to hear the words.

Tommy looked at his brother, part of his suit smeared with dozen of brown blood splotches and then back to the dead girl at his feet. Something cold snaked into the pit of his stomach and he shivered.

"She said, 'Thank you'."

"That's nuts."

"Yeah, I know."

"Well, forget it. Come on. We still got work to do."

They then proceeded to drop betting slips on the floor that came from one of Big Swede's racing joints. It would be just enough evidence to point the finger at Jorgensen. In all, the Bone Brothers had taken all of thirty-five minutes to do their dirty work. Walking away through the smelly back alley, Jack slapped his twin on the back and chuckled.

"Man, I'm starved. Let's find us a diner and get some chow."

"Okay, Jack. Sounds good to me." What Tommy didn't tell his brother was that he wasn't hungry at all. Rather he was ill at ease. The dead girl's parting words bothered the hell out of him. Why did she thank him for doing her? Was her life that goddamn bad that she was grateful to him for ending it? Now how screwy was that?

Screwy. Still, he heard the words in his head and they simply would not go away.

Two weeks later Tommy Bonello woke up screaming in the night. Since the hit on the bordello, the nightmares had come on a regular basis. Every single night it was the same dead hooker, smiling at him, her face cold and hard in death. And the words sliding over her gray lips were always the same benediction of the damned. Thank you.

Jack, who was aware of his brother's strange mood swing, questioned him one morning while they were cleaning their guns in their bungalow located on Boss Wyld's fortress like estate.

"I can't shake that girl thanking me for offing her," the younger of the twins confessed. "Every night she just comes out of the ground, her skin crawling with maggots and then she smiles and she thanks me."

Jack eyed his brother warily. He had never seen Tommy this upset before. "Hey, you ain't getting a conscience or something, are you?"

"Huh?"

"A conscience. You know. Feeling sorry about what we do and all."

It was such an alien thought to Tommy Bonello, he was confused for a moment. In all their years of mayhem and savagery, he had never once felt anything but elation. Suckers deserved what they got. If you weren't strong enough to survive, you died. Simple as that. It was the law of the jungle and he and Jack were the lions of Cape Noire.

"Bullshit," he finally blurted. "The day I get a conscience is the day dogs will fly and cats will swim."

He took a sip of his coffee and grinned. Jack responded with a chuckle of his own and they dropped the subject. Yet, Tommy felt the same ice in his stomach that told him something was not right. But he dared not share it with Jack. He was smart enough to know that would be dangerous.

Two nights later, the boys were called out to whack a crusading city councilman named Crammer. It seemed the man, a former cop, had started making investigations into the ties between the mayor's office and Boss Wyld. When the Mayor, who was on the payroll, informed the crime-boss, it was decided that the crusader should take a dirt nap.

The brothers shot him coming out of his garage and threw his body into the trunk of their black sedan. They drove up to Smoky Hollow, twenty acres of pines located along the coast west of the city. The boys had used it often as their personal graveyard and over the years had buried dozens of men and women among the silent firs. This night was just a routine job.

As Jack finished digging the four foot hole, Tommy paced around the body, chain smoking and staring into the inky darkness of the trees around them. On a boulder they had set an old lantern that gave off a weak, sick, yellow glow. In the distance an owl hooted and small animals skittered through the underbrush. Tommy's head snapped around trying to find their source.

"Jeezuz!" Jack said, seeing his nervousness. "It's just a freakin owl, is all."

"Right." Tommy tossed his butt and its burning tip made a tiny glowing arc as it died in the dew covered grass. "Are you finished?"

"Yeah. I am. Let's have the councilman."

Tommy grabbed the corpse by the ankles and dragged it to the edge of the hole where Jack took over. As the body dropped into the cavity, it made a soft, smacking sound. Jack handed Tommy the shovel and climbed out. That was Tommy's cue to start filling in the hole.

As the clumps of dirt dropped over the body, Tommy felt his heart starting to race. With each spade full, he could he feel his nerves tightening. Then, just as he was patting down the last chunk, he thought he heard a voice. Holding the shovel tightly, he leaned over the mound of dirt and he heard it again, a soft, eerie voice rising up out of the ground.

Thank you, it said. Thank you.

Tommy froze. His heart started racing wildly in his chest. Then he heard it again.

Thank you. But this time it was coming from behind him. He slowly turned around and sure enough the voice was coming from a nearby thicket. He remembered that was where they had buried old Judge Williams. Then he heard a woman's voice and it came from the rise where the woods sloped into a small valley beyond. Now there were lots of voices and they were speaking to him with soft, raspy words that were not of the living. Words spoken long ago by silenced voices. It was a cacophony of the dead.

"Make them stop!" Tommy cried, throwing the shovel to the ground and covering his ears with his gloved hands.

"Make who stop..what?" Jack asked, looking at his brother with a weird expression. "What's wrong, Tommy? What's the matter?"

With eyes bulging wide, Tommy looked at his kin with a wild desperate stare. "Can't you hear them, Jack?"

"Hear what?" Jack looked around the empty woods. "There ain't nothing out here but us and some critters."

"No," Tommy yelled back. "The dead are here, Jack. Don't you remember? They're all around us."

"Sure, they are, Tommy. But Tommy, the dead don't talk."

"Oh yes, they do. They talk to me!"

"That's bullshit, Tommy! Knock it off! You're starting to spook me."

"But I can't shut them out, Jack! They keep speaking to me. Here, in my head. Thank you. That's what they all say. Thank you, thank you, thank you…"

Jack rushed up and with a balled right fist, knocked his brother to the ground with a sock to the chin. Standing over him, he breathed hard, his fist ready to inflict more damage if necessary.

"I told you to knock it off! Damn it, Tommy, what the hell is wrong with you? Ever since we took out Sadie's place you've been coming apart on me."

"I'm sorry," Tommy managed, his voice a half strangled sob. "It ain't my fault. I didn't ask for this. It's just the voices. I hear them."

Jack reached down, took a hold of Tommy's arms and pulled him to his feet. He carefully brushed him off.

"Yeah, maybe so. But you got to stop hearing them, Tommy. Do you understand? If either Boss Wyld or Beest finds out you are hearing voices, it will not be good for either of us."

Tommy stopped his sniffling and wiped his nose with the back of his glove. "Right." Jack's warning was sinking in and its effect was sobering.

"If they think you've gone off the deep like this, you know as well as I do, it'll be all over for you! Then you'll be hearing the dead for sure cause you'll be one of them!"

For a second Tommy Bonello kept his eyes averted from his brother's face. He looked down at the new grave and then around at the trees with their mocking echoes. He shook himself and then raised his head.

"But what if they come back, Jack? What do I do then?"

"I don't know, Tommy. You'd just better figure something out and do it fast."

"Okay, Jack. I will. I'll make them go away. I promise. Somehow, I'll get it done."

For the next few days, the haunted killer kept to himself. He started taking long drives through the city. Aimlessly driving in and out of streets with no idea where he was going or what he was looking for. Then on the third day after the woods incident, Tommy Bonello drove past St.Michael's church. Seeing the giant bronze cross atop the high pitched roof, he instinctively realized the answers he was after might be found in a place such as this. He jerked the wheel hard and pulled into the narrow driveway along side the old, weathered structure.

Pulling his fedora down over his black eyes and flipping his collar up, Tommy rushed up the stairs and into the church. Through the shadowy interior, he proceeded down the main aisle, his passage noted only by one or two kneeling penitents. The interior was lit by candles decorating the side knaves and the main altar. It was there he spotted the little white haired man in the black robes.

For his part, Father Dennis O'Malley, age 72, had met many a strange soul as a priest in Cape Noire but the one he now faced was by far the most intimidating of all. The man was a veritable giant and towered over the old cleric. The man's face was lost in the well of his jacket and his hat brim covered all but his intense eyes that caught the sparkle of the altar's candles. Black eyes. Father O'Malley was scared. He silently invoked a prayer to St. Michael, God's fighting angel, and held his ground.

Then the fellow politely removed his hat and spoke in a voice sharp with agony and pain. "Padre. I need help."

The old pastor led Tommy to his sparse office behind the vestibule, offered him a chair and then poured them each a mug of bad coffee. Cooking wasn't the priest's forte.

"Go on, my son. You have obviously come here, to God's house, to unburden a heavy load. Tell me your story."

"Okay, padre, but it ain't pretty."

An hour later, Father O'Malley considered that the greatest understatement he had ever heard. He had spent a lifetime learning how not to pass judgment on others. His calling was to provide moral aid to all. Even the worse of sinners. Still, nothing in all his years as a priest had prepared him for this man's confession. Tommy Bonello was an agent of devil and clearly represented all that was rotten and evil about mankind.

O'Malley's initial fear had only heightened as he listened in horror and disgust as the murderer related his brutal history. When Tommy finally shut up, a silence heavy with dread descended on the small, square room. The priest's thoughts were a jumble. There was the fear that he had become a liability to Bonello. It was clear the man was a deranged monster. How soon before he realized he had told the priest everything! Still, Bonello sat before him, head hung down, looking pitiful and alone. Something about the man's plight triggered sentiments of concern in O'Malley. After all, this is was why he had become a priest in the first place. To help lost souls and, by God, was there anyone in the entire world more lost than this man?

"Hmmrr," the priest coughed at last to break the silence. "That is the most tragic story I have ever heard, son. Do you understand why you are hearing the voices of the dead?"

Tommy lifted his eyes. "They want to make me pay for what I did to them. I know that now."

"Then what you are telling me is what you did was wrong and you are aware of that fact. Correct?"

"Yeah, I guess so, padre."

"Are you sorry for what you've done?"

"I don't know? It's all too crazy in my head right now."

O'Malley nodded. "An honest answer. Good."

"Padre. If I have to stop killing to make the voices go away, I will! I can't go on like this. It's making me nuts. Can't you help me stop them?"

"No. I don't think I can…"

"Then this was a mistake…"

"But I think I know someone who can."

"You do? Who?"

"A very special man, Tommy. But if you agree to what I am going to suggest, it will mean the end of this life of killing. The man you are will have to die."

Tommy didn't hesitate. "If it will make the voices go away, I'll do whatever you say, padre. Just call it."

For the first time since their meeting, Father O'Malley smiled. The task before the young man would be a formidable one but the prize was nothing less than the salvation of his immortal soul. Could it be done? O'Malley had seen enough miracles in his days to believe anything was possible, if the angels were on your side. And besides, there was a real sweet pleasure in giving Satan a kick in the nuts.

O'Malley rang his hands. "Fine. Then I will make the call to my friend. The rest is up to you and God."

The next day, Tommy Bonello, killer and butcher, and one half of the infamous Bone Brothers, disappeared.

Gone. Just like that. As if he had been wiped off the face of the earth leaving behind not a single trace or clue.

For the next few weeks Jack Bonello went ballistic looking for his missing twin. Boss Wyld put his entire resources and considerable manpower into the hunt for the missing hitman but it was all to no avail. Tommy had vanished without a trace and the general consensus among the gang was that he had been eliminated by some old adversary. The brothers did not lack in enemies. It was a hazard of the job.

Finally, after turning the city upside, Harry Beest told Jack to give it up. Tommy was gone. He even hinted at the possibility that Big Swede had somehow tumbled onto the bordello affair and was responsible for Tommy's fate. As unreasonable an assumption as that might be, Jack was enraged enough to buy it, sales tag and all. Thus he was more than eager and ready to continue Boss Wyld's campaign against Big Swede.

So began one of the bloodiest gang wars in Cape Noire's less than illustrious history. For the most part, the police stayed clear of the conflict, no sane cop wanting to get caught in the crossfire between the two mobs. Raids started going down all over town and decent folks were keeping themselves locked in at night, when the bullets flew and the gutters were strewn with bodies.

For his part, Jack lost himself in his work and eventually came to accept the loss of his brother. He was not one to dwell on the past. Especially when there was a war to be waged.

What the older Bonello could never have guessed in his wildest dreams was that his brother had joined a monastery and become a monk, shaved head and all.

While Cape Noire was being torn apart daily, Tommy Bonello, now calling himself Brother Michael and living a life of peace and serenity in the Spanish style fort nestled in the hills overlooking the Crystal Cove. In fact the place was called Mt. Serenity and was very popular with the citizens of the neighboring town of Castle Harbor. The dozen monks at the abbey spent their days toiling in the lush vegetable and flower gardens, the excess of which they sold to the markets of the fishing port. The night hours were filled with prayer and silent meditation.

Late one hot, summer afternoon, Brother Jonas, the abbot of the community, was strolling past the pottery workshop, an open-air room located at the rear of the ground floor. Its back wall was made of louvered panels that slid open to reveal the gardens and allowed heat from the kiln ovens to escape.

Brother Anthony, a small black man from New Orleans, was carefully putting the finishing touches on a beautiful, bone white enamel mask. Brother Michael, carrying a heavy bag of fertilizer on his broad shoulders, had stopped on his way from the main shed to watch the artisan complete his beautiful piece of art. Neither knew the abbot was watching them.

"Hello, Brother Michael," the potter greeted without taking his eyes from the mask on the table. His skilled finger adroitly dabbing the hardened porcelain with the ivory colored paint. "It is almost finished."

"What is it?"

Brother Anthony finished his last swipe and put the paintbrush down. He looked up at the big man and grinned.

"It is an African spirit mask. When I was a boy, in New Orleans, my mama, she would make them all the time for the Mardi Gras."

Slipping his fingers under the hard mask, the monk held it up so that the rays from the sun played over its pale, smooth surface.

"Do you like it?"

"It looks like a skull head."

"Yes, I guess it does. My momma, she say, if you wear the spirit mask, it will protect you from the demons and ghouls."

"Ain't no such things."

"Do not be so sure, my friend."

Brother Michaels's face, brown with the sun, looked sad as if his mind were millions of miles away.

"No, Brother Anthony. You are wrong. There are no ghosts and such. Only death. That's all there is."

For a second, the man who was all too familiar with death remembered the red tattooed skull on his hand and he envied his friend. There were some things no man should have to know. He resumed his march to the fields leaving a perplexed Brother Anthony scratching his head.

Brother Jonas watched him walk off and wondered if the man would ever find the peace he sought. Looking around the small courtyard to his right, he could see the front entrance and the dirt road that led to the world outside. It was a place Brother Michaels had escaped from. Now if he could only keep it away. Maybe he would have a chance.

The old abbot prayed it would be so.

At the very same time, in a seedy, broken down Cape Noire landmark known as the Gridiron Saloon, Jack Bonello sat at his customary back corner booth nursing his third beer and doing his best to get drunk. It was still too early for the place to fill up with its usual assortment of lowlife and Butch Hammer, the owner/barkeep was busying himself getting supplies stacked away in the backroom freezer. The only other patron in the joint at this hour was a one-legged German sailor named Otto. He was sitting at the far end of the bar listening to a ball game on Hammers' battered old radio.

But none of this got through the haze that enveloped Jack at the present. His mind was muddled with events of the past few months. All of them bad. Very, very bad. And like some chain of bad luck, it had all started with Tommy's disappearance. After the loss of his sibling, Jack had turned to his mentor, Harry Beest, for guidance and support. For a while, both men were consumed with the business of warfare and things had gone along fine.

Then suddenly, in the middle of a planning session with Boss Wyld, Beest had gone into convulsions and collapsed. When Jack and some of the other soldiers started to go to his assistance, the Boss waved them off.

Instead, he walked around the long, rectangular conference table and stood over the fallen Beest with a smirk over his fat, beefy face. Clutching his stomach and groaning loudly, Beest continued to shake like some wind up toy gone berserk.

"My, my, Harry. Is there something wrong?"

But the man couldn't answer. He was twisting about in agony and by now it was obvious to all that he had been poisoned. Then, as if prearranged, an ambulance arrived at the estate bringing with it one of the strangest dude's Jack had ever seen. He called himself Prof. Bugosi and it seemed he and Wyld were old acquaintances.

Upon entering the room, Bugosi injected Beest with some kind of serum and then his two white jacketed assistants put the ailing man on a stretcher and removed him to the waiting ambulance. Prof. Bugosi and Wyld shook hands and the creepy doc with the thick, gray hair and eyebrows left without uttering another word. As for Boss Wyld, he resumed his place at the head of the table, looked at Jack and said quite simply, "You are now in charge, Jack. Don't disappoint me."

Jack never found exactly how his predecessor had messed up with the boss. There were whispers among the boys that Beest had embezzled cash from the war chest. Jack doubted that seriously. Whereas others put forth the scenario that the dabber Beest had been romancing the Boss's teenage daughter, Alexis. Now this was more likely the fact, Jack thought, having witnessed the raven haired beauty around the mansion many times. She was real easy on the eyes that one, with a look that meant trouble to any man who crossed her path. So, yeah, maybe old Boss Wyld had caught Beest sampling the goods of the forbidden fruit.

Hell, maybe it wasn't either the money or the girl. It really didn't make any difference in the end. Beest was gone, just like Tommy. Only this time, after seeing his final exit, his ultimate fate was a bit more determined. If that Bugosi character was a real doctor, then Jack was a cabaret dancer with flying feet. No, poor old Harry's lot was foregone the second he was wheeled away on that stretcher.

Which left Jack holding the bag. All of it. Sure, it was great to be the number one gun and Jack had the ambition to make it stick. Still, the added responsibility the position entailed was a full, twenty-four hour, seven days a week burden he had not been prepared for. The war with Big Swede had taken its toll and the current number of available men was at an all time low. Thus, as one of his first task as the new top lieutenant in the Wyld family, Jack had begun recruiting new talent.

Much to his dismay, he soon learned what was left on the streets was not the cream of the lot. Drunks, ex-cons and two-time losers were pretty much the bulk of the pool from which he had to draw. Among these was his own right hand man, a thin, rat-faced knife lover named Reed Vengel. The guy was pretty much a talent-less jerk, but he had the loyalty of a pit-bull and Jack was barely able to put up with him.

As if thinking of the gaudy dressed little crook was enough to summon him into being, the front door opened and Vengel came rushing in. From his look, he was agitated and his small, mean eyes scanned the place fast. Jack's booth left him comfortably in the shadows, which was he liked it.

Still, Vengel could make out a body and started coming closer. He had a handkerchief in his hand and was mopping his sweating face. Sure it was hot outside, but not that bad. Something was wrong.

"Jack! I've been looking for you all over!"

Bonello didn't reply. He didn't feel like wasting words. At his silence, Vengel slipped into booth across the Formica table from him and again ran the silk cloth over his rat-like face.

"I seen, him, Jack! I seen your brother!"

Jack was about to take another swig from his bottle. He put it down.

"Me and Louie had just come back from dropping our..ah, package. You know, for the fishes." Nervously the hood looked around to make sure no one was there. Otto still had his attention focused on a ninth inning tie out at Maxwell Stadium and Hammer was still busy in the backroom.

Vengel continued, his words chasing each other as if his breath couldn't keep up with the images in his head. "We was coming back when Louie says he needs to gas up the tank. So we stop at this pumping station.."

"Where?" Bonello's voice had dropped. It was hard.

"Out in Castle Harbor. You know, the little burg on the other side of the cove."

"Go on."

"Right. Well Louie pulls up to this here pumping garage and the kid comes out to take care of us. Turns out the place is also one of those off road side general stores, you know. They sell all kinds of things, mostly for the folks who live up in the hills.

"So I figure I'll run in a grab some smokes and beers for the ride back into town. While I'm doing that, I notice this group of holy joes talking .."

"Holy what?"

"Ahh…you know. Those guys who wear burlap and shave their heads."

"Monks?"

"Yah, that's it. Monks." Vengel pulled a pack of cigarettes from his jacket and lit one fast, continuing his story without missing a beat. "They was monks. Three of them. Seems they have some kind of place up in the hills and they grow vegetables to sell to places like that.

"Anyhow, they were so weird looking, you know. What it their cue-ball heads and all, I couldn't help taking a good look at 'em when they passed me on the way out. Especially the last guy in line. Jack he was a big mother and …" Vengel gulped, realizing the importance of his next few words. "He was the spitting picture of you."

Jack remained quiet.

"I swear it. It was you. Only you was bald and had this really good tan."

"Are you sure?"

Reed blew out a puff of smoke and then his eyes widened. "Shit, I almost forgot the most important thing of all."

"What?"

"Well, you know, I ain't ever laid eyes on that brother of yours. I only come on after he vamoosed. Still the boys have told me enough about him. You know, like the two of you are the same in almost everything..but.."

"But what?"

"But that tattoo, Jack. This here monk. When I saw he was your fucking double, I looked at his hands. He had the goddamn tattoo there."

"What was it?"

"It was a red skull. Jack. I swear, on the back of his right hand."

Jack took his glass of beer and drained it. Suddenly the taste was bitter. He wiped his lips with the back of his hand, the black ace visible as he did so. Reed took another puff on his fag and then ground it out in the glass ashtray.

"All right, Vin. Get Louie and Frank and tell them to meet us at the mansion in thirty minutes."

"You got it, Jack."

"Tell them to come loaded. Tell them we're going to a family reunion."

As the days were longer during the summer season, the brothers of Mt. Serenity took to reading their vespers, evening prayers, in the courtyard just inside the main gates. Here had been planted a small orchard of apple trees and although too soon for their fruit to arrive, the branches were lively with colorful buds. The sky was a soft rose color as the sun began its gradual descent into the western hills. A cool breeze wafted over the ground and the ten men who made up the community were relaxed and content in their prayers.

When they, as a group, heard the approaching motor car, they looked at one another in mild puzzlement. It was unusual for the group to receive company after dinner hours. Brother Jonas closed his prayer book and clasping his hands behind his back, strolled through the trees towards the gate to greet their unexpected visitors. He was nearing the gravel drive when the car, a huge, black sedan rolled into view. Brother Michael, still with the others, saw the car and immediately realized his time had run out. Clasping his own prayer book, all but forgotten in his hand, he started after the abbot, calling out to him at the same.

"Brother Jonas. Wait!"

The driver of the sedan saw the monk and veered the car to come to a stop before him. Simultaneously the two back doors and the front passenger door sprung open and from them emerged gun-wielding mobsters. The first, Vin Vengel, coming out closest to the surprised cleric, whipped his machine gun and fired a burst at point blank range.

"NOOO!" cried the man who had once been Tommy Bonello as he

watched his benefactor being cut down.

Lost in the shock of what they had just witnessed, the other brothers came running, heedless of the apparent danger they were rushing towards.

Brother Michael fell to his knees beside the lifeless body of the abbot. His hands were clasp in prayer. Then Jack Bonello came up and stood before him, a .45 automatic in his hands.

"Hello, Tommy. Long time no see."

As he stood in front of the sun's sinking rays, Jack was a wall of blackness to his kneeling brother.

"Jack," Tommy said, finding his voice. "Don't do this. It's wrong. They have nothing to do with this. It's me you want."

"Oh, you're right about that kid. I warned you what would happen if you ever tried to run out on me."

"I didn't have a choice, Jack. It was that or go nuts."

"Yeah, well, maybe that's true but it still don't change anything. We just can't have no loose ends hanging around. You know that."

Jack raised the automatic and shot Tommy in the head.

Brother Anthony gasped.

Like a sack of potatoes, Brother Michael fell over, his empty eyes skyward. The monks began to cross themselves, fully aware that they were next. To their honor, not one begged or pleaded as Jack's gunmen cut them apart with several long bursts from their Tommy-guns.

Satisfied with his handy work, Jack surveyed the dead and then pointing to them, ordered his men to drag the remains into the main building and torch it. The less evidence of a crime they left behind, the better. As Vengel and the others set about obeying his commands, Jack stared down at the man who had shared half his life. If there was any regret in his heart, he could not summon it. There were theories that professed a special life-sustaining bond existed between identical twins. Jack had wondered about that and come to the conclusion that the only true bond he and Tommy had ever shared was their homicidal natures. Having renounced that, Tommy had severed the only true connection they had ever had. Hell, it was only business, after all. And one corpse was just as dead as any other.

Jack fished into his coat, found a cigar and bit off the tip and spit it out. Sliding the two dollar stogie into his mouth, he turned his back on the monastery and gazed out at the horizon beyond. The sky was now a brilliant orange crossed with purple and pink shafts. It was one of the most breathtaking sights he had ever seen. Too bad Tommy hadn't lived long enough to appreciate it.

Jack chuckled at his own macabre humor and then using a silver, monogrammed Zippo, lit his cigar. With the mystery of Tommy's disappearance now to put the rest, maybe he could go home and finally get a good night's sleep. Now that was something to look forward to.

Eternal rest and salvation was the reward most good men aspired to all their lives. Regrettably Tommy Bonello had only come to his faith late in life and now had met his demise with his soul still in jeopardy.

As his consciousness floated in an ethereal wasteland between heaven and hell, he could not move on to either destination. He was trapped in a netherworld limbo and confused. Was he dead or alive? Was he awaiting some kind of final judgment or was this in fact his punishment, to linger throughout eternity as a lost soul?

The more his thoughts, for now he was nothing but pure energy, followed these tracks they seem to chase after each other like the wooden horses on a carnival carousel, never reaching answers but only continuing to spin round and round. It seemed a never-ending madness.

Then, just as he was about to succumb to a dark, enveloping despair, a light appeared before him. Slowly it began to shimmer until he realized it was taking on a vague, familiar form. A body emerged from the light filled with an inner incandescent that was so brilliant, it would have blinded him had he any eyes. But as a spirit, he could look upon the shape and watch its final materialization into someone he knew.

It was the girl from the bordello. The girl he had gunned down. The one who had thanked him for it.

Tommy wanted to speak but he had no mouth. Nor ears to listen if she spoke. But she was speaking and he could make out her words. Oh, not in any mortal, physical way, but inside his very being. It was as if each of her thoughts were being delivered by some arcane circuit of ectoplasm.

What she said was not to his liking. He was going back to the land of the living. To the land of pain and suffering. He was being sent as an avenging spirit to protect the innocent and punish the guilty. He had a choice and it was a very simple one. Accept the mission or continue on to eternal damnation. One chance to redeem himself. Whatever cosmic master was dealing the cards was not open to compromise.

The sweet young girl, now lovely in this after place, smiled and asked for his decision. The soul that was the late Tommy Bonello didn't really have a choice.

He gave her his answer and bid limbo farewell.

Blackjack Bobby Crandall was so afraid he might start screaming any second. Still, that act would have required he open his mouth and would have caused him to inhale, which would certainly induce vomiting. Of that, he had no thought in his young, fear numbed, twenty year old mind.

Bobby had good luck with the cards. He was a born gambler. It was a talent he had been blessed with from an early age. His parents called it a curse. He was betting by the time entered high school and quickly amassed a nice little sum of cash that made him quite popular with the other kids. All except those who lost to him in the after school locker room poker marathons Bobby orchestrated.

Upon graduation, near the bottom of his class, he wasted no time packing his bags and buying a one way ticket to Cape Noire. If he was going to be a big time roller, there was only one place to be, on the coast. His mother thought he was an idiot and warned him that coming to that western den of depravity and sin would be his ruin.

After six months working a blackjack table at the Gray Owl Casino, Bobby, now tagged with the new name, Blackjack Bobby, had all but forgotten his mother's warning. He was living the good life and loving it. Then the gang wars started and bit by bit it all went crazy. One set of bizarre circumstances following another that would eventually lead to him down a bad luck road to his current predicament.

Bobby was tied up, hands and feets, on the cold cement floor of an Old Town warehouse. In that condition, he was the only witness to the final moments of Big Swede Jorgenson, currently a lifeless hunk of meat hanging from the ceiling rafters by chains, his corpse a black charred, smoking nightmare. His death had been a long and gruesome affair that Bobby would most likely remember the rest of his life. Albeit that was to be a very short one now.

Bobby inwardly cursed God and all the heavens at the total unfairness of his lot. He was not suppose to be here. He was not a hood. Well, at least not a gun toting one for sure. He was a gambler. A man good with cards and favored, until the current situation, by the whimsical muse known as Lady Luck. But her favors were fickle indeed.

The same attrition that had so decimated Boss Wyld's army had befallen Big Swede's troops. Day after day the street warfare dwindle his ranks of soldiers until, in dire desperation, his lieutenants were forced to draft stooges from anywhere they could be had in Jorgenson's vast organization. When his personal driver was wounded in a gun skirmish weeks earlier, Blackjack Bobby had been drafted to replace him. When he tried to protest, he was told all he had to do was drive Big Swede. No one had expectations of him having to fight. Just drive. A chauffeur for a fancy, armor plated limo. That was all. How hard a job could that be?

Boss Wyld's men ambushed them on a rainy Sunday morning, on their way home from a rendezvous with some foreign dealers on the docks. While weaving their way through a tight, narrow back street, the lead car carrying the Swede's personal bodyguards had been taken out by explosives affixed to the underside of a manhole cover.

It started with a deafening explosion, sending the vehicle into the air, a massive hunk of twisted metal.

Crandall had slammed on the brakes and then shielded his eyes from the horrendous glare. By the time the wrecked car was slamming back down on the shredded asphalt, he was gunning his own machine backwards, his foot nailed to the pedal. Tires smoked on the wet street as Big Swede and his remaining bodyguard screamed frantically for Bobby to get them out of that alley. He almost made it.

Only yards from the lane's entry, the entire world was suddenly blocked off by a giant, orange sanitation truck. The kid never had a chance and they slammed into it hard, the rear end of the limo crumbling like so much tissue paper. Dazed, his nose bloody from hitting something, Bobby fumbled for the door and fell out of the car. Gunmen, wearing city coveralls, were all around the stopped car, guns at ready. Bobby was kicked along side of the head and fell into a puddle of brackish water. His last thought before passing out was that he might drown.

Perhaps that would have been a lucky thing. When he was revived, he was bound and in a huge, cavernous empty warehouse. He had been awakened by screams and the stink of burning flesh mixed with the sharp, pungent odor of gasoline. Big Swede was burning up, the fire devouring his clothes and the flesh beneath with an unquenchable appetite. All the while the big, blonde man, jerked and twisted in his chains, swinging high above the floor, trying to escape the pain that consumed him. His screams were raw notes of unadulterated madness.

Unable to watch any longer, Bobby surveyed his surroundings and for the first time had a clear look at his captors. He knew, of course, that they were Boss Wyld's men. That was a given and of the three present in the dimly lit building, he could only identify one, their leader, Jack Bonello. The killer was well known throughout Cape Noire and although the card dealer had never met the man face to face, he had seen him a half a dozen times patronizing various night spots in the town. Bonello wasn't the kind of character who lay low, no matter what the climate was.

Bobby knew there had been two of them a ways back, but the other one, Tommy, had disappeared a year or so back. Word on the street was that Big Swede's men had done the job. Which was obviously why the self-same individual was now a roasting carcass above them. From the smile on Bonello's handsome, hard face, Bobby knew this particular hit was giving the man lots of personal gratification. He was enjoying this, the sick bastard.

The two men with Bonello were standing on the other side of the burning man and Bobby could just make them out. One was a beefy type with a broken nose and wearing a fedora a size too small for his big head. The man beside him was a thin, rat-face character with a cheap, gaudy suit. He was sucking on a toothpick and grinning as much as Bonello was. Another wacko.

Blackjack Bobby Crandall tried to loosen his bonds but they were too tight. They had been tied by someone with experience in holding people captive. Frustrated yet resigned to the inevitable, he stopped struggling, laid his head on the cold cement and waited with his eyes closed.

When the Swede finally stopped screaming, Bobby knew he wad dead and slowly opened is eyes to confirm the fact.

Sure enough, the charred corpse was still at long last, the foul smoke curling up towards the steel beams overhead.

"I think he's done," the small, natty crook said.

"Oh, he's done, alright," Jack Bonello conceded with a laugh. He walked over and pushed the dead man's feet so that his body started swinging back forth. "I'd say he's well done!"

At that all three of them started laughing wildly.

"Boss, that's a good one!" broken nose chimed in, wiping his eyes. "Well done! What a hoot!"

Oh, yeah, thought Bobby. Hilarious. He was about to meet his end at the hands of bad comics. Now how sad was that. Life really wasn't fair at all.

"Well," Bonello continued, this time looking towards the boy on the floor. "Guess that leaves us with one final item to take care."

Bobby looked up at the merciless gunman and refused to let his fear show. If he had to die, then it would be with some degree of courage.

Bonello pulled the silver plated .45 automatic from his shoulder holster and pointed it at the Crandall.

"Sorry about this, junior. You just happened to be in the wrong place at the wrong time. Too bad."

Bobby swallowed, trying to keep his composure. Damn it, he thought, get it over with it. Shoot!

Suddenly a cold, chilling gust of air swept through the warehouse, washing over all of them. Reed Vengel looked around, trying to find where the blast had originated.

"What the hell was that?" he asked, his head twisting around. "Must be a broken window up there somewhere." Outdoors thunder crashed and a flash of bright, yellow light lit up the sky. It was enough to show there were no broken windows. All of them, situated high along the building's walls were intact.

Again the same cold wind swept over them. Bits of paper debris skittered across the floor and the little gangster jumped.

"Take it easy," Bonello snapped. "It's just a gust of air."

Then they heard the moaning.

"That's not just air!" Vengel said pulling out his own gun, a .38 Smith & Weston revolver.

The moan was coming from all around them. It was low and eerie, the voice of someone in agony.

Blackjack Bobby was instantly forgotten as the mob chief turned his gun around and likewise began trying to pinpoint the source of the creepy, low wailing cry.

"Who the hell is it?" he shouted. "Show yourself or get ready to eat lead!"

The moaning began to subside and the three mobsters looked at one another for some kind of explanation. None was forthcoming as each of them was totally mystified by what was happening.

"HOLY SHIT!" Vengel mouthed, his eyes going wide at something he saw behind Bonello.

Jack spun around, gun ready to fire and looked at a white, transparent image of himself. The ghostly specter flew across the space between them, arms reaching out in supplication and screaming, Jack fired at it.

Unaffected by the bullets, the pale apparition moved onward towards the other two men with the same outstretched hands. As it settled into a spot between them, it began its awful moaning again.

Completely unnerved, Vengel pointed his gun at the thing and fired off three quick rounds only to see his companion, he of the broken snoz, take all the hits and go down dead as a door knob.

The ghost moved in closer and Vengel could see it had no eyes. The sockets were empty black pools of nothing.

Insane with fear, he threw his gun at the spook and turning, bolted for the exit. He was gone in seconds leaving only Jack and the Blackjack Bobby to witness what would happen next.

For his part, Bobby was mumbling all the prayers his mother had thought him as a child. Words he had thought long forgotten were fresh on his lips as he mouthed them with all the sincerity he could muster. Dying was one thing. Being taken by a ghost was something else altogether.

But the spirit didn't want Bobby, it was after Jack and he knew it. In the few seconds since it had flown past him, Bonello realized he was dealing with his brother's ghost. It was Tommy come back from the dead to confront him.

"So, what am I suppose to be, Tommy?" he yelled at the floating, haunting figure before him. "Be scared? You think you can scare me? You couldn't beat me in life, kid and there ain't no way you can do it now. You got that!

"I ain't afraid of you!"

Then the ghost of Tommy Bonello glided forward and reached out its hand again. Jack fired the rest of his clip with the same useless results as before. As the thing from beyond fell upon him, he tried to bat it away, only to have his arm pass through it cleanly. Then the ghost reached into his body and grabbed his heart in its icy grip. Jack's face registered shock.

On the floor, Bobby had stopped praying, unable to look away from what he was seeing. The ghost was killing Bonello by squeezing his heart until it stopped.

Jack gasped, his eyes rolled upward, the gun fell from his lifeless hand and then he collapsed.

The white wraith hovered over the dead gunman and once again its mesmerizing wail started up. Then, like a descending cloud, it settled over the body of Jack Bonello and began to merge with it. Bobby gasped, his mind trying to grasp what it was he was seeing. That ghost thing was going into Bonello's corpse like a cracker sliding into a bowl of soup. Just like that, it was gone and with it the eerie crying.

Except for the booming storm still raging outside, a stifling silence filled the place. Crandall, now very much alone, began to tug at his ropes again. Somehow he had to loosen them and get out of here. Sooner or later that other hood would come back to see what had gone down. If he was still here, then it would really be kaput. Somehow, through a bizarre, supernatural intervention, he'd been given as yet another chance. He wasn't about to let it go to waste.

Frantically pulling and twisting, he managed to get the thick cords to loosen a bit after nearly ten minutes of non-stop effort. Buoyed by even this minor success, Bobby bit his lower lip and with all the strength he could muster, pulled his left hand free. Gasping with joy, he then tore the ropes away from his other hand and sat up on the hard floor. He rubbed his bruised wrists to restore the circulation to his hands. They were almost numb. Then, pulling up his knees, he started to work at untying the knots around his ankles.

There was a noise to his left and Bobby looked up. The dead man was moving! After everything he had already seen, Bobby was still not prepared for this final, unbelievable horror.

Like some marionette whose strings had been cut, the body of Jack Bonello began flopping around. Bobby thought of a dead fish he'd once seen his grandfather throw on the docks at the lake where he'd spent summer vacations. The corpse was doing the same kind of dance. But it was dead! It wasn't suppose to be moving at all!

Then the dead man was getting to his feet and now Bobby renewed his efforts to unfetter his feet. He had to get away from there! Managing to still his trembling hands, he undid the last knot and pulled his feet free.

"STOP!" The voice came from beyond the grave. Bobby all but jumped to his feet like a frog smelling a snake.

"RUN AND YOU'RE ARE A DEAD MAN!" A dead man's hand raised up and pointed to him. "HEED MY WORDS, BOBBY CRANDALL!"

Bobby was stunned. How had this thing, this zombie creature known his name? This was crazy. He should run as fast as he could for the door. No way this shuffling monster could ever catch him. But there was an implied warning in the words it had spoken. An unspoken threat that said no matter where he ran to, this thing would somehow find him. Right there and then, Bobby Crandall believe it could do that. Hell, it knew his name.

Slowly the dead man walked over to Bobby, the finger still pointing. As it neared, Crandall saw something happening over the man's hand. A tattoo of a black ace was fading and being replaced by one of a white skull. Now what the blue blazes was that all about?

"I have saved your life, Bobby Crandall. Do you understand that?"

"Yeah..gulp. I guess so."

The finger hit his chest, pushing him back a half-step.

"Good. Never forget it. From this day forth your life is mine to do with as I please."

Bobby kept his mouth shut. He wasn't about to start arguing with a zombie or whatever this thing was.

"You will obey my every command. Everything I demand of you will be done without question. In that manner you will remain in good health. Cross me once and you will die."

"Err, right, Mr.Bonello...."

The hand grabbed his ear and the dead man's face was suddenly in his.

"Jack Bonello is gone. My name is Brother Bones."

Then he was released as the figure went back to where it had dropped its gun. It picked up the automatic, its movement become more fluid with each passing second. In fact, if one did not know the thing was dead, it would be virtually impossible to tell. Only one thing hinted at something unnatural. The eyes were cold.

Putting the gun back in its rig, Brother Bones examined his tattoo and then wiped a mop of hair from his forehead. He looked at the frightened kid and smiled.

"Do you have a car?"

"No. But I can get one."

"Good. Do so. Brother Bones has places to go and things to do before this fateful night is finished."

By midnight the storm raging over the coast had started to diminish, although sheets of rain still fell on the city and the surrounding hills. It was a dark, lonely night and few people dared to venture out into its shadows.

Foraging rats were surprised and annoyed when the headlights of the small roadster came over the rise and drove onto the grounds of what had once been the Mt. Serenity Monastery. It came to an easy stop in front of the skeletal remains of the main house, now a broken erector set of burned timbers and piles of wet, dirty ash.

"Stay here and wait," Brother Bones commanded as he climbed out of the car. He pulled his fedora's wide brim down over his face, slipped his hands into the sleeves of his dark, greatcoat and began walking through the rubble.

As he moved cautiously over what had once been the home and sanctuary of Tommy Bonello, his mind replayed the movieola of memories. They were all of goodness and warmth. Strange memories for a thug like Tommy, but still his. Regardless of his new incarnation, they were still a part of him. So much so, that he was determined to make them part of his new life. But to do that he needed one thing and he was here to find it.

Remembering the floor plan to the work shop, he moved around fallen ceiling timbers until he saw the baking ovens. Millions of shards of broken clay were all over the floor and buried tables. Cautiously, he pushed aside debris and examined every nook and cranny. It was hidden beneath a heavy rag on the same table where Brother Anthony had last set it. The spirit mask was miraculously intact. There wasn't a scratch on it. As Brother Bones reached out and picked it up, a final flash of lightning split the horizon and the skull mask, wet with rain, shimmered.

Brother Bones held it up to his face and looked through the eye-slit with black, lifeless eyes.

The grandfather clock in Boss Wyld's study chimed that an hour had elapsed since midnight. Swallowing the sweet brandy he had been nursing, Topper Wyld went over to his elaborate liquor cabinet and poured himself another glass full.

It was late. Why hadn't Jack and the others come back yet? Had something gone wrong with the hit on Big Swede? No, that was impossible. Several of his other men had arrived after dinner to tell him the motorcar ambush had gone off without a hitch. The Swede, and some rookie kid driver, had been snatched and taken to the warehouse hours ago.

So why did it take so damn long to kill just two men?

Wyld took another sip of the rich, sugary liquor and started pacing in front of his huge, mahogany desk. Dressed casual in his pajamas, slippers and silk housecoat, he was an impressive sight. Wyld tipped the scales at well over three hundred pounds.

He had always been a big kid, from his early days on the docks. It was his strength that had brought him through the ranks to where he was on this night. A big man with big needs, as he like to put it. There was nothing wrong with ambition. It was the grease that made the wheels turn.

Now he was only minutes from realizing his biggest dream of all. Soon, when he knew for certain Big Swede Jorgeson was dead, he would become the true Boss of Cape Noire. He would be the single power that ran the entire city. No more deals with men who were below his intelligent. No more comprises. No more having to deal with half-wits to placate the status quo. There was about to be a new status quo. One that would bring stability to the underworld and make him a legend in his own time.

So where the hell was Jack Bonello?

He heard the footsteps seconds before the hidden entrance opened behind the bookshelf on the wall to the left of the room's entrance. Set on hidden hinges, the shelf covered the entryway to a passage that went to the garage in the mansion's lower, underground bowels. It was known only to Boss Wyld and his top lieutenants. Which was why he was startled by the figure that stepped out from behind the shelf.

Clad in a dark colored topcoat, with a matching fedora, the man standing before him wore a white mask carved in the shape of a human skull. In his gloved hands were two silver plated .45s.

Boss Wyld threw his glass at the ominous intruder and dashed around his desk in a desperate attempt to reach the gun in his top drawer.

Brother Bones fired once and the shot hit Wyld in the leg, felling him like a running stag.

"Aagh," he screamed, going down against the front of the desk. "Who are you? Who sent you?"

"I am Brother Bones. I have come to avenge all the innocent souls you have butchered during your reign of infamy."

"What? You're some kind of nutcase," Wyld rattled, his hands holding on to his bleeding leg. "Look, it don't have to be like this! I've got money. I can give you anything you want. Just name it and it's yours."

Brother Bones stepped over to the wounded crime-boss and then leveling both his guns, began to laugh.

"NOOO!"

The avenger fired point blank, sending round after round into the obese man at his feet. Each slug ripped through Boss Wyld and left him a bleeding, dead slug of humanity.

Brother Bones's laughter faded away as he stepped back from his handiwork.

Suddenly there was a loud scream from behind and Brother Bones whirled around. A young girl, beautiful with long, black hair, was coming through the front door and charging him with a long, sharp knife in her hands.

Before he could stop her, she drove the blade deep into his bosom.

Brother Bones cried out and slapped her with the back of his hand, sending her reeling back into a padded chair. She lost her balance and awkwardly fell onto the thick Oriental rug beside the bloody body of Topper Wyld.

Grim stepped over to the girl and dropping to one knee, shoved the barrel of one of his guns under her quivering jaw to press against her throat.

"YOU BASTARD!" she yelled, hot tears streaming down her cheeks. "YOU MURDERED MY FATHER!"

"Your father was an animal who got what he deserved. Nothing more. Nothing less. The same will happen to all who cross my path."

Then, almost as if an after thought, Brother Bones, using his free hand, pulled the knife out of his chest and held the blade in front of the crime mogul's daughter. It was clean. There was not a drop of blood on it.

"What are you?" she asked, her voice softening with the awareness that he was something macabre and not some mere gangster.

Grim tossed the blade away. "I am Brother Bones. I am the avenging angel from beyond the grave. Remember that, Alexis Wyld. Your soul is not yet corrupt to warrant my final justice. This night you are spared. It may not be so forgiving the next time we meet."

Brother Bones rose, put away his guns and then slipped away through the secret passage from which he had arrived.

"No." Alexis Wyld said weakly to no one but herself.

"Next time I will kill you, Brother Bones. I don't know how but if there is a way, I will find it. I swear it on my father's head."

Outside, on the small side street bordering the Wyld estate, Blackjack Bobby Crandall puffed away on his third cigarette in ten minutes.

Suddenly, without so much as footfall, Brother Bones was slipping into the seat beside him. Bobby almost dropped his butt into his lap.

"My work is done," Grim intoned. "Get us out of here."

Bobby tossed the butt out the window, started the engine and gave it gas. Switching on the headlights, he sent the roadster rolling down the lane.

"What the hell did you do back there?" he queried, afraid he already knew the answer.

"Brought justice to Topper Wyld. The only kind justice his kind can understand."

"You killed him!" Bobby said. "You killed Boss Wyld. Goddamn it, do you know what that means?"

Grim was silent behind his ivory mask.

"It means that both men who held this town together are dead! Both in a single night! That means that every two bit hustler and hitman will be making some kind of play to take over where they left off.

"Shit, man, the whole damn town is going to be up for grabs. It's going to be a bloodbath the likes of which no one has ever seen before!"

Brother Bones watched the sleeping streets roll by as they left the suburbs behind. Up ahead the lights of the city's skyline were coming into view. They were majestically grand in their nighttime display. But it was only a mask, a cheap cosmetic trick hiding the decay and corruption that would reawaken with the rising sun. It was a mask that Brother Bones was all too familiar with.

He turned to young Bobby Crandall finally and made one single comment. "Then let the games begin."

And then the dead man laughed.

THE BEGINNING....

SHIELD & CLAW

Sheila was something else.

That she was beautiful beyond measure was a given. Hers was an exotic beauty that radiated from every luscious pore of her body. It smoldered under her skin like a fire ready to erupt into a hot, all consuming blaze.

She was so sexy, tall and lithe. Perfect legs, long and graceful so that when she walked your mouth went dry and your hands began to sweat. The calves were taut and smooth so that her buttocks rocked with an unholy motion that invited temptation. Her waist was almost nonexistent but her breasts were things of wonder, full and shapely. Not too big as to be ridiculous and warrant jokes, but just the right shape and roundness to push against whatever fabric encased them. Sometimes when she sighed, they would rise ever so slightly and then fall again like the tide of a ocean storm. It was an apt description because she was indeed some kind of tempest in human guise.

But the real danger was in her face. That marble like image surrounded by her lustrous, black hair. She wore it like a crown, wild and silky, always whipping around her face and caressing her neck and shoulders. It was sinful to touch that hair and feel it on your fingers.

Her lips were full and she painted them with cherry red lipstick that left a sweet taste behind every kiss. Her cheekbones were high as if there was some kind of royal blood in her eyes, yet her mouth betrayed her gutter origins. Then there were Sheila's eyes that could doom a man within a second of gazing into them. They were dark green like the heart of the jungle and behind them lurked all manners of death and betrayal. At the same time it was the eyes that worked the magic and snared the poor fools.

It was her eyes that had sucked him in from the beginning and made his life both heaven and hell. To make love to Sheila was to live pure, unadulterated ecstasy. There was only passion in her touch. But like all addictions it was also a curse that once self-inflicted could never be erased.

Yes, sir, she was a woman like no other.

Which is why it was all her fault.

Detective Bruno Sancino slipped the pizza delivery boy a twenty, told him to keep the change and then gave the seventh floor hallway a quick look-see before closing the door and bolting it shut.

"Dinner's here," he announced to the other three men sequestered in the flea-ridden, two bedroom trap that was their secure base. Lost in the alleys of Old Town, the Sunshine Hotel was one the places the Cape Noire police had used several times in the past to hide people they did not want found.

People like mob enforcer, Trey Abelard, the skinny, hard looking man seated at the kitchen table with a bottle of beer in his hands. Dressed in slacks and a tee-shirt, Abelard had the look of an off-duty mortician. Even his thinning brown hair and pasty looking eyes added to the image. His true profession was that of a hired gun for the small time mobster, Reed Vengel, better known as Revenge Al. Having botched his last job and been picked up by the cops, Abelard found himself going up against a murder one rap that his gut said he was not about to beat no matter what kind of shyster the gang hired to defend him. The cops had his gun and his fingerprints. He was fighting a losing battle.

Thus, in the best style of street self-preservation, Abelard turned canary and decided to sing, provided he was given immunity and state protection. The D.A., one of the few public officials not on the mob's payroll, assigned the case to his best man, Chief of Detectives, Dan Rains.

Rains had a reputation as being the toughest cop on the force. Like his boss, he was also honest; a real sore point with the powers that ran Cape Noire.

Realizing the worth of his prisoner, Rains manned the safe house schedule with four veteran members of his squad of which Sancino was one. The other two blues present were Detectives Charlie Sites and Paul Castle. Castle was a big, ex-football guard with a pension for cheap cigars. He was puffing on one as he played a hand of solitaire on the coffee table in front of the old leather sofa where he had been perched for the last half hour. Sites, a middle aged sergeant with a walrus mustache was seated across from his partner in a torn, overstuffed recliner reading the evening paper.

The third cop assigned to the detail was off as Rains had set up a rotating shift which allowed each man some free time, while maintaining three with the target at all times. Rains had no illusions about the mob. If they thought Abelard's testimony would hurt them, then they would make some effort to silence him. Thus the Chief kept his men on a constant state of readiness for anything that might be thrown against them.

It was after eight on a Thursday night. Abelard was due in court on Saturday morning. The cops were starting to feel comfortable that things would go smoothly as planned. They had been on the job for nearly two full weeks and all of them were eager to see it wrapped up.

"What did yah get on them?" Castle spoke around his cigar, watching Sancino drop both cartons on the coffee table.

"A loaded and a veggie."

"A veggie? You're kidding, right?"

Sites dropped the top half of the Tribune and shook his head. "Huh, huh. It's for me. You know how the doc has been trying to get my cholesterol down. He says all those heartburns I've been getting lately are because of eating too much red meat."

"Geez," Castle said putting his cigar down on a glass ashtray. "That's too bad, Charlie. It ain't a pizza without some pepperoni or sausage."

"Tell me about it. I told him if this diet doesn't work in a couple of weeks, all bets are off." Sites put the folded paper down the floor by his chair. "I mean, what's a little heartburn anyways? Not like it's going to kill me or anything."

It was then the front door was ripped off its hinges and destroyed with a massive crunching noise. Everyone in the room was shocked into a momentary frozen tableau as four pairs of eyes all converged on the now ruined portal. Then the thing covered in fur leap into the room and snarled, its head twisting about, fangs exposed and drool spitting from its ugly maw. It was almost seven feet in height, massive in torso and armed with claws the length of bayonets.

The three cops went for their guns simultaneously, none of them believing for a second that bullets would have a prayer against the monster. Sites died in his chair, unable to make it to his feet before the werewolf leaped behind him and with a single swipe, tore off his head. Blood sprayed out of his neck as the head bounced off the wall, its eyes wide open all the while in disbelief.

Castle, gun out and firing, kicked the coffee table hard and it rocked into the thing's shins causing it a second of pain. It roared, its unholy cry vibrating the thin walls. Then it stepped on the offending table and smashed it like so much paper-mache. Castle's shots hit it in the chest four times without slowing it for a single breath. Now he was screaming, his mind letting go as the horror fell on him, claws flashing. It opened him up from crotch to breast and as his innards tumbled free, the monster bit off his face and spat it on the couch.

Sancino, to his credit, stood his ground, emptying his own magnum

.44 at point blank range. His eyes watched in wonder as each hole cut into the monster's back only to vanish beneath its thick, reddish brown coat of dirty hair.

It was as if the bullets were made out of wax and melted upon contact with the thing's hide.

Still, the bullet stings were enough to get its attention. Its head swiveled towards the cop, its fangs now covered in blood and bits of gore. There was a hellish gleam in the werewolf's red eyes. Deliberately it turned and came at him.

By now Abelard had wet himself in his chair and was crying like a baby. Detective Sancino somehow managed to keep his own wits and when his pistol clicked empty he threw it at the beast with all the power his muscles could summon. Seeing it smack into the werewolf's face with a sickening thud gave the officer a brief second of satisfaction, then the monster picked him up with one hand and tore out his beating heart with the other. As Sancino's body jerked in its death throes, the fiend chewed on the still warm organ with black delight.

After a few minutes, it dropped the dead man and went after its primary target. Poor Trey Abelard had finally encountered a nightmare from which there was no waking up.

Twenty-four hours later a soft, gray rain fell on the city making everything wet and clammy.

The police had arrived in ordered procedure to inspect and clean up what was now a bonafide crime site. The bodies had all been outlined in chalk, to include Sites' head off by itself in a corner, and photographed with half a dozen rolls of film. It was crucial that no detail, no matter how small, be overlooked during the investigation.

The county coroner had done his job and suggested all four men had been the helpless victims of some kind of wild animal. Hairs were found and collected and bloody foot smears on the tile floor clearly indicated some kind of paws. But then again, what kind of animal could go through the front door with such ease and then ravage four grown men so completely. Add to this mystery the status of weapons found at the scene. It was clear by the spent cartridges littering the floor that shots had been fired. Lots of them and still the cops were dead. As was Trey Abelard, his body strewn about the kitchenette in half a dozen pieces.

All in all it had been one of the messiest clean-up operations ever conducted. It was one the men in blue would tell their children about in the hopes of convincing them that real boogie men did indeed prowl the streets of Cape Noire. Fairy tales for the faint of heart.

Chief of Detectives, Lt. Dan Rains stood alone in the silent, empty apartment, his stance one of weary resignation and disgust. He had waited until everyone was finished and returned to the precinct house before returning alone and unannounced. It was a habit he had developed as a rookie on the beat. Somehow, amidst the chaos of the ambulance attendants, the bodies being bagged and hauled away and the evidence gathered, there was a lack of comprehension. It was if by merely gathering hard data, the true essence of the crime was forgotten. Pushed aside as if it didn't matter. It mattered to Rains.

The why was just as important as the who. So he came back when it was still and quiet. When he could move about slowly, his eyes taking in the surroundings with a calm, relaxed attention that missed nothing. It was this meticulous nature that had brought him up through the ranks so steadily. Among detectives, he was considered the most professional.

But none of that availed him now, as the rain slicked down over the kitchen window and the single light dangling from the ceiling painted shifting shadows on the dingy walls and the dirty floor. Even in his wildest imagination, he could not get a handle on what it was that had hit his men. A gorilla, the coroner had suggested in jest but no one laughed. But no normal gorilla could have done this. Not unless it was high on drugs and had somehow acquired the intelligence to commit crimes and then evade capture.

He had read Poe's MURDERS IN RUE MORGUE as a teenager and enjoyed it. Now, all he felt was a sick taste in his mouth at the slim possibility he might be actually living it. He rubbed his tired eyes and wondered how he could ever face the families of those three good men. Which of course led to a thought he had been avoiding since the call had first come in that something had gone wrong at the Sunshine Hotel.

"They needed silver bullets!" the icy voice offered from behind him and Rains twisted around while dropping into a crouch. His gun was aimed and ready to fire at the same time his mind was berating his inability to sense the intruder.

For a second all he saw were the shadows concealing the open door to the flat's single bedroom. Then slowly, as if materializing from an inkwell, the figure in black stepped forth. He wore an overcoat, hands stuffed in the pockets, and a wide fedora slouched down. It almost hid the bone white skull mask beneath the brim.

"Who the hell are you? Step into the light?" Rains' stomach tightened.

"I am Brother Bones," came the cold voice again and now, head raised, the stylized death mask revealing two cold and lifeless eyes. It was a notorious visage known throughout Cape Noire.

Rains stood straight and squared his shoulders. "I've heard of you. They say you only hunt mob boys." He kept his gun leveled at mystery man. "What's your business here?"

"It was a werewolf. Only silver can kill it."

"I don't believe in werewolves."

"Neither did your men. It's what killed them. I caution you not to make the same mistake, Detective Rains."

At hearing his name, Rains' ire grew. "Even if I gave any credence to what you're claiming, what's your angle in all this?"

"That is not important. I have my reasons. Rather you should concern yourself with your own misgivings."

"Meaning exactly what?"

"Only four men, beside yourself knew of this location. Now three of them are dead."

"How do you know that?"

"I am an agent of justice. The souls of the dead cry out for vengeance. With or without your help, I will settle their account."

The light overhead flickered and Rains shielded his eyes for a second. When he opened them, the dark apparition was gone.

"Bones!" Rains started to make for the bedroom but stopped in mid-step. Somehow he knew his visitor was gone as quietly as he had appeared. Putting his pistol away, he tipped his own hat back from his forehead and took a long, deep breath. The spook had read his very thoughts.

It was time to go see the fourth man on his squad.

He found Pete Henderson sitting by himself at his kitchen table killing a bottle of Jack Daniels. His clothes were a mess, the shirt torn, and Rains noticed the man was barefooted. There was blood on his feet.

Henderson and his wife lived in the bay district of a blue-collar neighborhood. Not the riches homes in the city but decent enough for most hard working stiffs. Oddly enough, in the three years the man had been a member of his squad, Rains had never once visited the place.

Now, as he shoved open the door after having knocked once, he wondered just how much he really knew about this man he had called a friend and brother in arms.

"Pull up a seat, Lieutenant," Henderson said, his words sounded heavy and slurred. "Misery loves company, they say."

Rains pulled out the chair opposite his subordinate and sat. He surveyed the room, a small, clean kitchen with two other doors leading to the rest of the four-room apartment. There was also an orange gym bag perched on the table's end as if carelessly set down and forgotten. Between the bag and the bottle was Henderson's shield, the silver badge laying face up. It too seemed to have been haphazardly set aside.

Although his topcoat was smelled musty from the rain, Rains' nose detected another odor. It was one he was very familiar with, that of blood. More than the smears on Henderson's feet. No, he was smelling a lot of blood. The hairs on the nape of his neck went stiff.

"What the hell's going on, Pete?"

Henderson was a handsome man in his late twenties but now he looked liked the survivor of a bad binge. His face was unshaven and his eyes, normally a bright blue, were bloodshot from the alcohol and an obvious lack of sleep.

"I sold out," were words Rains didn't want to hear. Henderson saw his disappointment and putting down the bottle, reached over and tugged the gym bag closer. Unzipping the top, he flipped it over and stacks of money spilled onto the table between them.

"See, I'm a rich man now. There ain't anything I can't buy."

"I don't believe this, Pete. It's too easy. What is this really all about? At least you can level me after letting three of your pals go down."

At the mention of the dead men, Henderson sat up and brushed a mop of sandy colored hair away from his forehead. He looked like he was going to cry.

Rains reached out and picked up Henderson's shield while the other tried to find words that were getting mixed up in his head.

"I didn't want that to happen, Chief. You've got to believe me. I was told it was only Abelard they wanted. That was all."

"Aw, come on, Pete, you're not that stupid." He slid the badge across the table and Henderson's hand jerked away at the touch of the metal.

"You don't understand."

"Try me."

Henderson's head turned to the closed door behind him to the left, a look of utter despair on his face.

"It was because of her, Chief."

"Her?"

"Sheila."

"Your wife?"

"Yeah, my wife." He paused, then looking back at Rains, grinned awkwardly. "That's right. You never met Sheila, did you Lieutenant?"

"No, I haven't."

"She's something else. I mean, like right out of those men's magazines. You know. So goddamn beautiful. I thought I was the luckiest man in the world when she said she'd marry me.

"And for a while I was. But then she started complaining."

"About what, Pete?"

"About everything. She wanted nice things. She said we should have a better apartment. She wanted new clothes all the time and jewelry and all sorts of things. Things I just couldn't swing on a cop's pay.

"At first I thought she'd get over it. She'd realize how things were and let it go. But she didn't. She just kept at it. Needling me more and more. Why couldn't I get her things? If I really loved her, I'd find a way."

"It's an old tale, Pete. Marriage and cops don't mix."

"Yeah, right. But she's so beautiful and all. And I wasn't the only one who noticed. I began to see how other men looked at her whenever we went out to dinner or a show.

"Hell, even some of the guys at the station started ribbing me about what a hot babe Sheila was and how I'd better make sure I kept tight reins on her.

"Sure, it was funny at first. Just kidding and all. But then I'd get home at night and she wouldn't be home. She'd come in after dark with some excuse about having been out with her girlfriends and had lost track of time."

Rains wanted to say things that would comfort the man but he didn't have it in him. Instead he let Henderson continue his confession in his own tortured style.

"Finally, she just admitted it. Just like that. Told me she was screwing around. If I couldn't keep her happy, then she was going to find somebody who could.

"Somebody with big bucks who could give her everything she wanted. Everything she deserved. And you know what?

She was right. She did deserve the best. And I was a bum for not being able to give them to her."

"So who bought your ticket?"

Henderson took a long swallow from the near empty bottle and then smacked his lips, the liquor calming his nerves. "Got a call from one of my snitches on the street.

Said Revenge Al wanted Abelard taken out and was willing to pay a hundred grand for the job."

"How did it go down? Did you meet with Vengel?"

"Are you kidding? Naw, in fact it was a whole lot weirder than that. I told the stooge he sent to meet with me, I'd pop Abelard during my next shift. Figured I could get him alone somehow and get away with it.

"But they had other plans. They wanted me to drink this stuff instead."

"Huh? What stuff? What are you talking about?"

"Seems Vengel had that creep, Prof. Bugosi whip him up some kind of mickey that was suppose to make a person go Pro-Ball. Sort of a super steroid cocktail."

"And you took it?"

"Well, yah. It was that or no deal. No cash."

Rains' thoughts were filled with images of the carnage he had witnessed at the Sunshine Hotel. "Jesus, Pete, you mean you did..that..at the hotel. That was you?"

Henderson nodded, his eyes beginning to swell with moisture. "At first it just made me sick. I thought I was going to puke my guts out. Then things started going really woozy. I stared changing."

"How?"

"I ..got bigger. Really big. Then the claws came and my skin got all covered with hair."

"Stop it!" Rains snapped. "This is all bullshit."

"No, it ain't. It's true. It all happened. They turned me into this thing, Chief. And all I wanted to do was rip them to pieces. And I..did."

Henderson hung his head down on the table and started to cry. Anguished sobs racked his body.

Rains got out of his chair and going over to the sink, poured himself a glass of water. He took a long swallow then set the glass down on the porcelain counter.

Henderson was still crying.

The stench of blood was getting stronger.

"Pete. What happened next?"

Hearing his name, Henderson looked up and his eyes focused on the present. "It was suppose to be all done. I drove down to a drop site in Old Town and found the money where they said it would be. Then I came home to show it to Sheila."

Henderson looked over his shoulder at the door then back to Rains. "They said it would only happen once."

"What?"

"My changing into that thing."

"The werewolf?"

"Yeah. But they lied. I should have known it. God, I was such a fool."

"Why? What happened?"

Henderson gave the door another glance and Rains realized whatever ending this tragedy held was behind that closed door. It was time to see what was hidden there.

"Sheila was so happy when she saw all that money. Oh, she was a little nervous about how I'd gotten it and all, but only a little. She just kept holding the bundles in her hands and laughing like she used to do.

"Then she starts kissing me and telling me how sorry she was for having treated me so bad lately. That she was going to make it all up to me."

Rains reached the door and twisted the black knob slowly, never taking his eyes off the distraught cop.

"So she pulls me into the bedroom, there, and starts getting out of her clothes. She does it nice and slow, like a dancer. Sheila always knew how to turn me on. Then she and I are on the bed and really getting into it hot and heavy.

"Sheila is an animal when it comes to sex."

Rains pushed the door in. The room was dark but he knew immediately he had found the source of the blood perfume.

"Go on, Pete. Finish it."

"I don't know how it happened. I mean, one minute I'm into her good and hot. I mean, it's so great, loving her like that. Then this red haze started coming over me. I started hearing all her lies like they were ringing in my head. All the times she laughed at me and hurt me. Just like that, I was there again. Only this time, I wanted to lash out and hurt her. I wanted to make her pay for all the pain she had caused me.

"I must have changed real fast because all of a sudden Sheila was screaming..and it wasn't the sex anymore. It was fear."

Rains flicked on the light switch and looked at what remained of Sheila Henderson sprawled on the red soaked bed sheets. Her face was locked in a death's grimace for eternity. There was blood everywhere.

He took a tentative step forward, weary of having to get closer to the still warm remains of Sheila Henderson. But he was a cop and it was what cops did. His feet took a zig-zag approach trying unsuccessfully to avoid the pools of blood. At the bedside, he looked down at the woman's shredded torso and could only think of what happened to meat when it went through a grinder. It became hamburg.

Fighting the rising bile in his throat, he tried not to breathe the foul stench around the body. He had to get out of there. Turning, he realized Henderson had stopped his crying. Not that he had shut up, but rather his sobs had turned to groans. Loud, unholy groans. He heard the chair fall over just as reached the door, in time to see the transformation in all its gruesome reality.

Henderson was no longer recognizable. He was almost seven tall now, his shirt in tatters over massive, fur covered body. His face had become an obscene thing of snout, long, sharp fangs and two, beady red eyes. Rains started for his gun just as the thing looked straight at him in the doorway. It roared and charged, claws extended.

Rains slammed the door shut and braced his shoulder against it, the gun forgotten. And he prayed half a second before the wolf monster hit his fragile barricade. The door caved in sending Rains onto his back. The blood pools caused him to slide all the way across the room into the bed where Sheila's left hand flopped down and hit his head, knocking his hat askew.

It was almost funny. Sitting with his ass in blood, a dead woman's hand on his head and a werewolf about to kill to him. Certainly not the way he had imagined he would die. Not even close.

The Henderson werewolf, crouched over the remnants of the splintered door, shook itself and growled again. Its shoulders hunched, preparing to leap across the gap that separated hunter from prey.

Brother Bones came in through the bathroom window, guns blazing. His first volley was all over the place. Slugs slapped into the walls over the bed knocking out chunks of plaster and dust. Another hit a lamp shattering the bulb within into a million bits of glass. The werewolf howled as one of avenger's missiles found its mark and sliced across the beast's right thigh, spraying fresh blood over old.

He's using silver bullets, Rains reasoned watching the wolf's reaction of immediate pain. It spun about and leaped away as Bones entered the bedroom still firing. Rains had never seen anything move so damn fast. It was a blur of fangs and claws hurling into the air and across the room. Then it was picking up the whole damn bed as if it were made of feathers. The mutilated corpse fell to the floor behind him, as the detective scrambled up on all fours to get out of the way. The werewolf threw the bed at the black clad specter.

Frustrated at not having hit his target with any damaging shots, Brother

Bones jumped back frantically. The careening bed, mattress, springs and all crashed into the far wall inches away from the avenger. Then, before he could regain his balance, the beast was on him, claws flashing. One of Bones' .45s was sent spinning away. The other almost useless as the werewolf tried to pin him against the room's corner.

"GET OUT!" Brother Bones screamed as he tried to ward off the sharp claws descending on him with lightning strokes. Unable to bring his remaining automatic down for a decent shot, he fired it regardless, the booming report only inches away from the man-animal's head.

As the werewolf howled once more, Rains managed to get to his feet and sprint through the demolished door and into the kitchen. But his luck gave out as his shoe, almost completely soaked through with blood, slipped and sent him into the kitchen table like a meteor losing orbit. The wooden table collapsed under his weight and he cursed aloud as he went down in a heap. The bundles of cash split open and hundred dollar bills fell over him as he tried desperately to regain his feet.

In the bedroom the werewolf, having seen his bolt for freedom, went crazy at the idea of losing its victim. It slashed Brother Bones across the chest, its claws cutting through layers of cloth to reach the skin beneath. Stunned, Bones tried to recoil but there was nowhere to go. Then the creature dug into his chest, picked him off the floor and threw him aside as if he was so much garbage.

Rains was sitting up trying to pull his gun from its shoulder harness when the hellish thing flew out of the bedroom and fell on him. Like some cat with a mouse, it sat on his chest, its weight constricting his lungs, and looked down him with perverted glee in its eyes. Rains's right hand flopped on the paper bills as his breathing shortened. Damn thing was going to crush the very life out of him. Drool from its open maw dripped onto his face.

Then his knuckles touched metal. He twisted his head around. The badge! It had fallen from the table into the pile of dollars. It was silver. Shaped like a spade, bottom half curving to a point. Rains managed to turn his hand and grab it. Then, without another thought save some measure of payback, he thrust the badge up hard into the beast's exposed throat like a dagger.

Blood gushed onto his hand as the monster's eyes went cold with hurt. It grabbed at it offending badge, a loud gurgling cough emerging from its mouth. Angrily it tried to pull the blade free, but its massive, clawed hands were too clumsy and it couldn't get a proper hold on the shield. It trembled mightily in its rage.

Suddenly Brother Bones was standing at the door, hatless, both silver plated pistols back in his hands. He fired and this time his slugs hit the werewolf dead center. It dropped back off Rains, who, free of its punishing weight, gulped air.

Refusing to give the beast a moment's respite, Brother Bones walked over Rains and continued to pour round after round into the creature. Rains thought he'd go deaf from the sound of the exploding shots. Within seconds it was over.

As he lifted up into a sitting position, Rains eyed the still shape of the werewolf. Then, like something from a magician's bag of tricks, the dead horror returned to its true shape. Detective Peter Henderson stretched across the broken table top, six gaping holes in his body and his shield embedded in his throat. As ghastly as the sight was, Rains thought the man's face contained some element of peace.

Brother Bones put away his .45s and looked down at the now exhausted detective.

"Bury him in hallowed grounds. It will guarantee he never returns."

Rains didn't know what to say to that.

"My work is done here." The avenger started to leave.

"Tell me something, Bones."

"If I can?"

"Who won here?"

"Justice."

Rains shook his head in puzzlement, looking up at Bones' skull mask.

"Four cops and a civilian are dead and the mob got what it wanted in the first place. The snitch was silenced. And you call that justice?"

Brother Bones laughed. The sound was unnerving like that of a cat when it's hit by a car. He started for the front door, stopped and turned back to Rains still chuckling.

"It's Cape Noire, detective. What did you expect?"

Then the undead messenger was gone leaving the cop alone with his thoughts.

Outside the rain continued to fall on the city like a cascade of endless tears.

THE END

SCALES OF TERROR

Paula Wozcheski clutched the shot glass of whiskey and her fingers trembled with agitation.

"Bobby, I don't know what to do?" her worried face, still layered with the evening's makeup that was part of her job, complimented the anxiety of her voice.

Bobby was Blackjack Bobby Crandall, one of six blackjack dealers at the Gray Owl casino. A young man with a freckled face and mop of unruly reddish hair, Crandall was easy to talk to. Which is why cigarette girl Paula Wozcheski was still hanging around long after her shift had ended at one a.m.

They were seated at a corner table in the adjoining lounge now deserted except for the clean up crew. Paula was nursing her second drink and chain-smoking a pack of unfiltered lung-killers. Bobby truly felt sorry for her.

"You think Janos is screwing around on you?"

"Yeah, I do, damn it." She sent out a gray cloud of smoke and stared into the shot glass as it were some kind of divination pool. "Why else would he be out every other night of the week?"

Paula was a lovely girl with auburn hued hair that was cut short to the tips of her ears and her eyes were a jewel bright green. But now that prettiness was hardened by worry and doubt.

"Paula, he's stevedore. You know as well as I do most of the big rigs come in at all hours and when they do, the dock handlers have to unload them quick."

"Look, Bobby, we've been married two years now. I know Janos's routine like the back of my hand. Which is the point. Dock work is hard and dirty."

"Yeah. So?"

"So, he comes home just before dawn and his clothes are squeaky clean. Not a smudge of dirt on them anywhere. That's not right, Bobby."

Crandall took a sip from his beer and wished he didn't have so friendly a face after all. As much as he wanted to help Paula, domestic problems were really none of his business.

"Look, Paula, why don't you just ask him outright?"

"I have."

"And?"

"He told me to shut up and drop the matter. He scared me, Bobby."

Janos Wozcheski was a Polish seaman who had settled in Cape Noire six months prior to meeting Paula at the club. He was a big man, Bobby recalled, with arms like telephone poles and hands to match. He had never seen the man angry, but it was not an image too difficult to conjure.

"Look, Paula, why don't you just leave him."

"But I don't want to leave him. I love him. I really do."

"How long has this been going on?"

"About two months now. It started after he joined that club thing."

"Oh?"

"You know, like some fraternal lodge or some such, only it's made up of dock workers. They call themselves the Order of the Dark Ocean or some such. Seems like he started acting strange right after he joined."

Crandall felt a familiar itch at the nape of his neck and did his best to ignore it. Words like acting strange made him very uncomfortable considering his new relationship of late; one who dressed in black and wielded two silver plated .45 automatics.

"You know what, Paula," Crandall was reaching at straws. "Why not just hire a private snoop and have Janos followed. That way you'll find out what you want to know and then you can make whatever decisions you have to.

"There's this guy named Spade downtown. I hear he's pretty good at this kind of thing."

The harried redhead set down her now empty glass and shook her head. "Naw. I don't have the money for a private snoop. I mean, why should I pay a total stranger for following my husband when I can just as easily do the same for free."

"Whoa, hold on just a minute." Crandall slid his hands across the table to cover hers, only to regret the impulse immediately and withdraw them. No need to complicate matters with his own private feelings. "That's really not a good idea. You don't know what those docks are like at night. It's not safe. Believe me."

"Well, maybe you're right. Still, I've got to do something. We can't go on living this kind of sham."

To that Crandall had nothing further to add. Sometimes life just handed you a bad hand and you had to fold before it was too late.

"I'm sorry, Paula. I'm not much help to you, am I? Paula rose up from her chair, collecting her gloves and handbag and gave him a tired smile. "You were here to listen, Bobby. That's more than lots of people would do.

Thanks."

Then she was gone, twisting her way through the round tables towards the exit and the night outside.

Desk Sgt. Mike Anderson looked up from his stack of paperwork to see Sally Paige.

"Ouch. Now what did I do wrong this morning to deserve the presence of the city's ace crime reporter scaling the battlements of my nice, quiet desk?"

Paige, petting a stray strand of black hair back into place with the help a small hand-held vanity mirror, gave him her best, winning smile. "Ah, come on, Anderson, is that the way to greet a lady this early in the morning?"

"The clock on the wall there tells me it's almost noon. What time do you get up in the morning, lassie?"

"Well, a girl does have to get her beauty sleep, you know. Especially a working one like me."

The bulldog Irishman groaned and waved an index finger down at her from his high perch over the desk front. "Tsk, tsk, Sally dear, but I wouldn't be using terms like working girl in the confines of this establishment. It has a certain negatory ring to it, if you be catching my meaning."

"Oops. Right indeed. Which, now that you bring that up, reminds me of something that I've been hearing on the streets lately."

"Oh, and what might that be?"

"That working girls of that persuasion have been turning up missing, or make that not turning up, in the docks of Old Town."

Anderson was too experienced to bite on any hook the comely reporter would feed him. "There you go again, trying to get me in trouble with me bosses."

"So it is true? Something is happening to prostitutes in Old Town?" The spunky journalist was pulling a dog-eared notebook and pen from her huge all-purpose handbag.

"Can I quote you on that, Sergeant?"

"Is Miss Paige giving you a hard time, Anderson?"

Chief of Detectives, Dan Rains, came sauntering down the stairs from his offices on the second floor, fedora in hand.

"Nothing I can't handle, Lieutenant."

"I wish you guys would lighten up," Paige said pointing her finger at Rains as he approached. "You know, we are all on the same side."

"That being the case, what do you say I buy you lunch, Miss Paige. I was on my way just now."

"What about this prostitute thing?"

"Excuse me?"

"Sally here has heard that working girls are disappearing off the streets and alleyways of our fair city," Anderson eagerly supplied.

"We should be so lucky, eh, Sarge?"

At that Rains nodded to the three gaudily and scantily clad women seated on a nearby bench awaiting arraignment.

"That would certainly lighten my load, sir."

Seeing that neither man was going to take her seriously, Paige put her away the tools of her craft and offered the detective her arm.

"Okay, Rains. You win. Lunch. Where we going?"

"You like hot dogs?"

"Geez, what a big spender."

They walked out arm in arm and Anderson went back to his papers. The bit about the lost girls was forgotten.

Paula Wozcheski pulled the old woolen coat tighter around her shoulders and shivered in the damp alley where she was hiding from her husband. It was nearly midnight and he had been in a seedy little bar across the street for nearly an hour. Paula cursed herself for the hundredth time, wishing she had had the sense to take Blackjack Bobby's advice of the previous night.

But she was too stubborn a girl for that. So here she was, somewhere in Old Town on a cold and windy night, crouched behind an alley wall looking over at a place called the Gridiron Saloon and hopping from one foot to the other to keep her legs from going numb.

Janos had come home from his shift at the usual time and at first she thought he was going to stay home. But just as she started getting ready to leave for the casino, he told her he would be working another swing shift and wouldn't be there when she got back. Paula had all she could do not to confront the issue right there and then. To yell at him and accuse him. But she had no real evidence. It was all supposition on her part. Thus, while on the bus ride downtown to the club, she made the decision to leave early and get back home in time to follow her husband. Which is what had brought her to this God-forsaken-hell-hole.

Initially, as Janos had started down the sidewalk from their apartment, she was happy to see him making for the docks that were only three blocks down Linden Ave. from their place. Maybe he was going to work after all and because he was on foot, she had no problems keeping up with him from a safe distance. Living in the city, they had no need of a car and didn't own one. It was only after she had begun trailing him that she realized, had he opted to call a taxi, she would have been stymied. Clearly there was a whole lot more to this snooping game then she realized.

It was only when he reached the Old Town district that his destination became suspect. Rather than continuing south towards the piers of Cape Noire, Janos had gone east and ended up at this particular locale.

For an hour, huddled in the shadows away from the corner street lamp, Paula had watched the bar's clientele come and go. They were a mixed lot of men and women, mostly of a desperate degree. Lost souls from the other side of the tracks. She had also spotted a few hookers plying their flesh trade on the two street corners to either side of bar. She was disgusted by their skimpy outfits and vulgar invitations, which they hurled at perspective johns rolling by in their automobiles. They were so open and brazen. Paula realized here, in Old Town, people did not concern themselves with the law. It was a stranger on these streets.

Looking at her wristwatch and seeing that it was now ten after twelve, Paula began to think she should give up and go home. She and Janos could have it out tomorrow. This waiting around was ridiculous and if the sniffles she was developing were any warning, she was giving herself a good cold in the process.

Just then Janos walked out of the bar. He was still alone. Slowly he surveyed the surrounding area and she ducked back further into the alley. What was he looking for? Did he suspect she had followed him? Or was he cautious for other reasons she could not fathom? From her position she could still see him clearly. He looked at his own watch and then glancing towards the corner to his left, turned and strolled over to two of the girls stationed there.

Janos began talking them. The brisk night air carried his voice easily.

He was looking for a date. Paula felt her stomach go sour. The two girls were both blondes, one tall and leggy in a tight skirt with black stockings and an over developed chest. The other was a bit stockier and older wearing a red leather mini-skirt that only enhanced her cheapness. Janos was interested in the tall one and after a few minutes of routine banter, took her arm and they walked off together.

Paula came out of the alley and dashed across the street not wanting to lose sight of the pair. As she went past the remaining prostitute, the woman gave her a passing look. "Hey, sugar, looking for a job. You got what it takes."

Paula ignored the whore and turned the corner in time to see her husband and the blonde turn enter another small, narrow lane. They were heading back towards the harbor again. Running along behind them, Paula was glad she had worn her flat-heeled shoes from her locker at the club. This would have been murder in heels.

She assumed the hooker was taking Janos to a hotel where she plied her trade.

She was wrong. Instead, after a good twenty-minute-hike, the couple arrived at the front of a nondescript warehouse. It was one of many such square, gray buildings along the wharf front. The overwhelming salt smell was everywhere and off in the blackness was the sound of the ocean as its waves slapped back and forth against huge, wooden pylons. A single, shade covered light bulb over the warehouse's entrance illuminated the scene.

Paula pressed up against the brick building at the corner and peeked out, not wanting to lose them now. They were standing in front of the entrance arguing. The blonde was not at all happy with whatever it was Janos was selling. Paula realized this had not been her idea. Janos had brought her to this place. But why?

Trying to keep the girl placated, she watched as Janos found his wallet and pulled out a handful of greenbacks. He held these up and the blonde reluctantly took them. She stuffed the cash into her small, black handbag.

Assured she was content, Janos then rapped on the big sliding door with his left fist. After a few minutes it was opened from the inside and another man appeared. He was big like Janos and Paula assumed he was another stevedore. He and her husband exchanged a few words, the man stepped back and Janos ushered the prostitute into the warehouse. The door slid shut behind them.

From her place of concealment, Paula rested her back and head back against the rough surface of the building and sighed heavily. Rather than find answers to her questions, what she had just witnessed only increased her confusion tenfold. Who was that other man that had been waiting for Janos and the hooker? What was this place and why was it important for Janos to bring the woman here? Was it part of some bizarre initiation of that club he had joined? Or was it something else altogether? Something sinister?

Her mind awhirl with these doubts and fears, Paula realized that she simply could not abandon her mission yet. She was driven to know the truth and somehow she would summon the inner courage to follow this course of action she had so recklessly embarked upon.

Looking back around the corner to the now still warehouse front, she eyed its architecture carefully. There was a small alley separating it from its neighbor to the left. Afraid she'd lose her nerve; Paula darted out into the open and ran across the road into the alley. There she quickly made her way back along the building's side in hopes of finding a window that would allow her a glimpse inside. Instead what she found was a rear door located at the top of a small, concrete dais. She inched her way up the two stairs to the square platform and gingerly touched the worn, porcelain doorknob. To her amazement, the door was unlocked and swung inward at her easy push. For a brief second she envisioned a curious fly buzzing near the beauty of a spider's web then she shrugged off her hesitancy and walked through the threshold.

Everything was pitch black inside. Vague shifting- shapes were all she could make out as she reached out her hands to feel her way along. There was the overpowering stench of fish and she recalled that long ago, before its fall from grace, Cape Noire had been one of the major fishing centers of the coast. Canneries of various sizes and output had provided employment for thousands of people. But then the catch had played out, the fleet had migrated further south and a once thriving district fell prey to the ravages of time and abandonment. Now it was just another jaded bird in the cage that was Old Town.

Somewhere at the end of the corridor she appeared to be following was a bright glow of light. The closer she came to this light she also began to hear voices, lots of them. They were chanting although she was still too far removed from the source to make out the words themselves. It was an eerie chant, full of dark rhythm and foreboding.

Once at the end of the corridor, she found herself at the outer edge of a huge, cavernous room that was obviously the buildings central shipping and storage area. Wooden pallets were stacked in rows to her right and left in over a dozen vertical stacks. Above these, suspended from the high ceiling were copper fixtures from which hundreds of halogen tube bulbs blazed giving the cold interior a harsh, unyielding light that hurt her eyes.

From this spot, Paula had a clear view of what had been the main work area. It was an empty space set around a square trap door opening in the floor. It was a large square almost twenty feet on each side. Although she couldn't see the water from her position, she could hear it lapping at the pillars beneath the floor. Over this section was a heavy-equipment winch, chain and hook set-up. It was all connected to a hand crank located against the back wall.

Around this area were two-dozen figures all wearing identical green robes. On these garments were painted odd-looking symbols Paula did not recognize. They were the people chanting. The robes, made out of a heavy material hid most of their bodies so that she could not easily discern their genders but she guessed they were all men. The voices were masculine. This had to be Janos's so called club.

The group was milling about some activity going on by the floor opening. Then Paula heard a woman's scream and nearly jumped. Slowly she moved in closer, using the pallet stacks as cover. The screaming continued, the woman now frantically begging to be released.

Within thirty yards of the assemblage, Paula could see it was the hooker making all the commotion. Three of the clan were on the cement floor wrestling with her as she struggled to free herself from their grasps. Most of her outer garments had been ripped off and the woman was almost naked save for her stockings and underwear.

"Quick, tie her up!" A big man, standing beside the trapdoor was speaking over the chanting. He tossed back the hood of his robe and Paula saw that he was bald, with a strange gray cast about his face. There was also something surrounding his wild eyes that gave Paula a jolt. The way the overwhelming lights shone down and sparkled off them, they appeared to be scales, green, shiny scales.

Now the trio handling the prostitute had her up on her feet, which were bound together with iron chains, as were her hands. The poor woman was crying and still begging them to stop whatever it was they were going to do. Paula was torn between running away or staying to see what would happen next. She realized there was absolutely nothing she could to for the other woman. Alone, she was as helpless as the desperate captive and were she to make her presence known she too would be lost.

"Hurry!" the leader snapped, pointing to the overhead hoist. "Get her on the hook! The master is almost here!"

Instantly obeying his commands, the three men holding the bound woman got her up and raised her arms in the air. A fourth man, controlling the winch, lowered the huge hook until it was level with the prisoner's hands. Then, with swift efficiency, one of the three slipped it under the chains binding the bruised wrists and gave a hand signal for the operator to raise the hook. Smoothly the well-oiled, heavy-duty chain went up and with it, the terrified, half-naked blonde. Her body twisted in midair as her feet left the floor.

As the woman rose higher, the hoist controller began maneuvering the winch so that it was swinging out over the open gap. Someone shut off the main lights and all that was left was a single spotlight over the floor gap. It was tinted red and painted the entire drama like some twisted, feverish nightmare. Paula rubbed her eyes, feeling the strain of her weary nerves.

Once the woman had been positioned directly center of the loading aperture, the winch stopped and she was left dangling there. Now the leader of the group extended his hands and began intoning some perverse summoning. The rest of the group ceased their chanting and all was silent save for the man's eerie prayer and the woman's now feeble protestations.

"Come, Unat-E-Rahk, answer the calling of your servants! Bring worth your wonder and splendor. Accept the blood offering of your chosen ones."

From below the water began to bubble and spray rose up hitting the edges of the floor. The woman stopped her cries and twisted her head to look below her feet. The water was boiling as if its temperature had been made to rise.

"Join me, brothers!" the bald priest directed. "Call our master forth from his deep domain!"

Then in unison, as one monotone voice, the group began calling, "UNAT-E-RAHK! UNAT-E-RAHK! UNAT-E-RAHK!"

The water became a bubbling froth spitting foam everywhere. Then something started to rise up of the sea. Along with it came a strange, keening sound that vibrated throughout the warehouse. Encouraged by this show of response, the green robed cultists continued their praying with renewed vigor.

A long, grayish-green tentacle came out of the boiling sea and slid itself around the blonde's legs. Her eyes widened with the contact of the slimy thing and now her screams were loud and raw. The tentacle itself was covered with small, tiny suckers and they affixed themselves to the wriggling woman's legs. Paula could see tiny rivulets, almost orange under the red glow, streaming down the girl's stockings and realized the suckers were actually cutting into her flesh. Paula gulped and slapped a fist into her mouth to stifle a scream and to check the bile rising in her throat.

A second and then a third followed the first tentacle. Each new limb attaching itself sinuously around the now writhing body. Then, like some great trophy fish on the end of a sportsman's line, the thing that was Unat came out of the water into full view. Its song filled the place and for the first time the men were quiet in their awe at the beast they had called into being. It was a giant, frog-like monster with scales the color of ochre. One giant, silver eye was set at its top, over a huge oval mouth filled with needle like teeth. Around the torso were the tentacles, to include the three now ravaging its prize.

As if it could float, the creature continued to rise up as blood from the tortured woman began to rain into its open maw. Enhanced by the taste, the demon bellowed a foul cry and opened its mouth wider. Snapping out of his reverie, the leader of the cult, turned to the man at the cable drum and barked, "Lower her, now!"

Slowly the prostitute's body began to sink down and after one last convulsive spasm; it went limp as the woman lost consciousness. Her head hung limp on her shoulder as the sea-thing began to close its mouth about her.

Paula fell back against the pallet and closed her eyes. There were loud crunching sounds from behind her and she bent over to hold her stomach. She wanted to block up her ears so that she wouldn't have to hear the obscenity that was happening only yards away. Thankfully the sounds ceased after only a few minutes and then silence filled the hall once more. There were splashing noises and then all was quiet.

This was it. She had seen more than enough. More than she had ever wanted to see in her entire life. She started to turn and slip away when a figure materialized out of the shadows before her. Paula gasped and stopped short. Then somebody switched the lights back on and in the glare she recognized the man under the green hood who was blocking her path.

"Janos!"

He looked at her and anger flared in his eyes. Eyes that were encircled by green, shimmering scales.

Paula screamed and he hit her with a balled fist. She dropped senseless at his feet.

Blackjack Bobby Crandall never went into Brother Bones' room. The man, if that was what he still was, gave him the creeps. It had been a year since the undead avenger had saved his life and drafted the young gambler as his mortal agent. It was a role Crandall did not enjoy in the least but fulfilled because he was too afraid not to.

Thus it took all the courage in the world for him to open that door and step inside his master's private sanctum. The room was lit by a single candle on a nightstand by a bed that appeared untouched in ages. Dust scented the interior, another clue to occupant's inactivity within its confines. Bones sat in an over stuffed chair on the small porch beyond the sliding French windows. A cool night breeze slipped into room flickering the candle's tiny flame. On the stand beside it was a porcelain mask. It was made in the shape of a human skull and was an ivory white color.

"Why do you dare enter?" Bones intoned without turning his head. In the distance the lights of Cape Noire beckoned seductively. "You know my rules."

"I..ah..Look, it's been two days since Paula reported in at work. Something's wrong. I think something bad has happened to her."

"I know." With that, the figure rose up and stepped towards the balustrade. "The ghosts of their victims have cried out to me."

"Huh? What are you talking about?" Crandall remained where he stood, having no desire to go any deeper into the chamber.

"There is a cult operating within Old Town called the League of the Black Water. Five prostitutes were given up as sacrificial offerings to a demon from the ninth dimension named Unat-E-Rahk. They cry out to me for vengeance."

Crandall had heard this litany many times before. Enough to know what was coming next. He just didn't understand how it addressed his personal concern about Paula Wozcheski?

Brother Bones turned and entered the room. Thankfully the darkness of the interior hid his features from Bobby. It was the face of a killer. Carefully Bones picked up his mask and settled it over the contours of his visage. There were no strings but somehow it stayed fixed. Another puzzle to credit the man in black with.

"Paula Wozcheski is to be the demon's sixth and final victim this night. With her death, he will have devoured enough power to enter our dimension permanently. That must not happen."

"Oh." Crandall's mind was hastily trying to play catch up. "I take it you want me to get the car out?"

"Yes," Bones said, pulling out a leather shoulder rig from a bureau drawer. There were two silver plated .45 automatics in each of the twin holsters. Bones slipped on the rig and then proceeded to check it each weapon.

"Do you know where she is? Paula, I mean?" Crandall's hands were sweaty.

"In Old Town. An abandoned cannery site. But we've two stops to make first." Bones threw his greatcoat on and then his black fedora. Done with his attire, he moved past Crandall, now intent on his new mission. Still, as he glided by his anxious servant, he fired off a single verbal reminder. "Do not enter my room again. Ever."

Father Dennis O'Malley, pastor of Saint Michael's Church was reading from his bible when there came a loud knocking on the rectory's back door. Pushing his reading glasses down over his nose, the priest, dressed in pajamas and a worn old house robe, glanced at the clock on the wall. It was nearly midnight.

Hurriedly he put the bible down on the seat of his rocking chair and hastened through the small apartment that had been his home for longer than his aged mind could remember. Flicking on the lights as he entered the kitchen, he could make out a man outside on the back porch. Father O'Malley hit the outside lights and opened the door to see a redheaded fellow with scores of freckles. He was holding a brown grocery bag and seemed extremely anxious.

"Father O'Malley?" the man asked.

"Yes, I'm O'Malley. What can I do for you, young man?"

"I'm sorry about the lateness of the hour, father. Really. But this is important."

"Late night visits to a priest usually are, my son."

O'Malley's craggy face was experienced and his smile ready to comfort even the most dire situations.

"Well, you see, I need you to bless what I have here," Blackjack Bobby explained, hefting up the brown bag in his arms. "My friend in the car said you'd do it for us."

"Friend in the car?"

Crandall stepped aside and Father O'Malley saw he had left a roadster parked at the street curb. The engine was still running and there was a man seated in the front passenger side. He wore a heavy coat and large hat that all but hid his face. All the pastor could make out was that it was unusually pale.

"I don't understand?"

"My friend said to tell you, father, to do it for the Brothers of Mt. Serenity."

The old cleric's eyes widened with surprise. Mt. Serenity had been the former home of a monastery operated by Jesuits monks. One horrible night they were all murdered and the place burned. To this day no one had ever been apprehended for the massacre. Yet, shortly after its occurrence, there had been born a new urban legend on the streets of the Cape Noire. It was the impossible tale of a dead monk who refused to accept his fate and still walked the earth.

Father O'Malley looked at the car again and the ghostly face. He shivered as a bizarre understanding came to him.

"What is it your friend wants blessed?" he finally managed, taking his tired eyes back to Crandall and his package.

Crandall stepped closer and opened the sack to show the priest his second surprise of the night.

Paula Wozcheski was hoisted up over the open trap door while the congregation of cultists sang their eerie chant. Like the blonde prostitute before her, she had been stripped to her underwear and now felt her skin shiver as cold air off the water embraced her. As the hoist lifted her higher, the tugging on the chains that bound her wrist was painful and there were already bruises from the rope marks. She had been kept tied in an empty office for the past two days.

It was where she had awakened after having been hit by her husband. She never saw Janos during her hours of imprisonment. Her only contact had been with the leader of the group, the bald headed man with the gray skin. He had called himself Krager and had brought her water and bread to eat. Both of which she threw back at him in a streak of pure stubbornness. Recalling the horror of the blonde woman's death, Paula refused to give these men another such show. She vowed if she were to meet the same end, she would do so silently. Now, dangling high in the air, her body weak and sore, she bit down on her lower lip to stifle the cries in her dry, aching throat.

There was a small jolt and she was no longer moving. The overhead lights went out to be replaced by the familiar red beam and the chanting rose in tempo. Krager, walking around the wide aperture, raised back the hood of his cowl and began his summoning prayer.

"Go to hell, you son of a bitch!" Paula screamed over his incantations.

Krager looked up her and a cruel smile appeared. "That, my dear, is your destination. Not mine."

Once more he raised his arms and began calling forth the outer dimensional demon.

"Come, Unat-E-Rahk and take the sacrifice we have prepared in your honor. Arise, Unat-E-Rahk, from the black waters of the netherworld!"

Suddenly two gunshots rang out and two robed acolytes collapsed where they were standing. The chanting stopped and everyone present turned to the source of the hostile gunfire.

Out of the shadows Brother Bones marched, his twin automatics leveled at the cultist.

"This travesty ends now! Lower the woman and untie her!"

Krager moved around the floor cavity and pushed back his men so that he was face to face with the masked intruder.

"Who are you that dares to interfere with our master's coming?"

"I am Brother Bones. Now, do as I say or more of your men will join their brethren in death."

From her lofty position, Paula had a clear view of the confrontation between Krager and her would-be savior. For a fleeting moment she began to feel hope. Then she saw that one of Krager's security guards had been hiding behind a stack of pallets and was now slowly coming up behind the masked gunman. The cultist had a shotgun in his hands.

"LOOK OUT BEHIND YOU!" Paula screamed but she knew she was too late.

The assassin, only a few feet behind Bones, shoved the tip of his weapon into the avenger's back and pulled both triggers. There was a muffled blast and Bones was propelled forward almost into Krager's arms. But the leader of the fanatics, side stepped and Bones went down hard, his guns knocked from his gloved hands. The back of his coat was shredded and smoke curled up from one, ugly massive wound.

Krager looked down at the still figure of Bones then turned to the man with the shotgun and nodded. "Good work, Disciple Janos. I will not forget this when the time for reward comes."

Janos peeled off his own hood and bowed slightly. "Thank you, Lord Krager. I only live to serve the master."

Paula hung her face down and began to sob. It was the final act of betrayal. Not only had Janos, the man she loved, brought her to this horror, but now he had also murdered the person who was about to save her. Everything was lost now. She had only minutes to live.

"Lord!" The man operating the winch was pointing to the water. It was starting to boil. "The master comes!"

Krager forgot about the body at his feet and hustled back to his original position. "Hurry, all of you. Resume the summoning prayer. Our glorious master comes!"

Below her chained feet, Paula saw the frothing sea bubbling up as if caught in a giant soda fountain machine. Then she saw the dark shape taking form beneath the mad surface. That the demon was near was heralded by its strange, unnatural keening. The noise filled her head and she tried to shake herself free of its influence.

Slowly a long gray tentacle, its hide covered with razor edged suckers, began to ascend out of the water like an undulating cobra in a snake-charmers basket. It moved towards her and started to slip around her feet.

Unable to contain her fear any longer, Paula opened her mouth and screamed. As if in answer to her cry, a shot rang out and ripped open the demon's hungry limb. The keening changed to one of pain. Paula looked down and had to blink her eyes in disbelief. The masked man was on his feet again, hatless, his hands clutching his silver coated pistols. He aimed his guns at Krager.

"So, you are an agent of the undead," Krager realized, refusing to be intimidated by what he was facing. "It changes nothing! Your bullets will only sting the master. They cannot harm him! Whereas you are alone."

If Krager thought Bones was insane for continuing his fight, that notion was reinforced as the dark avenger began to laugh. He stood there, laughing mirthlessly without moving.

Unat-E-Rahk was emerging out of depths, its torso coming into view. Now other tentacles were moving towards the helpless girl despite the pain in its torn member.

"Please," Paula begged. "Don't."

Brother Bones leveled his guns and fired. Both shots hit the man operating the winch and he crumpled. Krager was furious and pointed to Bones while yelling to his followers. "STOP HIM! NOW!"

But the zealots were not about to leap on a man with two guns in his hands. Especially one who had survived a point blank shotgun attack. Janos, meanwhile was quickly reloading his weapon in an attempt to obey his leader's command.

Brother Bones turned sideways, raised his left arm and shot Janos between the eyes. He fell back and the scattergun dropped to the floor beside him.

Paula was still crying out, as the beast was about to encircle her with its multiple appendages. Suddenly a figure appeared from behind the fallen cultist at the controls. It was Blackjack Bobby and in his hands was a small, heavy paper container. Krager, directly across the opening from him, was shocked at the sight of him. Then his eyes focused on the package in Crandall's grasp.

It was a bag of salt. Bobby ripped off the top and tossed a huge spray of the white particles onto Unat-E-Rahk. The second the blessed salt touched the foul, yellowish hide, it sizzled like the acid it had become. Being blessed, it was a purging element that would scour anything of unholy origin.

The demon's song went wild. Again Bobby tossed the bag in an arc and a new rain of salt fell over the monster.

Now nearly half of its skin was blistering with dozens of white fires. The demon thrashed about, its awkward body trying desperately to avoid the burning agent that was consuming it.

With a final toss, Bobby emptied the bag on the convulsing creature then grabbed the winch crank and began spinning it. Quickly he swung Paula away from the clutches of the scaly demon. Once over the floor, he started to lower her only to have Krager suddenly appear at his side.

"You fool!" Krager hammered at Bobby with his fist, knocking him down. "You will pay for this."

Brother Bones meanwhile was busy fighting his way through the cult members assailing him with clubs and knives. His guns kept blazing away and mowing down the crazed attackers. He caught a glimpse of Bobby going down under Krager's assault and brought his gun up. Just then one of his attackers slapped a heavy bat into his arm and his shot went wild. Bones shot the man with his other gun.

Krager pushed past the dangling Paula and yanked a long knife from his robes. He reached down and grabbing a handful of Bobby's hair, jerked his head back.

Madness gleamed in his eyes. "Your blood will pay for this blasphemy!"

As he was swinging his knife down for the killing stroke, Paula pulled her knees up and then lashed out with her feet hitting him in the small of the back. Krager spun about, releasing Bobby and waving his arms in the air tried to regain his lost balance. He fell back into space and landed on the monster's body. Tentacles wrapped around him and immediately proceeded to tear him asunder. Blood and gore flew everywhere.

There was a massive gust of fire, as the myriads torches all over the demon's body erupted into one huge blaze. The flame burst like a rotten orange, sending out heat flashes like sunbeams. Then it died and what had been Unat-E-Rahk was gone.

Brother Bones, his torn coat covered in blood and gore, looked up and realized his enemies were for the most part dead at his feet. Several, in the final stages of the battle, realizing their defeat, had fled. He was not overly concerned. With Krager dead and the demon vanquished, they posed no further threat to anyone. Over on the other side of the trap door, Crandall was rising to his feet and reaching out for Paula Wozcheski's form. She looked to be okay.

Bones put away his guns and scooped up his hat. He walked to the edge of the pit and looked down at the now calm blue waters. There was no sign of the beast.

Twenty minutes later, the three survivors exited the warehouse front. A thick fog had rolled in across the bay. Paula, still shaking, was wrapped in Bobby's sports jacket. He was holding on to her for support. Parked across the street was his roadster.

"Bobby will take you home now."

Paula, shivering, spoke, her voice strained. "Thank you."

Bones merely tipped his head slightly.

Bobby took her to the car, set her in the passenger seat and then climbed in behind the wheel. As they rolled away, Paula, looked back at Bones. He was just standing there on the sidewalk.

She looked at Blackjack Bobby. "Who is he?"

"Believe me, you don't want to know."

She twisted her head around and Bones was gone. Somewhere in fog she heard him laughing.

THE END

SEE SPOT KILL

Little Jamaica is the name given to a three-block district west of Old Town and set against the harbor tip of Crystal Cove. Here mostly blacks and mulattos from various islands have come seeking a better life. What they found was a newer version of the same old plagues, poverty, prejudice and despair. What they brought with them was a culture steeped in ancient magics whose origins were born in the dark jungles of a forgotten world.

Cody Daniels gripped the wheels of his convertible sedan as he raced through the night streets of Little Jamaica. He, his pal, Bradley Webster and his girl, Ashley Kent were partying on this hot summer night in Cape Noire. They had started hitting most of the dance clubs right after sunset and now, as the dash clock edged its way over the one thirty mark, the three of them were happily drunk beyond comprehension. In fact, as he maneuvered his long, gleaming steel chariot, Daniels held a nearly empty bottle of Old Kentucky bourbon between his knees.

As their car raced wildly through the quiet, narrow streets, they were observed by locals who were camped out on their front stoops trying to escape the relentless heat.

Nobody could afford air-conditioners in this part of the city. Not that they would have worked regardless. The wiring wasn't all that safe in most of the brick structures well over a hundred years in age.

Daniels was singing along at the top of his lungs with a new rock tune blaring over his radio speakers. Webster was hanging over the passenger door trying to catch some of the air whipping past them. Still it was hot air and offered no real relief. In the back seat, the girl was sitting back, her head on the padded seat half asleep.

Catching sight of her condition in the rear view mirror, Daniels twisted his head about and shouted. "Hey, baby! Don't crash on us now. The night is still young!"

As if to emphasize his point, he pulled the bottle up from his legs and tilting it to his lips, drained its remaining contents. Then he tossed it out of the car. It sailed past a lamppost and smashed on the broken sidewalk.

The girl, her face pasty from the alcohol, lifted her head and mumbled, "I'm tired, Cody. Can we go home now?"

"Home? No way, babe. We're just getting started! Right, amigo?" He jabbed Webster on the arm.

"You bet," echoed his equally inebriated compatriot. "Let's find someplace to eat. I'm hungry for some hot-dogs with lots of mustard and onions."

"Sounds like a great idea," Daniels laughed, yanked the wheel into a sharp right corner turn. The sedan tilted dangerously and then found asphalt again. "I know a diner up on the heights."

"Well, let's go!" Webster stood up, bracing himself with the top of the windshield and pointed his right arm out towards the lane ahead. "CHARGE!!!"

Suddenly, much to his total surprise, Daniels realized they were rushing flat out into a dead-end blocked by an old apartment building. Frantically his eyes swiveled about looking for an alternate route and spotted an alleyway to their immediate left.

"HANG ON!" he shouted as he tore the wheel hard with both hands. The car responded with a loud screeching of tires and once again defied gravity by making the near impossible course correction.

Now they were rocketing down the little street bordered by the seediest structures Daniels had ever seen.

"Man, where the hell are we?" Webster snapped falling back into his seat. "Shanty town?"

"How the hell do I know?"

"Cody, please. I think I'm gonna be sick."

At that, Daniels turned his head quickly. He didn't want no skirt puking all over his expensive upholstery. No freaking way! "Don't you dare!"

The sick girl brushed dirty blonde hair from her face and looked up at him. Suddenly her eyes saw movement to the front and she screamed a warning.

"LOOK OUT!!"

The big, yellow dog came out of a wall of trashcans, running straight across their path. The car hit it with a dull thud and continued over its body with a barely felt bump.

Daniels was pushing down on the brakes, fighting the wheel as the big machine came to a sliding, screeching stop that set it diagonally across the small roadway. The engine revving at a standstill, all three riders sat shaking at the thought of what had just happened. As if one body with three separate heads, they turned together to look back.

The dog lay still in the middle of the road.

"Oh shit!" Walters gasped. He was sobering up fast.

"You ran over him," Ashley said, covering her mouth with her hands to halt the rising sickness in her belly.

Daniels, still silent, shoved his door wide and climbed out of the car. The others followed his lead and with heavy steps they approached the canine corpse. It was, or had been, a big, golden retriever. Now it was in bad shape. The bumper had knocked the animal's head so that it rested in a twisted, impossible way. The dog's long, red tongue protruded out of its bloody mouth. The eye they could see was cold and glassy. The tire itself had finished the job by caving in the ribcage so that several jagged bone stuck up through the once soft hide like accusing fingers pointing at them.

"Oh, God," Ashley cried and stepped away to finally give in to her stomach's sourness. She vomited bent over double to ease the contractions. Daniels and Walters ignored her, unable to look away from the lifeless carcass before them.

"You killed my dog."

Both men jumped back, startled almost out of their shoes. The voice, that of a child, came from the corner of the nearest house. The same place the dog had emerged from only minutes ago, alive and vibrant.

Daniels looked into the darkness from which all his misfortune had come and could only make out the outline of what looked like a six or seven year old boy. He appeared black with a mop of curly hair over his small head. Daniels thought to get a better glimpse when the boy stepped into the area lit by the street light, but eerily the child came no closer. As if he preferred the comfort of the dark, he merely stood his ground and accused them once again with his tiny, wounded voice.

"You killed my dog."

"That tears it," Webster spoke up, his gaze going back and forth from the dead pet to its spooky little owner. "I'm out of here." With that he ran back to the car and jumped into his seat.

Daniels, now totally messed up, tried to move closer to the boy. "Look, kid. It was an accident. I'm sorry. Really."

"No. You are not. You are a bad man and you killed my dog."

"What?" The alcohol made it hard for Daniels to think clearly. "Look, I said I was sorry. Okay. I'll give you some money. You can buy another dog. What do you say?"

For a moment, he thought just maybe the kid was giving it some consideration. He was wrong. Dead wrong.

"You will pay for killing my dog. All of you."

Shit, now the little brat was threatening them. It was all Daniels could take. He twisted about and grabbed Ashley's elbow. Having finished her involuntary purging, she was weakly standing there, a mute and sympathetic witness.

"Come, on. Let's get out of here!"

Ashley never thought to protest. With one last look at the mangled dog, she allowed her boyfriend to lead her back to the convertible and put her in the front seat between Walters and himself. He started the ignition, straightened the tires and then gave her some gas. Smoothly the well kept machine nosed her front end back to the road proper and sped away.

Around the block, dozens of curious faces appeared through open windows along the street but none ventured forth when they saw the dead animal. And when the dog's master stepped out of the alleyway, they moved back into the safety of their homes. And they prayed.

Mama Tousainte came down the alley moving as fast as her eighty-year old body would allow her. That and the gnarled oak cane that kept her upright. Despite the cloying, humid night air, she felt a chill and knew it was Mr. Samedi that had come calling even before she reached the street.

Her grandson was kneeling in the middle of the road over the broken dog and she instantly crossed herself. Jesus, Mary, Joseph, she thought, help me now.

"Get away from it!" she ordered, stopping at the curb and putting a hand on the lamppost for steadying.

The boy turned his head and there were no tears. But she already knew that. She knew her grandson all too well.

"They killed Spot."

"Leave it be, Leon," she said his name at last. "Tain't nothing you can do for him now."

"No," he replied. "You can bring him back."

"NO!" She crossed herself again. "It is ..was only an animal. Leave it rest, boy. Please, listen to your old Mama and leave it rest."

The boy turned his back on her and with an effort she did not believe possible, put his arms under the carcass and then stood. Turning, with the dead dog in his arms, he walked to her, the overhead light drawing out his chubby features in sharp relief. She was afraid of what he would say next.

"You will do it for me. You will."

Two nights later, Cody Daniels worked a late shift at the bakery over on Sutton Drive. He worked as a shipping clerk and was responsible for overseeing two important operations. The first was receiving and stocking the tons of flour, butter and other food items the bakery used in the creation of their products from breads to pastries. The other was seeing that the delivery trucks were properly and efficiently filled to supply their hundreds of route customers; that being the stores and supermarkets throughout Cape Noire.

Daniels was one of three such clerks. His shift was usually noon to eight at night but today the tail end man had called in sick and he had been forced to stay over. Now it was past three in the morning and he was anxious to lock up and go home. In another forty minutes the day crew would arrive and he would punch out. Fortunately the evening's load had been light and his two crews had finished loading the trucks early. When this happened, the boys usually grabbed a few sodas and set up a card game using and over turned flour barrel to play on. They had asked him to join in, but being short of cash, he bowed out.

Instead he decided to light up a cigarette and take a walk around the building to get some air. Even though the loading area was wide open, little if any breeze ever made the place comfortable. Especially in this heat. It was Daniels beliefs that away from the hot warehouse lights, in the dark, he'd find some cooler air.

The bakery was an old, four story building that had seen better days. Around the corner from the loading docks was the main employee parking area. Located in a business district, the bakery was itself surrounded by other squat, ancient walls and narrow, pothole scarred streets.

Inhaling deeply from his fag, Daniels moved along the parked cars wishing he could change his life in some way to make it better. He had no illusions about his future. Not having finished school, there weren't many prospects beyond what he was doing now. Still, it was nice to dream. He was starting to turn around and head back to the docks when he heard the growl. It had come from directly behind him and he twisted about fast, his heart suddenly skipping a beat.

There, standing between two parked autos, was a big dog. At first Daniels had trouble seeing it clearly as the only illumination came from a distant lamppost standing at the distant corner. The dog was only a mass of gray and a growl. Daniels took a step back and flipped away his butt. As he did so, feeble light crossed his shoulder and the animal became clearer to his sight.

It was the same dog he had run over! The head was hanging at a weird angle off the still broken neck and from its belly the white bones were visible.

Daniels was stunned. This wasn't real! It couldn't be! He shook his head and took another step backward as the animal came closer. There was a dull red look in its eyes as it approached steadily. The growling grew louder and Daniels realized too late that it was about to attack him.

As the ghoulish creature jumped up, he tried to move away only to trip and go down under its slashing claws. On his back, the creature's foulness filled his nostrils and when he opened his mouth to scream nothing came out. The big retriever had sunk his fangs into his throat and ripped out a huge chunk. Blood gushed out and splashed over the animal but it would not be moved. Daniels tried to push it off but found his arms getting weak. Blood continued to flow and with it went his consciousness.

In the end, Cody Daniels had one final, ironic thought before eternity swallowed him up. He really liked dogs. Now wasn't that a gas.

Ashley Kent puffed on her cigarette and wondered why she'd bothered ordering breakfast. The eggs and bacon had long gone cold on the chipped diner plate and her juice glass was still half full. The only things getting any attention were the gradually rising pile of ashes in the ashtray and the empty mug once filled with coffee. Her third thus far.

Ashley set her lipstick smeared butt down and rubbed her forehead trying to forestall the headache she knew was coming. Her eyes were sore from crying and as if to mimic her, rain splattered the dirty window to her left. Outside the Wooden Spoon diner, the day was dark, wet and miserable. What few people braved the elements were misty shapes rushing back and forth along the street, some with umbrellas and while others were defenseless against the ceaseless downpour.

The tattoo on the glass was a steady drumbeat that only added to her anguish. Biting her lower lip, the grief stricken girl took up the cigarette again and this time took a long, slow drag. Maybe enough nicotine and coffee would eventually dull her senses and she wouldn't have to think about Cody anymore. Caught up in her melancholy reverie she failed to see the front door bang open and Bradley Webster come staggering in. His clothes were soaked through and the baseball cap on his head seemed plastered to his head. Water dripped from the brim like a faucet. He tore it off and ran a finger through his thick hair, at the same time twisting his shoulders around.

"Hey!" cried Milly, one of the two waitresses employed at the eatery. "Don't go getting the floor all wet, huh?"

Webster looked down at the smeared linoleum and then realized he'd been had. Still mashing her chewing gum, the haggard Milly smiled, "Gotcha."

"Very funny. Ha-ha. Hey, you seen Ashley?"

Using a can of ketchup, Milly pointed down the row of booths to the last one in the back.

"She's really in a bad way, Brad. Hasn't touched her food. Damn shame what happened to Cody."

"Yeah, right."

Webster started down the aisle not wanting to continue his conversation with the waitress. He knew it would lead to certain queries in regards to the manner of his best friend's murder and that was a subject he did not want to discuss with anyone. Anyone except the blonde in the back booth.

"Ashley?"

She looked up at him through a haze of smoke. "Oh, hi, Brad. Wants some breakfast. I'm not all that hungry."

"I'll, pass, thanks." He turned back and waved at Milly. He made a drinking motion and Milly acknowledged with a nod of her head and headed for the coffee urn with a clean mug.

"Shit, Ashley," he started after sitting down and dropping his soggy hat on the seat. "You've got to snap out of this."

"Oh, really. And just how do you suppose I do that?"

"I don't know. Maybe by admitting Cody is gone and something killed him."

The words struck her hard and he saw the old fire come back in her eyes. "Something? That's a good word. Cops say it was some kind of wild dog or coyote. Undertaker wouldn't even let me see him one last time. Said he was all torn up like a doll that's had the stuffing pulled out."

"Shit, Ash, don't any of this seem all too much of a coincidence to you?"

"What do you mean?"

"Well, it's been only a couple of days since Cody ran..I mean, we ran over that mutt down in Little Jamaica. Then he gets chewed up by some wild dog."

"What are you saying?" Ashley ground out her cigarette with a quick, mean gesture. The butt joined half a dozen others in the pile. "You think there's some kind of connection?"

"Damn right I.."

Milly appeared with his coffee and put it down before him. In her free hand was a pot of the black brew. She looked at the uneaten serving and picked up the plate. "You want anything else?"

"Just some joe," Ashley replied and Milly refilled her cup and then left them.

Bradley wrung his hands together nervously and picked up his argument. "Look, Ashley, this is weird stuff and I'm scared. Something got Cody and I don't think it was no wild dog. Damn, this is the city. You see any wild dogs out there roaming around. Or how about some beavers and bears while you're at it?"

"What's your point, Brad?"

"My point is, the cops don't know squat and there coming up with all these bullshits answers to make themselves feel good. But it don't wash and I for one ain't going to stick around and do nothing about it."

Webster unzipped his poplin jacket and peeled it open so that Ashley could see the snub-nose .38 handgun stuck in his waistband.

"God, Brad, what are you doing with that?"

"Protecting myself, that's what. Whatever killed Cody is still out there and I'm not going to let it get to me so damn easy."

"God," Ashley rubbed her head. "This is all crazy."

"Maybe it is, but I have to do something. Sitting around waiting is for the birds."

"You have a plan?"

"Not really. I'm just going to go down there and nose around. See what I can find out about that dog and that kid we saw."

Ashley took a drink of her fresh coffee and then lit another cigarette. "Okay. But how are you going to get down there?"

"I thought you had Cody's wheels?"

"Huh, huh. Cops are holding on to everything until the insurance folks settle his policy. He didn't have a will, so they have to look around for a relative or next of kin."

"Cody didn't have any folks."

"I know. But it's still going take a few weeks before they release his stuff. That's the way it is."

Webster zipped up his coat and looked out the window at the rainy world outside. Then a grim look of determination came across his swarthy features.

"Screw it. There's a metro bus that runs down there through Old Town every half hour. I'll just catch it at the corner of Clarke and Briar. It's only a few blocks away."

"I'm going with you," the girl decided, putting down her coffee. "If I sit around moping any longer, I'll go nuts."

Webster smiled for the first time since entering the diner. "Great. Come on then."

Ashley took her leather jacket from the clothes tree and slipped it on, then she grabbed her hand bag and started to fish inside for some cash.

Webster threw a fiver on the table. "It's on me."

"Thanks."

They waved to Milly and exited, Webster slapping his hat back on and Ashley wrapping an old cotton scarf over her hair. The storm assailed them as they started jogging down the sidewalk, side by side. After the brutal heat wave of the past few weeks, the rain was a much-welcomed reprieve. What was a little wet compared to the spirit sucking dryness that had oppressed them?

Still the downpour was like a sheet of water and made the sidewalk slick and treacherous. Ashley held on to Webster's hand as they worked their way down towards the Eight Street corner bus stop. Being mid-day, the traffic along Central Avenue was heavy and almost bumper-to-bumper as thin, over-worked windshield wipers fought a losing battle to keep rain from obscuring drivers' visibility.

The bus stand kiosk was occupied by a single, old man. He wore a natty bow tie and was clutching a tent-sized, red umbrella for dear life. With a bowler hat and thick eye-glasses, he looked like an accountant very sorry to have ventured away from the security of his desk cubicle.

Ashley gave him a polite nod and he returned one in kind.

"God, I hope it's not running late," Bradley grumbled, shaking his arms so that water slid off his shoulders. "We could catch pneumonia standing out here too long."

A yellow cab rolled by the curb cutting through a huge, dirty puddle and Webster jumped back in time to avoid the mini tidal wave that splashed up at him.

Ashley huddled close to him, glancing up and down the street in hopes of sighting the familiar shape of the downtown bus. She heard the growl from her left and at first thought it was the muffled sound of a stalled motor engine. When it repeated, she turned her head around and saw the killer-mutt. It was coming at them along the sidewalk, its ruined body making its gait lopsided and difficult.

Ashley gasped, her hand rising to stifle a scream.

"Brad," she finally managed, her back still to him and the old dude. "Look! It's the dog!"

Webster came around and looked over her shoulder at where she was pointing. The moving canine corpse was now only a dozen yards away and its growl getting louder.

"Oh, crap! I was right." Not that this fact now gave him any particular satisfaction. Hurriedly he fumbled at his waist and yanked his .38 free. "Get behind me!"

Without waiting or considering the few pedestrians rushing around them, Webster leveled his gun and fired.

Instantly people stopped, looked around and then scrambled for whatever concealment they could find. Gunshots in Cape Noire were not unfamiliar and when heard, the good citizens instinctively knew how to duck and cover.

This included the old clerk who backed immediately away from Webster and the girl to the furthest shelter the small kiosk could offer. In doing so, he tripped and went down on his butt, his glasses sliding off his nose.

At first Webster thought his hasty shot had missed the devil-dog, for it just kept coming. He aimed carefully and fired off a second round and saw the animal jolt as the bullet hit it. For a micro second it stood statue still, then it merely shook itself and started forward again, now it's growling an angry warning.

"Shit, I can't stop it!" he realized aloud. "Come on, we have to get out of here!"

Ashley could only shake her head affirmatively. She was too scared to speak and had a hard time taking her eyes off the coming horror on four legs.

Webster took her arm and shook her hard. "Make a break for it across the street. Maybe the traffic will slow it up!"

Grabbing her arm, he propelled her off the curb and there was a loud blaring of horns and brakes were suddenly applied. Cars screeched to jarring stops as the two tried to weave across the four lanes of moving traffic. Midway across was a dividing cement island, Bradley stopped to see if the dog was still behind them.

The undead animal had reached the curb and now was twisting its broken neck around in clear frustration. Then it stepped onto the road and came on.

"Go to the other side," Webster ordered. "I'll try to hold it off with a few more shots."

He started back across the lane they had just crossed and brought his gun up. He fired two shots in quick succession and the noise boomed out over the storm creating a loud din. Loud enough to drown out the sound of the oncoming bus that had just swerved around a stopped sedan.

Ashley saw it just as it bore down on Webster. The driver, struggling to right his steel behemoth saw the man just as they plowed over him with a loud whap. Bradley Webster disappeared under the wheels of the metro bus and Ashley Kent screamed. What the bus left behind was a gooey orange smear on the blacktop.

City reporter, Sally Paige grabbed her denim handbag off her desktop and waved to night man, Lou Potter, who was just settling in behind his own desk in the far corner. The city room was practically deserted as the evening's shadows descended through the plate glass windows fronting Main Avenue.

Paige was bone tired after spending an entire day chasing down leads on a new story involving political corruption. It was a big story and could win her a Pulitzer if she could bag it. Unfortunately most of her leads had turned out to be phantoms with as much substance as the steam rising from Lou Potter's first cup of coffee.

All dead ends.

Frustrated and angry with herself, the perky brunette decided what was needed was a tall whiskey and ginger and a long, leisurely hour in the tub. Bubble baths were one of Sally's secret pleasures. She was already starting to feel better just thinking of all those tiny pink bubbles caressing her skin by the time she slapped the elevator button. Just another hour and she'd be there, in bubble heaven.

The doors parted and Ashley Kent stood before her looking like something no cat would ever consider dragging anywhere.

"Are you Sally Paige?"

Paige wanted to lie but the dried tear tracks on the girl's face just wouldn't let her.

"Yes, I am." Good-bye bubbles. "Can I help you?"

The elevator doors started to cycle shut, and Paige stopped them with her left hand.

"Spill it, kid. What's the problem?"

"My name is Ashley Kent, Miss Paige, and I think I'm being hunted by a zombie dog."

Oh, yeah. Bye, bye bubbles for sure.

The girl sniffled and Paige knew she was standing on nerves alone. "You'd better come in and tell me the whole story. I'll get us some coffee. My desk is right over here."

Thirty minutes later, Paige sat with her legs crossed, chewing on the temple of her eyeglasses while the distressed young woman finished her third cup of coffee.

Paige's thoughts were spinning on a carousel called unbelievable.

Which had been her first impression upon hearing the girl's story. Then, like the veteran newshound she was, she had made a few phone calls to either corroborate or deny the facts. Each call had supported the Kent girl's tale but only along a thin line of reasonable data.

Fact number one, a man named Cody Daniels had been chewed to death several nights ago by what her police informant had labeled a wild dog of some kind. Now that was weird.

Fact number two, a second fellow, one Bradley Webster had been run over by a metro bus that very afternoon. From what she learned, witness had reported the man standing in the middle of the road firing a pistol when he was struck. No one, except Kent of course, had mentioned anything about a dog, alive or dead, on the scene. The mousy accountant who was closest to the brutal collision had said something about hearing a growl but since he'd dropped his glasses after hearing the first gun shot, he could not swear it was not a car engine he had heard.

So the facts braced Kent's story only so far. Still, what bothered Paige were the odds involved. How likely was it for a girl to have two close friends come to violent, dramatic deaths within days of each other? As a reporter, Paige understood the fickle whimsy of fate but this was stretching things even for dear old destiny. Paige's gut was sending off familiar signals that said she had a real story here. One she had to pursue, regardless of how fantastic it might sound.

And of course, there was one other element to consider. This was, after all, Cape Noire, and in her time covering the city beat, Paige had learned that nothing was too out there for this city of darkness.

"Okay, kid. I'm going to go out on a limb here and buy your story."

"It's all true, Miss Paige. Every word of it." The girl put down her coffee and brushed a lock of hair away from her weary face. "Which is why I came to you. I read your stories all the time. You always help people when they have nowhere else to turn."

Sally shrugged off the compliment. "It's a job, kid. Don't go putting any glitter on it."

She nibbled her plastic temple then abruptly sat up, slipped the glasses over her nose and reached for her phone. "If we're going to get to bottom of this, there's somebody I have to call."

Paige dialed from memory, then drummed her sharp fingernails on her desk blotter while the connection was being made at the other end.

"Countess Selena's resident," a deep, male voice intoned from the receiver.

"Hello. This Sally Paige calling from the Tribune. Is Countess Selena available?"

"Please, wait."

There was silence on the other end and Paige saw Ashley's look. She cupped the speaker and explained, "If anyone in this town knows the bizarre, it's the Wicked Witch of the West."

"Hello, Miss Paige." The voice was syrup and arsenic. "What a pleasant surprise. To what do I owe the pleasure?"

"Good evening, Countess. I'm doing a feature on occult practices in Little Jamaica surrounding the voodoo religion."

"Indeed. Now there is a very dark subject. I would advise you to proceed with caution, Miss Paige. Voodoo is not something to approach lightly."

"I agree wholeheartedly. More specifically, I was hoping you might be able to tell me something about a zombie dog."

"Really? How odd."

The taxi dropped them off at the corner of Morneau and Edgewater. The driver refused to go any further into Little Jamaica.

"Sorry, lady, but this is as far as I go. Ain't enough money in all Cape Noire to make me go in there after dark."

Sally Paige shoved a ten spot into his calloused hand and told him to keep the change. The meter said $9.25.

Cursing under his breath, the cabbie pulled away leaving the two women under the street lamp. It was nine o'clock. Ashley hugged herself, shivering more from fear than the weather, which was once again hot and humid.

"I don't like this, Miss Paige. Did we have to come right here now? Couldn't we have done this tomorrow morning or something?"

Sally adjusted the strap of her handbag, taking a second to double check the .38 snub-nose hidden beneath a folded handkerchief, then put on her reporter's confident smile. "Look, Ashley. Either we get to the bottom of this or we wait and see what happens next? Do you understand the implications of that?"

Ashley nodded. "You mean I could still be ..ah, the thing's next target."

Paige took hold of her shoulder. "Exactly. If there is some kind of monster dog out there, we've got to find a way to stop it now. Not tomorrow. Tomorrow may be too late."

"Alright. Let's go. But I'm scared of this place."

"Honey, so I am."

They started down the broken, dirty sidewalk heading north.

As they walked along, people seated on the stoops and balconies along the street eyed them coldly as if they were bug-eyed aliens from another planet. Strangers, especially white ones, did not often frequent the byways of Little Jamaica after dark. Still, the residents left them alone and soon enough they were at the site of the collision where the entire affair had begun.

"It was right over there," Ashley said pointing to the alley behind them. "That's where the dog came from and then the little boy who gave Cody the willies."

Paige dug a scrap of paper from her jacket and confirmed it was the same address she had scribbled down back at the office. "Right. This is the place Countess Selena said we should go to. This Mama Tousainte supposedly lives in an apartment back in there."

The reporter started down the narrow passage with Kent following close behind. "Then the boy was her what? Her grandson?"

"Huh,huh." Paige was having trouble seeing, as the light from the street behind them could not penetrate the alley's interior more than a few yards. All she could make out ahead were gray, block like shapes. Luckily there were lit windows indicating the apartments to the rear of the alley. They were looking for 3-B.

"Selena told me something weird about that too."

"About what?"

"The little boy."

"What?"

Suddenly Ashley stepped on something alive and she screamed. Paige turned and grabbed her.

"What is it?"

"I stepped on something!" the girl gasped, feeling her heart racing.

Paige looked about at the trashcans lining either side of the small lane and could make out shifting outlines. Rats. Lots of rats.

"Come on, kid. We're almost there."

Reaching the back wall, they found a makeshift porch like structure enclosed with chicken wire. At the flimsy screen door, Paige pulled a Zippo lighter from her purse and snapped the flame on. The painted address 3-B was faded and the B nearly invisible with age.

"Bingo." She put the lighter away and knocked on the door. Nothing happened. Beyond the screen, she could see an open door and a gray, dingy room that seemed deserted.

She tried knocking again, this time a bit louder.

"Hello? Is anybody home?"

When she failed to get a response, Paige pulled the screen door and it opened with a soft creak. Ashley knew she was going to go in and started getting a familiar queasy feeling in her stomach. This was not a good idea. None of it. Still, she couldn't let Paige go in alone. The reporter was here on her behalf. Like it or not, Ashley knew she had to follow her and simply bit her lower lip to keep from mumbling.

The front room was lit by candles and the light they provided was soft and wavering. It danced over second hand furniture, a dirty linoleum floor and wall shelves were crowded with some of the strangest knick-knacks Paige had ever seen. Everything from rag dolls to African shaman masks made of dark teak wood. There were also toys one would associate with a little boy. A miniature dump truck, its bed filled with marbles and plastic soldiers. There was a stack of baseball cards and a few comics with their covers missing.

There was a sweet smell to the room that she identified with that of fresh fruit gone bad. She continued moving through the room to what she guessed was the kitchen beyond.

"Hello, Mama Tousainte? Is anyone here?"

Mama Tousainte, or what was left of her mortal remains, was sprawled out on the kitchen floor, half hidden by a rickety table built with aluminum legs and a Formica top. Most of her throat had been shredded and a mass of small, black flies were feasting on the congealed blood between her old breasts.

Paige stepped back and covered her mouth before the bile in her throat could progress beyond her initial shock.

"Sweet saints alive!" she gasped.

Ashley stepped beside her, saw the remains of the old woman and turned her head away fast. "Oh God! Oh God! It got her too!"

"Sure looks that way." The lady newshound surveyed the kitchen with a quick glance, not wanting to be surprised by what had ravaged the body on the floor. There was a plate of half-eaten chicken and mashed potatoes on the table and an open bottle of sherry by an empty glass on the sink counter. She had obviously been attacked while opening the liqueur bottle.

"But I don't understand," Ashley broke the eerie silence. "If she made the zombie dog, why did it go after her?"

"That's the thing," Paige began to explain. "When I told Countess Selena about the boy and the dog she told me something really weird."

"What?"

The porch door banged behind them and both women spun around in unison. Coming at them across the living room was the zombie mongrel, its twisted neck bone gleaming visible in the candlelight. A soft growl emanated from its throat as it approached them.

"We've got to get out of here!" Ashley choked, backing away from the animal. There was a back door to the left of the sink cabinets and she was going to bolt for it. But what if the door was locked? Paige's mind frantically tried to find some solution to their predicament. Anything that might slow down the furry undead. Somehow she knew the gun in her purse would be useless against the thing. Now confronted by the reality of the monster, her survival instincts were kicking into high gear.

The buzzing flies brought her attention back to the corpse under the table and she knew what she had to do.

As Ashley Kent reached the back door and turned to grab its steel knob, the dog went for her with a burst of unholy speed. To do so, it had move past Paige and the busted-up table. Without thought, the gutsy reporter grabbed the edge of the Formica and upended the table onto the animal, driving it to the floor. Dishes, utensils and cold food spilled over as the creature barked with maddened frustration under the overturned furniture.

"Come on!" Paige screamed at Kent, now frozen by the door. "We've got to get out of here the way we came!"

As Ashley moved past her, the upended table shifted and the trapped dog began crawling out, its lifeless eyes blazing with evil fury. Paige's glance fell on the half filled glass of sherry and quickly she picked it up. She threw its contents on the animal while at the same time charging after the frightened Kent. In the living room she swiped a candle from one of the wall sconces and then turned to face their attacker.

The zombie dog was moving through the upright legs of the table, its dirty fur wet with alcohol.

Saying a silent prayer, Paige tossed the candle at it. The dog barked as the wax stick landed on its backside. The tiny flame sparked and caught with a whoosh. Suddenly the creature was one huge ball of fire.

The women rushed outside. The burning beast followed on unsteady legs. When it reached the alley, it stopped as the fire consumed more and more of its hide. Its head was a grotesque, charred ball, twisting to and fro trying to shake off the flames.

"SPOT!"

Leon came out from behind the corner of the porch where the trashcans were stacked. Moving towards his fiery pet, the boy's face was revealed to the women. It was gray and pasty, the eyes devoid of life.

"Oh God!" Ashley stumbled, the full realization finally dawning on her fevered mind. "He's ..!"

"A zombie too," Sally nodded. "That's what Countess Selena suggested. When I told her of your confrontation with the dog's owner, she was puzzled. Said the old woman lived alone. That her only grandson had died about a year ago."

"She made him a zombie!" Even though Ashley was saying the words, she couldn't believe them. Not completely. It was all a crazy nightmare that she would soon wake up from. Someday.

"Right. My guess is the old woman refused to do the same for the dog and the boy went ahead and did it himself. Then he turned it on her when she discovered what he had done."

By now the fire had finished its work and the husk of the animal collapsed and was still. The boy stood over the smoking heap and shook his head in denial.

"You burned up Spot. You bad people killed him and now you burned him up." He turned towards them. "You bad people must be punished."

Paige was about to grab Kent and start running for all she was worth. Dealing with a zombie dog was one thing. A zombie child was something else.

Just then a huge black figure dropped from an overhead fire escape and landed behind the boy. Paige saw the bone white skull mask under the wide brim of a fedora and knew she was looking at Cape Noire's mystery avenger.

"Brother Bones!"

With his gloved left hand, Bones took hold of the zombie's hair and jerked him off his feet.

"Child of Satan, it is time to pay for your sins."

From under his greatcoat, the night agent produced a long, silver machete and held it up poised for a mighty stroke. Seeing the weapon, the undead boy twisted desperately in his grasp, trying to break free.

"The souls of your victims cry out for justice. Now it is served."

The blade swung down and cut through flesh long turned cold and hard. The head came off and the body dropped to the street where it lay unmoving.

Sally gasped and closed her eyes, as Ashley buried her head in her shoulder with a similar shudder at what they had just witnessed. There was the stench of smoking fur and silence.

Something rolled and touched the tip of her shoe. Paige summoned her resolve and opened her eyes. Bones was gone. At her feet was Leon's head looking up at her with empty eyes.

THE END

THE ROOT OF EVIL

The undead avenger sat in his chair looking out the open window at the city that was Cape Noire. A butter colored moon glided across the night heavens and somewhere in the far distance, traces of heat lightning sparked the horizon. Another storm was fast approaching.

It had been an oppressively hot summer with little rainfall and the city was chafing under all that heat.

Petty crime was up in every borough, as the weather edged tempers over normal restraints. People were hot and miserable and it showed.

The crime fighter who had once called himself Tommy Bonello watched as a stray gust of air played over the treetops in Veteran's Park and he heard a voice whispering his name. The ethereal figure of a young girl materialized before his open portal like a cotton candy sculpture. He recognized her with little difficulty. After all he was the man who had killed her.

"The Ivy League returns," she said to his mind without moving her lips. Floating there before him, a ghostly messenger with the sweet, innocent demeanor of one taken too soon. "Be prepared, Bones. The Ivy League returns."

Then like so much smoke, she was gone and he chuckled to himself. Be prepared. Ha! What else did he have to do? Sometimes he wondered if the entire universe was nuts.

Across town in the city room of the Cape Noire Tribune, reporter Sally Paige was wiping her eyeglasses with a tissue, while seated cross-legged on the edge of her boss's desk. For his part, city editor, Hank Anderson sat back in his swivel chair biting on an unlit cigar admiring Paige's long, shapely limbs.

"When is this heat wave suppose to let up?" the ace newshound asked for the millionth time that day as she slipped the lenses back over her eyes.

Anderson averted his stare before she could catch him ogling and glanced back over his shoulder at the light show raging outdoors. Heat lightning weaved its way through the concrete towers like dozens of elemental demons playing hide-and-seek.

"How the hell am I suppose to know?" he growled, wiping sweat of his blocky forehead and then smoothing out his iron gray hair. "All I do know is that maintenance had better get their sorry asses up here and fix the goddamn air-conditioners or heads will role."

Paige looked at the old stand-up fan clanking away in the room's far corner and nodded. "Cheer up, Hank, at least the heat seems to be keeping the city quiet. People are so miserable no one has the energy to do anything. Good or bad."

Anderson pulled the wet stogie out of his mouth and scowled. "Least you forget, Miss Paige, we are a newspaper and slow news days are the kiss of death."

"Excuse me?"

"Circulation, sweetheart. Sales are down five percent since last week."

"Since when do you give a shit about circulation?"

"Since the publisher called an hour ago and proceeded to rip my eardrums asunder with his monosyllabic tirade."

"Meaning, no sales, no paper, no jobs. In that order."

Paige slid off the corner of the desk, then twisted sideways to look at the back of her legs. She bent slightly, hoisted her skirt and examined the seam in her nylons.

Anderson's eyes smiled. God, but he enjoyed a nice pair of gams. Of course Paige was all too aware of that fact and considered her peep show harmless flirtation. Never hurts to keep the boss smiling.

"What about that story on the Ivy League boys coming home for their annual reunion?"

"Fluff stuff," the bulldog chief snapped. "Bunch of old Cape Noire rich kids who all graduated from the same prep school out on Riverhead thirty years ago, then went off to conquer the world. Yada, yada, yada."

Paige dropped her hem and straightened up. "Right. But when six of those silver-spoon-fed nerds, from the same class mind you, are now considered the six most powerful men in the business world, you have to wonder."

"At what?"

"At how they did it? What's the secret? What was it about that particular class that made them all so successful? And why, when they have homes scattered all over the world, do they return every five years to that abandoned old estate where the school was located?"

"Geez, Paige, now that sounds like a story, doesn't it?"

Paige's eyes sparkled. "You bet. Want me to check it out?"

"Sure." Anderson grabbed the bottle of warm soda on his desk. "But first finish the horse racing expose. I want that to be our lead in Saturday's morning edition."

"And the Ivy League boys?"

Anderson took a small swallow, grimaced and then wiped his lips with the back of his hand. "They're in town till next week. No rush."

Paige picked up her purse from the desk corner, opened the door and waltzed out. "Okay, you're the boss."

He caught one quick final flash of shapely calves before the door swung shut. Damn, to be thirty again. He'd give that little filly one hell of a run for her money. Ha.

Dolores Desire came off the stage, beads of sweat speckling her tall, statuesque figure. Ignoring the catcalls, whistles and cries from the other side of the curtain, she made her way through the shadowy passage heaving a long sigh of weariness. A thirty-minute routine was brutal enough, but in this heat, it was murder. Sure, the place had central air, but it was nearly a hundred years old and never worked right. Halfway through the night, loud clanking sounds would emit from the club's dungeon like basement, almost keeping tempo with the drummer's back beat cadence.

And there you stood, if you were a class act stripper at the Sexcat, center stage in a hot room filled with cigarette smoke and the smell of weak men too stupid to be anywhere else. You strutted, bumped and shimmied back and forth as they howled and yelled, liquor making their voices oddly tinged with sadness. Businessmen out on the town, college boys looking for a cheap thrill and the others, quiet men with an obscene hunger in their eyes.

Back and forth you moved, showing the goods bit by tantalizing bit until, with the timing of a pro, you dropped your last stitch as the house lights died and you did the vanishing act.

Dolores had long black hair and breasts the size of ripe pineapples. Her money machines, as she liked to call them. Clutching the pleaded skirt, high school jersey and snowball white pompoms that made up her naughty cheerleader costume, she marched her way back to the long, crowded dressing room.

As she neared the door, Babette emerged. She was a vixen blonde in a black and white French Maid's outfit. Both women wore six inch heels.

"How'd it go?" Babette asked, adjusting her tight little apron while clutching her white feather duster and still managing to hold the door wide at the same time.

"The usual," Dolores fired back catching the door edge. "You're typical bunch of animals."

"Oooh, Babette likes zee boys wild," the stripper laughed, her accent as phony as a three dollar bill. Then she was rushing into the curtain shadows as the announcer was calling her name.

Dolores chuckled and made her way through the double rows of vanity tables where half a dozen other working girls were busy either putting on or taking off their make-up. The Sexcat employed of a total of fifteen strippers, with at least eight on parade week nights and ten on Saturdays and Sundays when the house was packed.

Still the heat had been keeping customers at home and the boss was bitching at the diminishing profits these past few weeks.

Dolores sat down in front of her own lighted mirror located midway along the right wall, between Lacy Chavez, a slim waisted black girl who did Cleopatra and Monica Silvers, the just departed Babette. She dropped her costume on the table with a tired moan. Lacy was applying body lotion to her own magnificent breasts, as Dolores picked up a cigarette from her table top and lit up with a diamond studded lighter.

"Ooeee," Lacy sang out eyeing the expensive lighter. "Another present from your new sugar daddy?"

"Huh, huh. He gave it to me after dinner last night. At the Falmouth Inn no less."

Lacy put down the bottle of lotion and wiped her hands on a terry cloth towel. "The Falmouth! Landsakes alive, girl, that's the fanciest eatery on the East side."

"Don't I know it. The place was filled to the brim with swells. All of them worth millions."

Dolores sent a gust of smoke past her red lips and held the lighter up to examine the three diamonds set on the gold plated finish. She smiled. "Hiram says there's nothing too good for his little baby."

At that Lacy pounded her table and laughed. "Deedee, that man of yours best get those glasses of his examined as there ain't nothing, and I do be mean nothing, little about you."

The raunchy humor got both of them laughing momentarily. Still, Dolores' thoughts floated around the strange, gaunt man who had come into her life only days before and pretty much turned it upside down. He was a skinny, frail type with thick brown eyebrows. She guessed his age about forty. Not a bad face, if you liked them thin and serious most of the time. In fact the only time his expression would alter in the slightest was while they were making love. And then he would actually smile. Thing is, it looked sadly awkward on Hiram, like a foreign thing that just didn't belong. Dolores felt more sympathy than true passion for the rich man. Although passion was as yet another mystery about Mr.Hiram Woodbrige. He had it in abundance.

For a skinny body that looked like so many matchsticks stuck together with glue, his sexual prowess and endurance were amazing and had left her both totally satiated and deliriously fulfilled. The man was a sexual dynamo between the sheets. Then add to this the fact he was wealthy and for Dolores, all her dreams were on the verge of coming true.

Which was what scared her now, on the brink of a yet another evening with sweet, strange Hiram. What if it were all a dream? What if she woke up suddenly and he didn't exist? And worse yet, what if he did and somehow this fling was merely an infatuation for him? One that he would soon tire of. What then?

Lacy was sharp enough to see the questions buzzing around her eyes and tenderly reached over and touched her arm. "Hey, relax, Deedee. It's okay to be happy."

Dolores blinked and shoved back a tear starting in the corner of her eyes. "Yeah, right."

"I mean it, sweetie. You've paid your dues like the rest of us. Why shouldn't you land a nice fat sugar daddy and move out to the Heights? Don't let go of your dreams, Deedee. Never do that."

She was genuinely touched by Lacy's support. "I won't. I promise."

"Excuse me, I'm looking for a Dolores Desire?"

The girls all looked to the door. A woman wearing a long, tan colored trench coat and a man's fedora was standing there, hands in her pockets. At first Dolores thought it was a guy, then as the head under the wide brim turned, she saw the spillage of long, jet black hair on the stranger's shoulders.

Mona, the busty redhead closest to the door, gave the stranger a quick once over. "Hey, sister, no one's allowed back her."

"It's okay," Dolores said, holding up her hand with the cigarette. "Over here."

The Brunette nodded and came over. As she did, the fold of her coat parted to show long, fine legs in fishnet stockings and high heels. Lacy's eyes took in the outfit and she commented. "Whoa, girl, that's some theme you got going there. Sort of a Dan Rains-in-drag affair, right? But I got to tell you, sister, those fishnets are tacky."

The Brunette smiled. "Thanks, but I find they wear longer in my line of work."

"Which is what?" Dolores asked, taking another drag from her smoke.

"Helping people," the Brunette replied her voice soft but with an edge. Her eyes, hidden in the shadow beneath the long brim were dark but somehow vibrant with an inner fire.

"Oh. And who are you helping now?"

"You, if your real name is Gladys Sullivan."

Dolores sat up and involuntarily coughed.

"Hey, are you alright?" Lacy looked from her friend to the stranger and back again.

Crushing out her cigarette, Dolores shook her head affirmatively and then coughed once in her balled fist to clear her throat. "I'm okay, Lacy. Really, it's okay." Then she stood up and squared off with the mystery woman. "Let's take this out back."

The Brunette nodded as the stripper slipped on a silk teddy and followed her as she walked quickly to the room's back door exit. They emerged into a dimly lit back alley. To their left was the main street boulevard, to their right a larger door for beer and food deliveries. A naked light bulb over the service door cast the alley in a gray gloom. Across from them were dozens of over filled trashcans now being scouted by a scrawny looking feline who hissed at their presence then went back to digging in the fly-infested heap.

Having escaped the relative comfort of the dressing room, the two women now found themselves enveloped by the night's cloying humidity.

"Shit," Dolores mumbled, feeling the heat immediately. "Okay, lady, what gives? How'd you come by that name?"

"Are you Gladys Sullivan?"

"What if I am? What's it to you? Who put you on my case? Was it my folks? Cause if it was, you can tell them to go straight to hell! You got that?"

"I got it. Now if you'll just calm down for a second, I'll explain everything for you."

But the Brunette never got the chance to elaborate for at that moment a gaunt, haggard looking man in a tailor made three-piece suit and wearing a bowler hat materialized beside them. In one hand he carried an ivory handle umbrella and in the other a huge bouquet of roses.

"Is there a problem here?" Hiram Woodbridge peered through round, wire-rim glasses at the two women with an innocent puzzlement.

"Hiram, dear," Dolores's nervousness went up a notch. "You're early?"

"Well, we did have a late dinner, my sweet, at Chez Antoines and you know how I hate to be tardy."

Hiram handed her the flowers. "Is there something wrong?"

"Oh, ah, no. This woman was looking for somebody else."

"Really." The thin man studied the Brunette. "Someone you know, dear heart?"

"No," Dolores looked over her flowers at the Brunette. "I was just telling her I can't help her. I don't know the girl she's looking for."

"Then the matter is settled. Now shouldn't you go and change. I've a taxi waiting out front."

"Please," the Brunette interjected, positioning herself in front of the door. "This will just take a second."

"Young lady, Miss Desire has told you she cannot assist you further. What more do your require?" There was an agitation in Woodbridge's voice. One that spoke volumes.

Before the Brunette could retort, the door opened behind her and Bennie Morton, the assistant club manager popped his small, bald head out into the alley. He spotted Dolores and stepped out.

"There you are. I just got off the phone with Alice. Her kid's home with a stomachache and she can't make her midnight show. How's about filling in for her and saving my neck?"

"What?" This new wrinkle addled Dolores. Too many things were all happening at once.

"Come on, Deedee," the manager persisted. "Be a trooper and help me out here. I need somebody to fill that slot or the boss will have my neck."

"Excuse me," Woodbridge's voice seemed to have risen in timber. "But we have a reservation to make."

Bennie looked around. "Who the hell are you?"

"I am Hiram W. Woodbridge!"

"Terrific. Now get lost." Bennie turned his back on the dandy. That was his mistake.

Woodbridge stepped up and with a motion that was blur, brought the handle of his umbrella down on the back of Bennie's head. Bennie groaned and fell to his knees. Dolores jumped back and screamed.

"No, sir!" Hiram raged, bringing up the umbrella for another blow. "It is you who will be gone!"

As the handle came down, the Brunette stepped in and caught his wrist. The contact pushed her back a half step in surprise. The power in the man's arm was immense and even though she was no weakling, the pressure she fought against was formidable. For himself, Woodbridge's face flared as he locked eyes with the woman who had stopped his attack.

"Why don't you just back off a little," the lovely mouth gritted. "There is no need for this."

"I'll be the judge of that!" he snapped and suddenly his left hand took her by the throat before she realized what was happening. Then, as if she were nothing by a rag doll, he lifted her into the air and began to squeeze.

Gasping, the Brunette let go of his hand and tried to pry his hold off her throat. His fingers were like clamps of steel welded shut.

"I'm sick and tired of people interfering where they don't belong! Sick and tired of it!"

Whipping her around as if she were a feather, Woodbridge continued to apply more pressure and the Brunette felt the blood draining from her head. Stars popped up in her vision that was quickly receding into a deep, black tunnel. A tunnel she knew would be a one-way fall.

"NO, HIRAM!" Dolores begged, coming up along side him, her face registering total fear. The Brunette's face was going gray. "You're killing her!! STOP IT!"

Dolores grabbed his free arm and the skinny man reacted like a kicked dog. His arm shot out and hit her across the face hard. She was flung backward into the brick wall and her head hit with a loud smack. Her eyes glazed over and she slumped to the pavement unconscious, the forgotten bouquet coming to rest in her lap.

Hearing the impact, Woodbridge turned and saw her laying still, her torso slumped over. On the wall was a small stain of red.

"DOLORES!"

His momentary distraction was all the struggling Brunette needed. Holding onto her own awareness with her last ounce of strength, she managed to slide her right hand into her coat pocket. There she found what she prayed would be her salvation; a nickel plated .45 automatic. Slowly, as if through a sea of molasses, she pulled the gun out and tilted its barrel at her maddened attacker. Then, seconds before the descending black veil ended her world completely, she squeezed the trigger.

The shot fractured the silence of the alley and Woodbridge rocked back, his hold on her throat released in shocked surprise. The Brunette landed on her feet wobbly, her fedora falling askew over her back to reveal her angry face. Her lungs filled with air and it hurt to breathe, but it was a really good hurt. It was the kind of hurt that said I'm alive and still kicking. So go on and breathe the hurt baby. Let it hurt and hurt and hurt.

For his part, the thin man stopped his backward motion, then looked down at the smoldering hole in his expensive suit.

Chasing the spots away from her eyes, the Brunette brought the gun up and wondered what was keeping the guy standing. She had nailed him at point blank. Yet, there he stood, dazed, but no worse the wear for the slug that had to be nesting in his gut.

Then Hiram Woodbridge looked down at Dolores and shook his head in genuine sadness. "I'm sorry." With that he turned and ran out of the alley. The Brunette lowered her gun and tried to stand straighter. She saw a taxi zip by the alley opening and knew the mysterious suitor had made good his escape.

"Oh, shit. Dolores, baby." Bennie knelt beside the stripper, his hand trying to support her head. There was blood on his fingers.

He looked up at the Brunette. "We got to get her to hospital fast!"

The Brunette put away her pistol, picked up her hat and went back into the club get help. As she took one last look at the comatose figure, she mouthed a silent promise that Mr. Hiram Woodbridge was going to pay for this. One way or another.

Daryl Fernell was both scared and excited. As chief accountant for Baxter Industries, Inc. he was somewhat familiar with his employer's history of eccentric behavior. It was weird enough that old man Baxter rarely visited the corporate headquarters in Cape Noire. What was even more disconcerting was the fact that when he did, his arrivals were totally unexpected and generally caused all manner of chaos among the managing staff. This was peculiar enough but that Baxter only arrived late in the night after most of the crew had left for the day was really perplexing. Fernell had been sent a telegram informing him not to go home at the end of the day. He was to stay at his desk until summoned by the big man himself, Charles Warren Baxter. That was the first time poor, anxious Fernell was even aware the man was back in Cape Noire. Guessing what the purpose of this summoning could mean was pointless and thus, after all the hired help had made their normal exodus, the senior company officer had settled himself in with a bottle of gin and his rich Cuban cigars to await his fate.

At midnight, alone in his top floor office, Fernell, now somewhat tipsy, heard footsteps outside in his secretary's outer office. Then his door swung open and a giant of man with ebony skin and wearing a chauffeur's livery was before him like the angel of death.

"Come, now," was all the giant said. Fernell took a last swallow of liquor, wiped his mouth and like a good and faithful employee, did as he was told.

Five minutes later he was sliding into the back seat of a Rolls Royce to sit beside Charles Baxter.

"Mr. Baxter, so good to see you again. You're looking well." Fernell's voice was tinny, unable to hide his doubts and fears.

Baxter, a handsome man with a chiseled profile only sneered. He reached out and handed Fernell a silk handkerchief.

"You're sweating like a pig. Here, clean yourself up."

"Yes, sir." He clutched at the silk scrap and mopped his face. It was weird, but Baxter did not seem to have aged a day since the last time Fernell had seen him. And that had been many years ago. Then again, the old boy was rich enough to afford any kind of counter-aging treatment out there. The perks of the high and mighty.

"Johnson, crank up the air back here."

"Yes, sir." The chauffeur obeyed, adjusting a cool stream of air, even as he wheeled the big auto onto the empty street.

Fernell watched them roll out of the city. "Where are we going, sir? If I may ask?"

Baxter, his hair a tawny brown with errand streaks of gray turned and looked at the beefy Fernell. "All will be explained shortly, Daryl. Be so good as to keep your mouth shut."

"Ah..er..yes, sir. I'm sorry if I..er.." Finding a small ounce of will, Fernell clamped his mouth close. For his reward, Baxter once again offered his stony profile in silence. The nervous accountant sat back into the padded leather seat and began twisting the piece of wet silk in his pudgy hands. Outside the dark city was left behind and soon the small hills of Riverhead began to rise under the moonless sky ahead.

Half an hour later the Rolls snaked its way up a long and twisting private drive that led to the abandoned grounds of the Excelsior Academy for Boys. There, in the center of a six building complex, the auto came to a stop beside four other such vehicles. Fernell came out the back door looking for human activity and found very little. Each of the expensive chariots was manned by a lone driver, none of which bothered to greet the arrival of Baxter's car. There were no lights in the buildings themselves, although floodlights affixed to a series of poles skirted the huge front campus.

"Isn't this your old alma mater?" Fernell said, thoughtlessly forgetting his orders. Baxter, coming out of the other side, with Johnson holding the door, looked over at him and brought his finger to his lips to remind him.

"Oh, sorry," the round man whispered, hoping he hadn't upset his boss. Whatever the hell was going on, he knew it was prudent to simply play along. Sooner or later Baxter would have to tell him what this was all about. He had to. Or so Fernell's rational mind reasoned.

Baxter told his chauffeur to wait and then signaled to Fernell. "Come along, Mr. Fernell. We've a short walk ahead of us." Fernell hurried to keep up with him, as Baxter started up a small dirt path that went off away from the buildings and into the wooded hills beyond.

They had reached the tree line when a taxi came racing up the drive and came to a screeching halt in the parking area. Both men turned to look as a very agitated man jumped out and handed the angry driver a wad of bills. Then adjusting his bowler hand, the man, swinging an ivory handled umbrella, raced up to join them.

"You are late, Hiram," Baxter all but snapped. Fernell could see his displeasure even in the faint light of the lamps behind them.

"It couldn't be helped," the other man replied and Fernell instantly recognized him as being Hiram Woodbridge, another millionaire recluse. And if his memory was right, another famous alumnus of this very academy. What was it the press called this group of royal tycoons? Oh, yes, the Ivy League. He knew stories about their rather odd reunions. It seemed he was about to witness one up close.

Baxter accepted Woodbridge's tardiness without further comment and once again started off along the path. Woodbridge motioned for Fernell to go second and then took the rear.

As they marched along the incline, the accountant was puzzled by Woodbridge's appearance. For a man supposedly in his sixties, he looked damn fit, almost youthful. Maybe he and Baxter belonged to the same health club. Fernell made a mental note to check that out later. If any kind of program could guarantee the kind of vigor these old farts seemed to possess, he very much wanted to look into it. Of course he'd have to shed a few pounds and get back into shape first. Even now the small slope they were crossing was an effort for his overweight body. He prayed they wouldn't be going much further.

Cresting the hill, the trio looked down on a small orchard of apple trees at the center of which was a blazing campfire. Around the burning stack of wood were four men, all richly attired like Baxter and Woodbridge. As they neared the fire, Fernell noted the sorry condition of the orchard around them. The drought of the past few weeks had taken its toll and most of the fruit trees looked withered and dead. Which was why the massive bulk near the blaze was so impressive. The tree was a huge, leaf covered monster rising there in the midst of its skeletal brethren.

A big fat, giant of a tree surrounded by a dying, dried up orchard. Fernell suddenly remembered the story of the dream-speaker Joseph from the bible. How Joseph, while in an Egyptian prison, had been called to interpret the Pharaoh's nightmarish visions. One in particular dealt with a group of seven fat cows devouring seven emaciated cows. Having heard the story as an impressionable child, Fernell now recalled the imaginary image of that bovine cannibalism when looking at the single, healthy tree before him. It gave him the creeps.

As they joined the men around the fire, Fernell recognized them as well. Peter Ambrose, Darren Goodhardt, Stephen Bennett and James Chambers. The remaining members of the so called Ivy League club. There was a fifth person standing behind the quartet as they welcomed Baxter and Woodbridge but Fernell couldn't make him out. No one paid him any attention and he felt as if he were purposely being ignored. Typical of the snooty rich, he thought. Still, he kept trying to see who it was hiding in the background near the bole of the massive tree that still unnerved him.

Fernell realized that the businessmen were holding small tin cups in there hands and cut into the tree was a tap to collect a clear, thick sap into an old steel bucket affixed to the bark. Now that was really weird, as Fernell knew most sap trees only ran in early spring. This was late summer. It should have been impossible for sap to flow now.

Somewhere in the woods beyond an owl cried "WHOO!" and Fernell jumped nervously. Nope, wrong question, he thought. Rather what, as in what the hell was going on here?

As if in answer to his mental quandary, the gathered

millionaires moved aside and the mysterious fifth person stepped forth into the firelight. Considering the bizarre tone of the entire evening, Fernell was not the least bit amazed by the fellow's appearance. Here was a small little oriental chap dressed in what appeared to be loose, dirty gray pajamas and his feet were bare. Small of frame, the man was bald, his skinned dried like worn leather and his head was centered by two almond shaped green eyes. Except for those orbs, the man looked ancient.

So exotic was the old man's face, it was near impossible to guess his lineage. At first Fernell had thought him Chinese, but upon a closer inspection, recognized a different strain to the man's cheeks, nose and temple. Eurasian perhaps. Even Mongolian?

The small man bowed to the newcomers then held up two tin cups to them. One each to Baxter and Woodbridge.

"Ah, Jararo," Baxter bowed slightly, reaching out for the cup. "It is good to see you again."

The diminutive fellow merely folded his leather like hands into the voluminous sleeves of his tunic and giggled a high pitched keen, "Heee, heee, heee." Fernell loosened his tie unnerved. This close to the fire, the night's heat was doubled.

Baxter and Woodbridge brought the tin cups to their lips and swallowed their contents. As Woodbridge was lowering his container, Fernell spotted a drop of pasty liquid on the edge of his bottom lips and realized it was the tree sap. They had each swallowed tree sap. Weirder and weirder.

"I see by your look of consternation, Mr. Fernell, that you are fairly bursting with curiosity." Baxter smiled coldly.

"Well, yes sir, I suppose I am."

"Then it is time you were told what this is all about." Baxter looked at the others. "Are we agreed?"

There was a unanimous nodding of heads and Baxter stepped closer to the accountant, continuing his narrative.

"I am sure you recognize our fellow school alumni?"

"Of course, Mr. Baxter."

Baxter patted his shoulder. "Good. That simplifies matters greatly. You see, Fernell, all of us came to Excelsior many, many years ago. All of us at the time, bright and eager young neophytes ready to take on the world. Sometime during our senior year, Mr. Jararo arrived to take the position of grounds keeper."

At the mention of his name, the odd man giggled again.

"Hee,hee,hee."

"He was truly an amazing man," Baxter went on. "He is a student of oriental sciences regarding the botanical. The so called secrets of nature. Mr. Jararo brought with him the tree you now see before you. At the time it was a mere sapling, but under his loving care, it has grown to this fine, arboreal stature.

"Prior to our graduation, Mr. Jararo informed a handful of us, the members of this fraternal order, about the tree's amazing ability to produce a life sustaining elixir."

"The sap!" Fernell blurted out.

"Excellent, Fernell. Glad to see you are paying attention."

Fernell beamed. Maybe this wasn't so bad after all.

"Indeed, the sap of this particular tree contains certain chemicals found nowhere else in the world. Chemicals that effectively retard the aging process. Of course, at the time we learned of this, we were all of us, skeptical. I mean, imagine it, a group of young boys, at the prime of their physical well being, learning of such a potion. Why it was pure fantasy, we thought. Still, Mr. Jararo invited us to sample a single taste before our departure.

"We acquiesced. What was the harm? Ah, that fateful night, all of us decked out in our caps and gowns, rushing out here to taste the first yield from the Source. That is how he refers to her, Fernell." Baxter pointed up at the tree.

"She is the Source. Well, I could go on and on, but let's cut to the chase here. Five years later, all of us returned for a school orchestrated reunion and discovered, much to our complete amazement, that none of us had noticeably aged. Whereas our classmates were clearly five years older. Of course it was too early in the process for anyone to stumble on to our secret. It was thought that the six of us were merely more energetic in our personal health care, blah, blah, blah.

"We had no such illusion. On that night, we met here and took our second taste of the tree. As we have been doing now for well over seventy-five years."

Fernell wanted to rub his eyes. Seventy-five years! He quickly did the arithmetic in his mind. Considering they would have been seventeen or eighteen upon graduation, that would mean each of these men had to be ninety-three years old!! It was fantastic.

"Ah, I see you grasp the significance of all of this, old boy." Baxter went on. "Good. You see, Fernell, it is important you understand exactly what this is all about.

"None of us harbors any ill will towards you in the least."

"Ill will?" Fernell blinked. Had he heard correctly? "I don't understand, sir."

"Of course you don't, dear boy. Let me explain. We know you've been embezzling the firm to the tune of several hundred thousand dollars annually."

Fernell gasped. "No! That's not true!"

"Ta, ta, sir. Please don't waste time with silly denials. We've had independent auditors inspecting your records for several months. We know about your secret bank account and villa in Mexico City. I must say, when you steal, Mr. Fernell, you do it with panache."

They knew everything. Fernell's ample stomach rumbled and he thought he was going to be sick. Exposure had never once entered his greedy, criminal mind.

"Alas, we simply cannot allow you to continue in this fashion."

"Look, I'm sorry. Really. I'll pay it back. Please. Just don't call the police. The scandal would destroy my family."

"Police? Why, you misunderstand me, sir. We are not going to say a word about this to the authorities."

"You're not?"

"No. You see, Mr. Fernell your crime has, in its own way, provided us with a useful purpose. You see, the tree, that is, the Source, has certain requirements to maintain its continued growth. More than the normal sunshine and rain. As you can see, it is clearly much healthier than the rest of the trees about us."

Fernell could only stand there. He had no idea where Baxter's lecture was going. He felt nauseous.

"The Source requires a special nutrient, my dear chap." At that, the oriental man pulled his hands from his sleeves and with them two long, elegant paper fans. These he flipped open with a quick, easy twist of his wrists. He held them out at arms length and Fernell saw that their tips sparkled in the fire's glow. Fernell squinted. The tines on each fan were capped.

Suddenly Mr. Jararo sprung forth and slapped one of his fans across Fernell's face. He screamed and fell back, his cheek suddenly stinging with hurt and wet. His fingers felt the twin cuts and with horror he examined the blood pouring forth. It came to him instantly. Razor blades. The fans were edged with thin, sharp razors.

He looked around him and saw only cold, determined faces. He took another step back only to have a hand grab him by the nape of the neck, jerk him off his feet and propel him forward towards the fire. He barely managed to retain his balance, twisting his frightened face around to see Hiram Woodbridge staring at him like an evil scarecrow.

"Oh, I forgot to mention something else. Repeated dosages have added to our stamina and strength? Each of us possesses the power of an Olympic athlete."

The circle moved in closer.

Jarora struck again. Fernell threw up his hands to hide his face. There was an awful pain and three of his fingers were neatly severed. He screamed, his voice reaching a fever pitch.

"Blood, Mr. Fernell," he heard Baxter's voice droning on through his screams. "The Source requires blood."

The fans were coming for him again and again and again.

Lacy Chavez paced back and forth across the linoleum aisle in front of the Emergency room's nurses station. Still attired in her Cleopatra costume, she made quite a picture with her silk see-through pants, red pumps and bronze halter-top. Never mind the asp shaped gold band that encircled her head. Orderlies and nurses alike had a hard time ignoring the black beauty as she stormed up and down, nervously biting her nails and looking towards the double doors that led to surgery.

She and Bennie Morton had followed the ambulance in Bennie's car and had rushed in only minutes after attendants had wheeled the still unconscious Dolores through to gray doors. Now Lacy paced and Bennie sat on a plastic chair in the waiting area sipping on tepid coffee from a vending machine.

"God, Lacy, will you sit down and be still?" It was the fifth time in the last twenty minutes he had tried to make her stop and sit down. He didn't really expect this new urging would work any better. It didn't. Lacy just turned her head to him and made a face.

The wide, glass doors to the emergency entrance slid open and two uniformed cops walked through. They saw Lacy and approached her. The lead uniform was older and wore several chevrons on his sleeve. He removed his cap before speaking and Bennie, still unnoticed, appreciated the gesture. Somebody with manners. Now there was a novelty in Cape Noire.

"Miss, are you with the girl they brought in from the Sexcat?"

That stopped Lacy. She pulled a fingernail out of her mouth and hugged herself. "Yes, I am. I'm Lacy Chavez. I do Cleopatra."

The cop raised a whimsical eyebrow and smiled. "Yes, I see that. Can you give me the name of the young lady who was assaulted?" He pulled a notebook and pen from his shirt pocket.

"Her name is Dolores Desire," Bennie offered and he joined them by the desk. The sergeant turned and his look implied the question. "I'm Bennie Morton. I'm the assistant club manager. I was there when it all happened."

"I see? And how long ago was that exactly?"

"Gee, I'm not too sure. Maybe a half-hour? Why don't you ask the Brunette. She came in the ambulance with Dolores."

The sergeant looked around. "What Brunette?"

"She was something else," Bennie explained. "She was talking with Dolores in the alley behind the club when that weirdo showed up. Hell, she even plugged him."

"She shot him?"

"You bet. Not that it did any good, mind you. But blam, right in the chest, with a .45. Saw the whole thing."

Now the two cops were definitely interested. The young one spoke up for the first time. "Where is she? This Brunette with the .45?"

"Gee," Bennie thought aloud. "She was right here a minute ago."

"I think she went to the lady's room," Lacy said pointing to the corner behind her. "It's just around there to your right."

The senior cop put away his pad and turned to his young partner. "Wait here and stay sharp."

He then walked around the corner with his hand falling to the butt of his own revolver. The public rest rooms were only a few yards away. Quickly he walked over to the door marked WOMEN and reached out with his left hand. Suddenly the door opened from the inside and out walked a very startled, familiar brunette with glasses.

"Why Sgt. Sprague, I never would have figured you for the little girl's room?"

"Sally Paige!" Every cop knew the dark haired dynamo from the Tribune. "What are you doing here?"

"Hey, who's the reporter here? You or me?"

Sprague stepped past her and shoved the door wide.

"Is there anybody else in there?"

"Huh, uh, Sarge. Just me. So tell me, what gives? Is this about the stripper from the Sexcat?"

The cop let the door close. "And what do you know about that?"

"Not a whole lot as yet, but I catch up quick. I was on my way home for the night when I saw the ambulance leaving the front of the club with a good size crowd gathered there. Figured there was a story in it and followed."

Sgt. Sprague considered her explanation was solid enough. He started back for the nurse's station. Paige fell in step beside him, pulling her own notebook from her shoulder purse.

"So, come on, Sarge. What gives here? Did one of the girls get shot? Or stabbed? Was it some crazed customer losing his sanity? Was it a crime of passion?"

"Sheesh, Paige, give it a rest, will yah. Me and my partner just got here ourselves."

When they reached desk, the others gave Paige a once over.

"Who the hell are you?" Lacy asked directly.

"Sally Paige. I'm with the Cape Noire Tribune. And what might your name be, huh..Cleopatra?"

The young cop moved over to Sprague. "What about the gun packing Brunette?"

"Gone. She split. These two say anything else?"

"Only that the perp was some kind of rich dude who'd started coming around a few days ago. He was giving this Dolores girl lots of expensive gifts."

Paige's news ear was picking up the dialogue fast. She started scribbling into her notepad. "Does anybody have a name on this sugar daddy?"

"Oh, yeah," Lacy chimed in. "His name is Hi..."

The portal to surgery flew open and a tired looking doctor came out removing his surgical mask. Everyone standing by the desk stopped talking and waited for him to say something. Lacy had no such patience. She pushed the two cops aside and confronted the doctor.

"Well, how is she? Is she going to make it?"

The doctor smoothed his thinning gray hair and answered, "I think so. Miss Desire suffered a severe concussion. There was fluid build up which we were able to drain and relieve the swelling. Pending no further complication, I think, with a few days of bed rest, she is going to fine."

Lacy threw herself onto the doctor, wrapping her arms around his neck and planting a long, loud kiss on him. "Oh, thank you, thank you, thank you."

His cheeks turning beet red, the doctor politely peeled her arms off his neck. "Er..yes. You are quite welcome."

Paige turned to Bennie, her reporter's instinct still very much attuned. "The name of the guy who did this?"

Bennie tore his gaze from Lacy and the doc. "What? Oh, right. It was Woodbridge, I think. Hiram Woodbridge. Yeah, that's it."

"Holy smokes!" Paige mouthed, recalling her earlier conversation with Hank Anderson.

"Do you know that name?" Sgt. Sprague inquired, his own interest still pressing.

"Oh, you bet I do, Sarge," Paige replied with a Mona Lisa grin. "And so do a whole lot of other people in this town!"

She started writing again.

Bobby Crandall had just managed to slip his hand under the cigarette girl's blouse and was fondling a very round breast when the door to the cloakroom opened.

"Hey, Blackjack? You in here?"

Paula jerked away breaking their tongue-lock as well as removing the bra-covered treasure from his grasp.

"Yeah!" the young, freckled faced card dealer snapped angrily, turning his head to see the senior pitman, Larry Miles, standing there. Miles had a canary-eating grin on his long, horse like face.

"What?"

"There's a call for you on phone. Guy says it's urgent."

Looking back at Paula, now hidden by the hanging coats, as she straightened her tight, skimpy costume. Her fingers nimbly buttoning her blouse, her lipstick slightly smudged.

"Sorry," he whispered. Paula gave him a hasty kiss, then rushed out without giving Miles a passing look.

Watching her go, Crandall cursed his bad luck. There went weeks of coaxing and flirting. Paula Wozcheski had become widowed several months ago and was just now starting to come around to his advances.

"Thanks a lot, asshole!" He shoved past Miles who was having a hard time controlling his laughter.

"Hey, I was just trying to do you a favor. Besides, a friendly word of warning, Blackjack, don't let the boss catch you diddling on his time."

"Yeah, yeah." Bobby made his way through the almost deserted Gray Owl casino to the front lobby. After midnight was always a slow time in the joint but with the current heat wave, the place had as much life as morgue.

He saw the dangling receiver in the middle of the five mounted phones and pulled it up to his ear. Only then did he think about who would be calling him at this late hour.

"Hello."

"Bobby." Brother Bones. Shit. Just once it could have been somebody... hell, anybody else but his nocturnal employer.

"What's up?"

"I have an errand for you to run tomorrow morning."

"Okay. What's the deal?"

"Drive out to Riverhead. I wish you to investigate an old boy's school long abandoned."

"Yah. So what am I looking for out there?"

"Evil. Bobby Crandall. And pray it doesn't find you first."

At the very same time, at the Excelsior School for Boys, the members of the Ivy League were departing the grounds. Walking together, Charles Baxter turned to his oldest friend, Hiram Woodbridge, and offered him a ride back into Cape Noire.

Minutes later, the Rolls was moving silently along the highway, Johnson, the black giant at the wheel. In the rear, Baxter puffed slowly on a Cuban cigar while, Woodbridge, staring straight ahead finished recounting his earlier confrontation at the Sexcat. Thick cigar smoke wafted out of Baxter's partially opened window.

"What is wrong with you?" Baxter asked his displeasure clearly evident. "You are jeopardizing everything we have worked for all these long years."

"A house of cards, Charles. Built on shadows with absolutely no substance whatsoever."

"What about power? Does that count for nothing?"

"You call this power? This living in the shadows of society, never able to lead normal lives for fear of exposure."

"Normal lives, bah!" Baxter all but spit out the words. "We are the richest men on the planet. We control billions. Leaders of the world jump when we snap our fingers. And we are virtually immortal. I consider that everything."

Woodbridge turned to Baxter and opened his jacket where the bullet had ripped through the cloth. "Immortality at what cost, Charles? I was shot and there was not a single drop of blood. What kind of monsters are we becoming? For God's sake man, we don't even bleed!"

"Enough of this, Hiram. All of us have put up far too long with these self-serving, reckless deeds of yours. Do you understand me? I am now speaking for the group. We demand you cease these shenanigans at once."

"Meaning exactly what?"

"Do not return to your hotel suite. It is a sure bet the police will seek you out once the girl, or one of her friends, identify you. Find somewhere else to stay until you can straighten it all out."

"And how am I do that?"

"Hiram, you were intimate with her. She is now a threat to the group and must be eliminated."

"No. I won't do it. I love her."

Baxter turned on Woodbridge and brought the glowing end of his cigar up to his face.

"There is no such thing. Do you understand me, Hiram? Make no mistakes about this. You take care of the girl or else you will be excluded from the group. Permanently."

"You wouldn't dare!"

Looking over the red-hot ash, Baxter's eyes were hard and demonic. "Do not mistake friendship for weakness. The group will be protected no matter what the cost."

Baxter sat back, rolled down his window and threw away his cigar. The earthy tobacco smell lingered between them for the remainder of the ride back to the city. Neither said another word.

The temperature had risen to ninety-five degrees Fahrenheit by ten-o-clock the next morning. Wearing a short sleeve shirt and slacks, Bobby Crandall felt as if he were roasting like a peanut in a street vendor's cart. He had walked around the deserted grounds of the Excelsior School for Boys twice and for his efforts found zip. As he made his way back to the parking area, he pulled his shades off and wiped sweat from his face with a pocket handkerchief.

He also cursed Bones for the hundredth time. What the blazes did Mr. Undead expect him to find out here? The place was locked up tight, the windows boarded up. By the dust and cobwebs, it was clear there hadn't been any activity in this place in years.

Still, there was one troubling element Crandall just couldn't ignore. Upon arrival, he had noted that the surface of the cracked and pitted concrete was laced with recent tire tracks. Like fine dirt lines, they painted an abstract image that testified to recent visitors. Within the last few days, if his eyesight wasn't failing completely.

Okay. So there was the puzzle. Cars had come up to the place but the buildings looked untouched. Crandall moved along the sidewalk path to its end by the brown, pathetic field beyond. His mouth was dry and he began thinking how good a cold beer would taste.

Bobby didn't like being out in daylight. It just wasn't natural for a nighthawk. People like Crandall worked the city's night scene because they liked the twilight world. Most days he'd sleep most of the morning away, have a late lunch and go to the job just before dusk. This being about under a grueling sun was no fun.

He spotted the path immediately and upon closer inspection, the faint outline of footprints. He looked up toward the hill and sighed. What the hell? Might as well do a thorough job it and make like Daniel Boone. He did not feel like getting Bones' tempter up.

Over the rise, he spotted the skeletal orchard and finally the remains of the campfire from the previous night. The charcoal chunks were still warm when he knelt down and touched them. What kind of idiots had a fire during a heat-wave? He continued to inspect the area but it was only when he stepped completely into the shadow of the big tree did he realize its size and difference.

Cautiously he moved in towards the bole. His right foot sank into wetness and he froze. Looking down, he cursed aloud. "What the fuc..? What the hell is mud doing here?" He backed up, shaking his foot to clean of the bits of sticky dirt. Annoyed, he crouched down and looked at the soft spot where he had stepped. Gingerly he reached down and touched the wetness with his index finger. Bobby was no medical expert, but one quick sniff of his fingertip and the redness of the soil were enough to convince him.

"Blood."

Suddenly something white emerged out of the gory mud at his feet. He thought it was a grub worm. It wiggled and rose further out of the earth, its round, twisted form moving jerkily towards him. It was a tree root and it was now slithering towards his shoe. Bobby stepped back, his nerves totally frayed. He rubbed the bloody finger against his pants and moved further away from the extending root. It was almost a foot long.

Ground soaked with blood and roots that moved as if they were alive. He had seen enough. Hurrying back to his car, Bobby mused at how in-tuned to the supernatural Brother Bones was. Once again, from a great distance, he had divined the macabre. What it could all mean, the young gambler didn't have a clue. That was the boss's deal. Now, he was simply anxious to get home and give his report.

And to finally get out of the damn, hot sun.

Seated in the darkness of his inner sanctum, Brother Bones listened as Bobby Crandall finished his account of what he had found at the old academy on Riverhead.

The window curtains were drawn tight, as Bones detested daylight for his own particular reasons. When not out on the streets scourging miscreants, the agent of death preferred solitude and quiet. This room was the only place Bones did not wear his ivory, skull shaped mask. A fact Bobby was all too aware of us. Not that he was unfamiliar with the true face of his master rather he was all too personal with it. It was the face of a murderer who had come very close to ending his life. Now it was the face of dead man. A dead man who still walked the earth.

Bobby was grateful Bones demanded darkness.

"Remove your shoe," Bones said.

"Huh..my shoe?"

"Yes, the one with the mud on it. Set it on the table and then get a candle."

Crandall had worked for the ghoulish avenger long enough to accept his often eccentric requests. He lifted his right leg, slipped of the shoe and set it on the small card table at the room's center. Then he hastened to the kitchen pantry to find a candle and matches. When he returned, Bones had donned his mask and was standing beside the table holding his shoe.

"Good. Now set the candle down and light it."

Bobby complied and as the small flame hungrily fed on the air about it, a soft glow ballooned over them. Bones, holding the footwear in both hands, had it upside down to reveal the dried, dirty coating. Using his fingers, he pinched of a piece and holding it over the flickering flame, ground it to a powder.

"Now let us see what blood will tell us?"

As the mud dust hit the fire, the flame burst outward and swelled into a fiery, orange and yellow shimmer. Bobby, his eyes squinting, backed away, holding his hands up from the intense blaze. Bones stood unmoving, his gaze never wavering from the occult torch. Then, as if drawn from deep within its core, the fireball produced the image of a face. It was the anguished shell of a man in agony, his mouth wide with a scream drowned in the bowels of hell.

Then the fireball dimmed and within seconds all that remained over the tiny candle flame was a wispy, quickly vanishing haze.

Bones handed the shoe back to Crandall. "It is as I suspected. There was murder of the foulest kind."

"Yeah, so does that mean we've got another case?" Bobby held the edge of the table and put his shoe back on, his voice still shaken by the suffering soul he had just seen in the occult fire.

"Yes, but I need more. Go out and get a copy of the morning paper. Bring it to me."

"Okay. Anything else?"

"Yes. Go to the nearest hardware story and buy a can of kerosene."

"Kerosene? You planning on starting a fire?"

"Yes. We must exorcise the roots of this evil."

"Right. Whatever you say. Maybe I should get an axe while I'm at it?"

"Yes. Do so. But make sure it is sharp, very, very sharp."

By late afternoon the weatherman on the radio had promised rain was on the way. He just didn't promise exactly when. As the station went back to big-band music,

Sally Paige lowered the volume and took a swallow from her tall glass of ice tea.

Maintenance was still working on the air-conditioner. Yeah, right, and the Cape Noire Bats would win the World Series any day now. Laughing to herself, she began to pound away at her typewriter just as the phone on her desk jangled.

"Paige, who's calling?" She spoke loudly to beat out the cacophony of the noise around here. Newspaper city rooms were anything but quiet.

"Huh, huh," she said after a few minutes. "Thanks. I owe you one, Sarge. Right, keep me posted."

She was cradling the receiver as Hank Anderson materialized in front of her desk. He was holding the paper's morning edition, with her small feature on the lower front half.

"Nice piece on the Sexcat incident, Paige."

"Thanks, Boss."

"What's the follow up?"

"A dead end, I think," she nodded to her phone. "That was my contact at Police Central. The boys in blue didn't get around to Woodbridge until late mid-morning. He had a suite of rooms at the Columbia."

"Let me guess, they we're too late, he'd already skipped town."

"Bingo. Night clerk said he checked out around two in the A.M. and that's that."

Anderson fished a cigar out of his shirt pocket and waved it like a baton. "What about the stripper he assaulted?"

"Dolores Desire," Paige looked down at her notebook. "I called the hospital this morning. They say she's out of danger and doing okay. But they want to keep her for another day just to be sure."

"Okay. Give the girl a rest and then go see her first thing tomorrow."

"That was the plan."

"Right. Okay, stick with it. You did good last night, following that ambulance. You've got the nose, kid."

Caught flatfooted by the unexpected praise, Paige put down her notepad and grinned. "Thanks, Boss. Now about that raise I was…"

Anderson threw his hands up in the air and took off grumbling. "Reporters!! Can't give them a lousy compliment without them getting their hands in your pockets. My mother always said I should have been a doctor. Then all I'd have to do is cut up people. Now there's a job with instant gratification."

Lightning continued to stitch the purple sky like a maddened weaver, creating an elaborate aerial quilt as the night descended. The temperature fell to a balmy seventy and the day people went home to their sanctuaries.

By ten o'clock, things on the fifth floor of St. Mary's Hospital were still under the glare of the overhead florescent lights. The desk nurse, an experienced staffer was making her rounds of the ward when the elevator at the far end of the corridor opened its door. A tall man holding a cane and bowler had stepped out and seeing the nurse, smiled politely.

"I a relative of Miss Dolores Desire."

"She's in room five-ten, but I'm afraid visiting hours are over."

The man made a worried face then transferring his cane to his left hand, hit the nurse with his right. She fell unconscious into his arms and he quickly carried her into what appeared to be an empty room. Gently dropping her on the unoccupied bed, he whispered an apology for his rudeness and then exited, closing the door behind him.

Back in the hall, Hiram Woodbridge proceeded to the door marked 510.

As he started to push the door inward, a familiar voice stopped him. "Now that wasn't very nice, Mr. Woodbridge."

The Brunette in the trench coat and fedora from the club stepped out from around the corner. Her hands were filled with two identical automatics.

"You certainly do have a problem with manners, don't you?"

Woodbridge stepped away from the door and faced off with his opponent. "You again."

"Yes, I am quite the nuisance, aren't I?"

"Oh, you are much more than that, young lady. You have no idea what you've gotten yourselves involved with here."

"Maybe not, Woodbridge, but I'll be damned if I'm going to let you waltz through life thinking you can manhandle people any time you have an urge to do so."

"Is that all you think this is about? That I'm some kind of rich spoiled dandy out to have a good time."

"Isn't it?"

Woodbridge shook his head in resignation. "To a certain point, I suppose you are right. But there are other things at play in all of this. My feelings for Dolores for one. I really do care for her."

"You have a funny way of showing it, Woodbridge."

"I have no time for this," he pointed his cane at her pistols. "Those didn't stop me last time. What makes you think they will now?"

The Brunette realized too late his words were a faint as Woodbridge suddenly whipped his round hat towards her face. The Brunette instinctively raised both guns and fired, ripping the bowler apart with deafening blasts. It was all the diversion Woodbridge required as he flung himself off the opposite wall and rushed her.

The Brunette spun around, her mind reeling at how fast he moved. It was uncanny. Then before she could squeeze off another shot, his cane slapped against her shoulder and sent her careening backwards. There was a window behind her and she hit with the back of her head.

Woodbridge was on her fast. The Brunette fired again, but her shots went wild to either side of the enraged attacker. Using his cane like a sword, he hit both her wrist in quick succession, knocking her guns away effortlessly. As they clattered to the floor, he pushed her back against the window pane, dislodging her fedora. The cane came up under her throat as he applied pressure.

The Brunette snarled. Nose to nose, Woodbridge returned the sneer. "You really are quite beautiful, aren't you. Too bad such beauty has to be wasted like this, but it was of your own choosing."

With that he continued to push and the Brunette felt the glass shattering behind her. It would break in a second and she would tumble through a heartbeat later on her way to the hard concrete five stories below.

Then a specter, big and black rose up behind Woodbridge and something metallic caught the glimmer of the overhead lights. The Brunette's eyes registered the act. It was her mind that had trouble believing.

The axe in Brother Bones' hands bit into Hiram Woodbridge's neck at the collar with a loud wack! He cried out, his hold on the Brunette immediately released. Savagely Bones yanked the axe head free and liquid gushed out. The Brunette blinked. It was clear. It wasn't blood at all!

Woodbridge turned slowly, his hands reaching up to his ruined neck just as the avenger of dark justice raised his arms again. Seeing Bones and the axe, Woodbridge screamed just before the blade swooped down and cut off his head. It bounced off the corner wall and then hit the floor and rolled several yards before coming to a stop in front of the nurse's station.

Meanwhile the headless torso took several steps away from the Brunette, its arms whipping around frantically in search of direction. Then, as if finally accepting its fate, the body dropped to the floor, pasty ichors seeping from its open neck.

"What the hell is going on out here?" The door nearest the desk opened and from it emerged a heavyset woman with glasses. "This is suppose to be a goddamn hospital!"

Mrs. Bernard Atwater, a forty year old patient awaiting surgery to remove ingrown toenails, looked across the hall at the decapitated head of Hiram Woodbridge. Then she turned and saw Brother Bones, axe in hand with the headless corpse at his feet and she fainted.

Bones turned to the Brunette as she bent down to scoop up her guns. "Are you alright?"

"Yes, thanks to you, Bones."

She holstered the pistols and then brushed back her long, dark tresses. "That wasn't blood in his vein, was it?"

"This is no longer your concern. I suggest you depart immediately if you do not wish to deal with the police. They will be here soon."

Brother Bones handed the Brunette her fedora.

"Right. Word on the street is you use to be one of the Bone Brothers that worked for Topper Wylde."

The white ivory mask under the slouch hat was incapable of revealing anything. It was a shield she could appreciate.

"Don't always believe what you hear on the streets."

As the Brunette adjusted her hat, Bones disappeared around the corner, axe in hand like some mad woodsman. She could hear other patients moving about and knew the avenger's parting advice was sound. She raced to the stairwell to make her own speedy retreat. There would be time to sort things out later.

Bobby Crandall dropped the five-gallon can of kerosene in front of the giant tree and stretched his back in an arch. "Damn, but if I had to carry that any further, I'd have a hernia for sure."

Forty-five minutes after picking up Brother Bones at the hospital rear entrance, Crandall had driven them to the Riverhead site. Then he lifted the kerosene from the trunk and they'd made the five-minute hike to the orchard under a starless, black sky.

Bones had led the way holding a lantern in his left hand while the right hefted the gore smeared axe. Crandall, upon seeing the residue on the blade, did not bother to ask how things had gone back at the hospital. The gore was enough.

"Get on with it, Crandall. This is unholy ground and it is not wise to tarry overly long when dealing with such forces."

"Sure, sure. Just give me a minute to catch my breath is all. Okay?"

Holding the lantern high, Brother Bones moved around the huge arbor, light ripples sliding over his sleek mask.

"There is much evil in this nature. It is like nothing I have ever felt before."

Bobby, ignoring Bones' remarks, ripped off the tab to the round steel can and once again lifted it off the ground. He began to pour the contents over the base of the tree and circled it as he did so. Brother Bones backed away to allow him sufficient room to splash the ignitable liquid.

"Continue to widen your circle so that the kerosene will soak into the very roots around the trunk."

"Right. God, this stuff smells to high heaven."

"Be careful not to get it on your clothes or shoes."

"Thanks for the concern." Crandall, now moving in larger circles, stopped and looked beyond the lantern's light. "Did you hear that?"

Brother Bones raised the lantern higher to extend its glow. A tinny laughter reached his ears.

"Hee,hee,hee,hee." A small figure detached itself from the night gloom and entered the light. Jiraro, still dressed in his loose cotton garb, casually approached them, his hands hidden in the folds of his sleeves. The light played off his tiny, button size eyes.

"Who the hell is that?" Bobby asked, setting down the now empty container.

"Be wary!" Bones warned tightening his grip on the axe shaft.

Jiraro continued to get closer, a thin smile on his yellow face.

"Halt," Bones commanded. "I know what you are, witchman. Come no closer!"

At that, Jiraro did stop and looking at Brother Bones, laughed again. "Hee,hee,hee,hee."

"What is he?" Bobby whispered, still cautious of the unexpected intruder.

"A Burmese witchman. Their skills in the black arts are legendary."

Jiraro pulled his hands from their concealment and revealed the paper fans each held. With a flick, the fans opened and he went after Crandall. Bobby fell backwards under the attack, yelling as razor tips tore through his shirt and cut the skin beneath.

Brother Bones dropped the lantern and lifting the heavy axe with both hands, set after the oriental killer. But Jiraro was ready for him.

Forgetting the cringing boy for a moment, the witchman spun around waving his arms towards the massive tree, uttered guttural incantations at the oncoming avenger. Just as Bones was about to throw the axe, a thick branch dropped down and slapped it out of his grasp. It fell useless to the dry earth. All the while a second, larger limb reached out and encircled his body from behind. Before he could react, Bones was lifted off his feet and jerked upward into the twisting maze of the great tree.

"AAGHH!" he cried, as the snake like member tightened around his middle. Unless he could break free quickly, the possessed tree would crush him into a second death. If that were at all possible.

Crandall, witnessing Bones' plight, ignored his own predicament and grabbed the empty gas can. He hurled it at the foreign shaman only to have Jiraro, by some magical sixth sense, twist his body out of its path at the last second. Laughing his grating cackle, the yellow man returned his attention to the bleeding lad.

Bobby threw up his hands to protect his face as the fans descended on him for a second time. The dozen razors ripped the sleeves of his jacket to shreds.

High above, twisting in the clutches of the unholy tree, Brother Bones struggled to reach his guns. As he did so, several new branches began wrapping themselves around his kicking legs. A third, smaller limb slid menacingly around his neck. He would never reach his guns in time.

"Hee,hee,hee,hee,heee.."

BLAM! BLAM!

The gunshots shattered all other sounds. The first bullet took Jiraro in the side of the neck, punching through completely with a spray of blood and bone. The second, coming a second later tore off the crown his forehead.

Looking up through his folded arms, Bobby saw the killer's eyes go blank in their sockets and the man died as he collapsed.

At the exact time Jiraro's heart stop beating, the arcane tree lost its animation and a released Bones fell ten feet to the hard ground. Dazed, he looked to the path as the trench coat Brunette stepped forth, her smoking automatics still aimed at the witchman.

"You!"

"You were expecting somebody else?"

"How?"

"Saw you drive away from the hospital and figured there was still another chapter left in this story so I jumped in my car and followed you.

I guess I was right."

"Then we are even," Bones intoned, getting to his feet and brushing dirt from his coat. Bobby Crandall joined them, eying the Brunette with both gratitude and curiosity.

"Lady, I don't know who you are, but I think I love you."

The Brunette used one of her guns to indicate the state of his clothes and the blood smears. "Curb your passion, Romeo, until you get yourself patched up. You look like you just went fifteen rounds with a meat grinder."

"I feel that way." Crandall looked back to the body of the diminutive assassin. "I ain't ever seen anything like those fans of his. And I hope I never do again."

Brother Bones put a hand on his shoulder. "Come, let us finish what we came here to do."

The Brunette put her guns away, as Bobby went to get the fallen lantern. "I take it you're going to torch the thing?"

"That is the plan."

"How did it pick you up like that? Was it some kind of magic?"

"The darkest of all. The magic of a corrupt soul."

Bobby brought Bones the lantern. "What about the witch guy?"

"Drag his body against the tree. It is fitting he suffer its fate in death as he did in life."

Crandall, although unnerved at even touching Jiraro, complied with Bones' order and hastily dragged the corpse to the kerosene-drenched tree.

The trio stepped back away from the area and then Bones, with a mighty heave, sent the lantern smashing into the tainted monstrosity. The glass broke against the tough bark and instantly there was a whooshing sound and flames appeared. In a sliding rush, they moved both up and down along the surface of the tree until every inch of it was engulfed in a mighty inferno. Even the ground itself began to smolder as the fire fed into the roots hidden beneath the surface.

The dancing pyre sent its fingers high into the sky as snaps and pops of exploding branches resounded unendingly like a symphony from hell.

Like sentinels of the righteous, Brother Bones, Crandall and the mysterious Brunette bore witness to the final climax of a vanquished horror finally put to ashes.

They would be there until the first rays of a new dawn appeared.

Bobby Crandall wrapped the last strips of surgical gauze over his chest abrasions. Bones, his unlikely nurse, joined him in the bathroom carrying a mug of tea generously laced with bourbon.

"Drink this and then get some sleep. You need it."

Bobby took the offered mug and sipped it carefully. "Hmm, good stuff. Say, can you answer some questions for me about what we just went through?"

The hatless Bones stepped back against the door and folded his arms across his chest. "If I can."

"Fair enough. First of all, what exactly was that stuff in Woodbridge's veins that made them him and the others so strong?"

"I am not a chemist, but my best guess is it was their own blood. But somehow evolved into a purer glucose state. Thus its different viscosity and color."

Bobby put away the antiseptic ointment and closed the medicine cabinet. Bones' stark white mask looked at him via the reflection.

"Okay. So it turned to some kind of super-blood thanks the tree sap."

"Yes, although I am sure it was much more complicated than that."

"And it gave them, besides this wild strength, a certain longevity."

"Yes. One of the oldest dreams of mankind, immortality."

"Yeah. You'd know all about that, wouldn't you?"

"Hear me, Bobby Crandall, it is not something to be sought after."

"Okay. So one final thing. If Woodbridge in fact did get intimate with this stripper, ah..Dolores Desire, then isn't there a chance her own body will be altered by their sexual contact?"

"That is within the realms of possibility."

"Then don't you think we should watch her?"

"That is not our mission. For us, the matter is closed."

It wasn't the answer Crandall had expected. Bones was moving out into the hallway ending their conversation. But the youth had one final puzzle to bring up.

"What about the Brunette with the guns? Who is she and what was her role in all this?"

Bones stopped in mid-step and looked back over his shoulder. "I don't know. Perhaps you should ask her."

He left Bobby alone with his thoughts and his warm elixir. The card dealer shrugged, took another swallow of the spiced tea and recalled the Brunette's lovely face under the fedora. Now there was a dame. Maybe their paths would cross again some day. He would certainly like that. Yes, indeed, a whole lot. He headed for his room whistling.

Outside rain clouds began to gather over the city.

Dolores Desire packed her costume in a small carrying case and prepared to leave her hospital room. Lacy Chavez had stopped by earlier that morning to bring her some clothes. All she'd had on when first admitted had been her costume and a housecoat.

Lacy had also told her of Hiram's brutal end the night before in the very corridors outside her door. Police detectives had questioned her as well, after Lacy's visit. She cooperated to the best of her ability. Hiram, although very dear to her, had still been pretty much a mystery and she really didn't know all that much about him.

Now it didn't seem to matter. The cops had departed, clearly still baffled by it all, but at least willing to accept her non-active participation in the drama.

Dolores picked up the bag and reached for the door just as it started to swing inward. It was the Brunette from the night of the attack.

"You! Hey, can we give this a rest? I'm tired of all this. Whatever it is?"

The Brunette closed the door behind her. "Two nights ago I asked you a question and you never really answered it. Please, Dolores. Hear me out. Then after I've finished my say, you can go and I'll never bother you again."

Dolores studied the other woman and saw a genuine sincerity. "The cops think you were somehow involved with stopping Hiram from hurting me."

"I simply did what had to be done."

Dolores tossed the valise on the bed. "Okay. You got five minutes. Make it good."

"I was hired by Jack and Mary Sullivan to find their missing daughter, Gladys. Gladys was a rebellious soul and she ran away from home when she was only sixteen."

Dolores's eyes tightened at the sound of a name she had buried long ago.

"The Sullivans have had many years to reflect on the mistakes they made with the girl and they are heartbroken about it."

"Sure. Just like some cheap melodrama on the radio."

"It's more than that. Much more. You see, Gladys isn't their only daughter. There was another, younger, girl."

"Dotty!"

"Yes. Dorothy. She was only ten when her big sister flew the coop. She is part of the reason her parents have changed. Realizing their rigid mores and standards had driven Gladys away, they vowed to not to repeat the same mistakes with their remaining child."

"Is she alright? Dotty, I mean?"

"No, Dolores. Your sister is suffering from a kidney disease and will die unless she gets a transplant."

Dolores fell back against the bed. "Oh, no."

"This is why your parents hired me. The doctors say you should be a perfect donor."

Dolores shook her head and then tears began to fall from her eyes. She rubbed at them without being able to staunch their flow. "She's such a sweet kid. She doesn't deserve that kind of luck."

"No, she doesn't. What are you going to do about it?"

The dancer looked up at the Brunette with her tear streaked face, sniffled and then stood straight and determined. "Whatever it takes. Where is she?"

The Brunette smiled and pulled open the door. "I had a hunch you'd say that. Come with me."

Dolores grabbed her bag and followed as the Brunette let her out through the hospital ward.

"You mean she's here? In this hospital?"

"Yes. She was brought in a few days ago. When your parents told the doctors of their inability to find you, one of them, an old friend, was able to contact me. That's how I was brought in on the case.

The Brunette turned several corners and then came to a halt before a door similar to all others on the floor. Dolores Desire, once Gladys Sullivan, stopped before it and froze. Suddenly she was afraid of what she would find beyond its portal. Or more exactly, what she wouldn't find.

The Brunette slid next to her and whispered, "Go on, kid. You'll do fine."

"You think so?"

"Believe it."

Dolores pushed open the door and there they were, familiar faces. Altered by time, but still her mother and father, a bit grayer with more lines in their faces. Between them, sitting up in the bed, propped up with pillows was Dotty. Loving, sweet, kid sister, Dotty. It was Dotty who spotted her first.

"SIS!"

Her parents turned and at the sight of her, rushed forth, arms opened wide. Dolores, her heart suddenly fracturing, dove into their love.

The Brunette let the door to the reunion close and with a whimsical grin, strolled away. Sometimes Cape Noire wasn't such a bad town after all.

As the first burst of thunder unleashed a torrential downpour over the waves of Crystal Cove, the luxury yacht, Pandora, made its way through the channel towards the open sea.

Gathered on its forward deck, oblivious to the rain that fell, the remaining members of the Ivy League stood together watching the city diminish behind them.

Charles Baxter addressed them, the water rolling over his hard face unable to soothe the rage that simmered within him.

"Tonight we leave on a journey of utter most significance to our very survival. We must locate another Source tree if we are to maintain our continued existence through the years.

"It is our due and we will not be denied."

At this declaration, the heavens sent forth a bolt of lightning that flared across the harbor. Baxter looked back at the somber shaped buildings and thought about their mysterious foe. Prior to evacuating their haunts, he had sent out agents and their hasty reports were unclear and confusing.

There was an entity inhabiting the night streets of Cape Noire. An avenger the like of which he had never encountered before. It would take time, but Baxter and his colleagues planned on having an abundance of that.

"Our second objective," he pressed on, again facing his companions, "after finding and renewing our strength, will be to return and destroy the cause of our defeat."

As thunder boomed, he raised his fist to the storm and cried, "We will find this Brother Bones and we will destroy him. So do we swear."

Four voices echoed the oath and the craft sliced effortlessly into watery blackness of beyond.

THE END

GORILLA DREAMS

He was dreaming again of the jungle. It was always the same jungle. Vividly colored every shade of green imaginable, with exotic flowers painted in rainbow watercolors. Now most people dream in black in white. Somewhere in the catacombs of the dreamer's mind, he had heard that. But it was a dream and the thing about dreams was there were no rules that couldn't be broken in a damn dream. So he dreamed his dream in color. Maybe it had something to do with the emotions that played out in the dream. Whatever. It was his dream and his jungle. So there.

Now the air was sticky hot and humid in this jungle which made it doubly oppressive. What he wouldn't give for a cold beer along about now.

Then the girl appeared all sweaty and breathing heavy from her flight through the confining foliage. She was a stunner, with long blonde hair that gave the flowers competition and a voluptuous body any man would kill for. Tall and leggy in her leather boots, her safari pants were torn as was the dirty white blouse that had been dwindled into a scant rag barely able to cover her bazooms.

Her naked arms, long neck and exposed leg flesh were covered with hundreds of scratches and tiny cuts were blood smeared all over. The jungle was not kind to intruders unfamiliar with its ways.

The girl broke through the thick wall of fern and fell to the mossy ground of a small clearing. Panting for breath, she leaned against a massive tree and tried to catch her breath.

It would have been one hell of an erotic dream up to this point. One he would have enjoyed mightily. But no matter how many times he had it, it always continued into the bizarreness of what came next.

A great roar erupted from the jungle and into the clearing a massive, silverback gorilla emerged. Hunched over and walking on his ham-sized fists, the hairy brute with small, marble eyes sought out the frightened woman and roared again at the sight of her.

At the exact same time, the god-like jungle man appeared at the opposite side of the bare patch dressed in a tiger skin loincloth, his body a magnificent example of human perfection. He was naturally the King of the Goddamn Jungle.Handsome of chiseled face, his nostrils flared in a primal snort as he pounded his fist against his muscular chest and snarled at the giant gorilla.

The woman, her chest heaving, watched in fearful silence as the two enemies eyed each other with anger and contempt. She was the prize both coveted. Both desired. Suddenly the jungle man launched himself at the powerful ape, his hands shaped like claws.

The gorilla swung out and knocked him off his feet. The Jungle Lord flipped over and slammed face first into the ground. He was dazed. Before he could recover, the gorilla snorted, jumped and landed on his back. With relish, the silver-back reached down, took hold of the man's head twisted it around. The neck snapped like a dry twig and the hero died, his eyes glazing over instantly.

The busty blonde and climbed to her feet.Walking in a rolling side to side gait, the victorious gorilla approached the damsel. He was ready for her to start screaming blue-bloody-murder. That would have been okay by him. After all, he had just killed the hero of the piece. After all, everyone knew how these jungle tales went.

Which is why the damn dream was so stupid.

The woman didn't scream. Nope. Instead she peeled off the remaining cloth from her chest to expose herself before the man-like creature. Then, caressing herself, she wantonly came into his arms and began making out with the gorilla.

All the time. The dream always ended with the girl giving herself to the gorilla. French kissing the hell out of the dumb shit, all the while pressing her soft, ripe body against his hairy chest. It was sick!!

Harry Beest woke up with a cry filled with anguish. He hated that dream, more than he hated himself. Sitting up in the oversized bed, his seven hundred pound frame trembled with revulsion and sweat beaded his knobby brow. He raised gnarled and horny gorilla fingers to his forehead and scratched. Sweating always made him itch.

The sun was long gone from the streets of Cape Noire when the dapper, elegant looking man with the straight black hair and pencil thin mustache stepped out of the Chandler Arms Hotel.

He stopped under the red canvas awning to taste the night air. Slipping his hands into the folds of his Hong Kong tailor-made suit, he found a silver cigarette case and extracted a filter-tipped Regent. As his slender fingers flipped the butt to his lips, Theodore, the evening doorman, moved in and produced a lighter-flame.

"Allow me, Mr. Knight."

"Thank you, Teddy." He inhaled and let the heavy nicotine blanket his nerves.

"Thank you, sir. It is good to have with us again."

"Yes, it is good to be back in the city. Be a good fellow and hail me a cab, Teddy. The evening is young and I feel particularly lucky."

"Right away, sir." Theodore liked the sophisticated Brit. The class the gentleman exuded was what the Chandler Arms Hotel was all about. As he went to the curb and raised his arm to flag down a passing Yellow Star, Teddy wondered what far-off places the slick Temple Knight had visited since his last stay.

A dented, dirty cab screeched to a halt inches from his left foot and the doorman swung into action, opening the rear door for his patron. As the stylish Englishman bent over to enter the cab, he slipped the doorman a folded twenty-dollar bill.

"Have a good night, sir," Teddy said as he deftly hid the gratuity in his palm and tipped his hat.

As he closed the door, he heard Knight say, "The Gray Owl club, old man and don't spare the horses."

Once the hack had rolled off into traffic, the burly hotel greeter retreated to his work alcove. It was a small room located to the left of the glass doors. Inside was a table with his work sheets, a coat rack and on the wall beside the key holders, a telephone.

Theodore picked up the receiver and dialed a familiar number. There was a ring and then a gruff, "Yeah?"

"It's me, Teddy. Yeah, yeah. Right. He just left. He's on his way to the Gray Owl. Okay."

His call over, Theodore cradled the phone and then reached into his pocket to fold his new twenty around the hundred-dollar note he'd just earned. Whistling, he went back to his station outside. For a fleeting second he thought about his call and sincerely hoped Mr. Knight wasn't in any kind of trouble.

That would be a real shame.

Bruno St. George watched the streets of Cape Noire roll by as the night arrived like a familiar whore; used but still worth a tumble. The streets whizzed by as his driver, Joey Molton kept his foot flat on the gas pedal. Joey loved to drive fast, especially when they were on a job.

St. George patted the machine gun in his lap and contemplated what the next few minutes would bring. A big man, he had started his criminal career on the docks when he came to the attention of Boss Wyld as someone good with his mitts and a taste for head-bashing. He'd been recruited by Harry Beest and never looked back.

It was also the reason for his fervent loyalty to the tragic mob boss. Even after Beest had been transformed into the hairy monstrosity, Bruno had come back to him. Like a bulldog, he had ever only known one master and saw Beest's furry new body as no excuse to change. Actually, working for a boss who inspired fear throughout the city wasn't really a bad thing in their line of employment.

"So Jackie boy is skimming off the top, heh, Bruno?"

The speaker was one of the two shooters seated in the back seat of the gray sedan, Don Mackoy. Beside him, cradling his own Thompson submachine gun was Baldy Dave Tackman.

"That's what the boss says," Bruno confirmed. "And he thinks it's time we made an example for the rest of middle management to see and understand."

"Middle-management, ha. That's a good one," Joey laughed as he jerked the wheel into a hard left turn. City traffic was picking up as the various nightspots started to come alive. At one intersection, the car raced through a red light nearly taking out an old model T with an elderly couple scared out of five years of life. The maddened senior made a gesture with his fists as they continued on their course.

A parked radio police car saw the near collision and the young rookie cop at the wheel started to shift gears only to have the weary sergeant riding shotgun stop him.

"Go easy there, rookie. That was one of the apeman's goon squads. We ain't got no cause to be messing with them."

The young cop was green, but not that naïve to understand what most Cape Noire's finest knew from day one on the street, best to leave the mobs to themselves. You tended to live much longer that way. So the car, a fairly new model with a powerful engine, continued to wind its way through the mazes of the lower East End; destination murder and mayhem.

The Grey Owl Club was just starting to come alive when the dapper figure of Temple Alan Knight walked into the vestibule of the brightly lit casino. He winked at the cigarette girl passing by in the skimpy costume, fishnet stockings and stiletto heels.

"Good evening, Mr. Knight. It's nice to see you again," she greeted, a warm smile brightening her cover-girl good looks.

"Why, thank you, Trixie. It's good to be back. How's the action so far?"

The tall brunette nodded towards the crap tables where a loud, rhinestone blazing cowboy ruled a growing coterie of curious players. "An Arizona oil king, from the way he's been throwing the green around. He's been on a hot streak the last few rolls."

Knight smiled knowingly. That wouldn't last long. The house always had the advantage in that it could wait out any streak. As a professional gambler of sorts, the debonair adventurer was well aware of how fickle Lady Luck really was.

"I think I'll stick to the cards," he said handing Trixie a twenty. "Be a doll and have one of the girls fetch me a gin and tonic. You keep the change and tell whoever you send I'll match the tip if she finds me in ten minutes or less."

"You got it, champ." Trixie snatched the folded twenty and sashayed away, her shapely rear leaving a pleasant visual behind.

"Pleasant visual behind," he mumbled, amused with his own pun. "Looks like it's going to be a fun night."

Knight went to the cashier and exchanged five thousand dollars into multicolored chips. Then he made his way to a crowded blackjack table where a freckled faced dealer with a candy-apple smile controlled the table. Blackjack Bobby Crandall was a master card handler and he worked the three players, two middle-aged matrons and one tuxedo draped business type with charm and aplomb.

Knight edged in among the crowd of gawkers, the kind who watch the action like vultures, but are too timid to take a chance and play. "Excuse me, may I get by please. Thank you."

"Mr. Knight," Blackjack greeted him. "How you doing? Long time no see."

Throwing his cuffs and adjusting his cravat, the sophisticated gambler nodded. "Indeed it has, Bobby. So tell me, can a lonely traveler ensconce himself in this contest or must I await a turn?"

"Table limit is four," Bobby grinned. "Welcome aboard."

"Yeah, jump in," the pale man to the right chimed in as he turned over a ten card to bust his hand. "Misery loves company, as they say."

Knight put down a hundred dollar chip and smiled. "True enough, my friend. But I prefer another adage on these occasions."

"Oh, yeah, and what's that?"

"Lady Luck never shares."

Bobby laughed and dealt out the cards. Knight looked at his hand, winked at the society matron beside him and threw them face up. A queen and ace of spades.

"I believe that's what they call you, isn't it, Bobby? Blackjack."

The businessman groaned. Some people certainly had all the goddamn them luck.

The Handy-Dandy Laundromat was open twenty-four hours a day. Which was why it proved to be a solid front for Jackie Cinolla's bookmaking operation located in the back room. But at eight o'clock at night, the place might as well have been a morgue, so quiet had it become. A few old women knitted in the far corner by the bulky driers while a greasy, pimple-faced college kid sat behind the counter drinking beer, smoking cigarettes and reading the latest issue of ARGOSY.

Molton parked across the street from the nearly deserted shop and shut off the engine.

"Place looks dead," he commented, dropping his hands from the wheel.

"Which suits us just fine," St. George admitted, jacking back the feed-bolt on his Thompson. "You just keep a look out, especially towards the alleys to either side. If there's gonna be trouble, that's most likely where it'll come from."

"Gotcha, Bruno."

The three killers climbed out of the car at the same time. Crossing the street, Bruno gave them their orders. "Baldy, you go round back and cover the rear entrance. When the shooting starts, get ready to slap down any rats who might think of slipping away."

"You bet." Tackman jogged across the street and into the darkened alley at the right corner. In seconds he was lost in the blackness beyond and all that remained were the fading echoes of shoe leather slapping asphalt.

St. George kicked the front door open to the laundromat and went charging in like a fullback. Mackoy followed his machine gun moving back and forth like an antenna tuned for trouble. The kid on the stool chocked on a swallow of beer and his eyes grew double with terror. He figured he was dead. Somehow he was more offended by the idea than scared.

"Keep it shut!" St. George whispered harshly as he moved past the counter to the back door. "And you'll live to see tomorrow."

Without further instructions, the reprieved youth dove behind the counter, disappearing from site. Meanwhile the two old women, after looking to see if the commotion concerned them, continued their knitting. They had accepted the gospel of destiny a long time ago.

Within seconds pandemonium erupted.

It was a busy betting night in Cinolla's parlor and when Bruno and Mackoy entered, there were seven men seated around various tables counting stacks of money. Cinolla, a tall, wiry figure wearing glasses, was at the blackboard erasing the latest racing numbers.

"Ah shit," was all the doomed man said before the two killers opened up. The noise from the machine guns was deafening and the only other sound competing with it were the high-pitched screams of the victims. One man, short and stocky, his sleeves rolled up past his elbows, managed to elude the first hail of slugs and drop to the floor. Using overturned tables, he raced to the back door on his hands and knees. Wood splinters from the tables being chewed up rained down on his head and back, along with the confetti made from shredded currency. All of this giving him the impetus to reach the exit quicker.

The slippery felon pushed the door ajar and coming up on one leg, bolted through the narrow gap like a sprinter at a track meet. He made it to the collection of trashcans lining the rear wall when Baldy appeared from the alley and let him have it. Flames spit out of the muzzle as dozens of lead slugs tore into the startled escapee. His body convulsed like a marionette suddenly cut loose and as blood gushed out of his mouth, he gasped his last breath and fell dead on his face. Baldy stopped shooting and gave the back lot a quick once over. A building adjoining the alley went completely dark as late night dwellers were quick to recognize the sounds of murder and put out their lights.

Baldy grinned, stepped over the dead man and went to join his compatriots inside.

The smell of gunpowder and a thick haze of gun smoke wafted across the small, square room as St. George and Mackoy moved around to give the bodies a better inspection. It would never do to simply leave without asserting the actual demise of their intended target. They were not sloppy killers.

Bruno was crouched over the dead Jack Cinolla and marveling at the man's stupid look of surprise that would go with him into eternity.

"You shoulda known better, Jack," he admonished the dead man.

"Hey, Bruno," Mackoy called out from where he stood next to a tilted green topped table riddled with bullet holes. "You'd better come see this."

St. George rose and walked over to his friend, just as Baldy came in from the back door.

"Jeezus, you guys really burned them good," he laughed. "This place is a wreck."

But Bruno wasn't listening to Baldy's wisecracks. He was more concerned with the small body crumbled at the feet of Boss Mackoy.

"It's a freaking kid," the rattled Mackoy identified. His foot kicked a rectangular wooden box by the boy's body. "I recognize him. He's Jake Kingman, the shoeshine boy who always worked in front of the train station."

"So what the hell was he doing here?" Baldy asked, now as annoyed as his partner who looked anxious.

"Old Cinolla was probably using him as a numbers runner," St. George guessed. Blond hair, in tight curls peeked from under the still boy's baseball cap.

"This ain't good," Mackoy continued. "He shouldn't have been here like this. We weren't suppose to kill no kid."

"What's done is done," Bruno snapped. "You got that?

Both of you! It's too bad about the kid, but it ain't no skin off our noses. He was just in the wrong place at the wrong time.

"Now let's grab the loose cash and get the hell out of here before someone has the balls the call the coppers."

Without further comments, the two hoods began to move around the room collecting the money. Bruno took a last look at the lifeless boy and then backed away from the body. He wiped his mouth with the back of his hand, suddenly very thirsty for a good, stiff drink.

There is a run down, two-bedroom coldwater flat on the other side of town. In it a dark figure stirs as newly born ghosts begin to wail in his soul. He is the zombie agent of justice raped, of innocence destroyed. He is the dark wanderer, one with the night; the dead man who dreams.

The twin silver-plated .45 automatics remain undisturbed on the dresser drawer. The dream is shapeless and the ghost-victims, for now, unintelligible. But he is patient and has all the time in the world. He is Brother Bones and he dreams.

Knight walked out of the Grey Owl Club two hours later and two thousand dollars richer. The cards had been good to him on this, his first night back in familiar haunts.

Going down the cement steps of club, he mentally imagined the various world capitols that were his playground. All of them had their own identities and ambience that attracted his sense of adventure and risk taking. But none of them had the aura of danger that so permeated the streets of Cape Noire.

The sky overhead was clear of clouds and somewhere beyond the high-rise steel mountains he could smell the evening brine of the sea. Even the moon looked skeletal in its pasty whiteness as it gave off an eerie, cool light.

Traffic at three in the morning was virtually nonexistent, save for the cabs, street-sweepers and various retail trucks delivering their goods for the coming day's business. Knight stopped at the curb and wondered if he'd have to hoof it back to his hotel. He needn't have worried.

A gray colored sedan rolled up and two men, each bulging out of their cheap suits, popped out of the rear and approached him.

The nearest, a bruiser with a prize-fighter's mug and missing a front tooth, gave him a silly smile, while pulling a pistol from his pocket. "Mr. Beest request your company at his home."

Knight knew these men were idiot goons with no compunctions about shooting him on the spot. The thought of eluding them flitted across his mind only because it would have been easy enough. In fact, with his past commando training, the Brit could have disarmed both gangland soldiers without breaking a sweat.

But then again, where would the fun in that be? Here he was, on his first night in Cape Noire, being summoned for a private audience with one of the city's most infamous crime figures. Knight had heard the rumors of the man whose brain had been transplanted into the body of a gorilla. He had always considered it a fanciful urban myth like the alligators in the sewers of New York. Now he was being offered the opportunity to learn the truth for himself.

Knight reached a hand into his jacket and the stooge whipped up the barrel of his gun.

"Easy, old chap," the handsome foreigner cautioned and withdrew his pack of Regents. "I'd be honored to meet the famous Mr. Harry Beest."

"Oh," the gunman muttered. "Good. Get in the car."

Both men put away their pieces, as Knight slid into the plush and comfortable back seat. They took their places beside him. Once inside, missing-tooth tapped the front seat and the driver got the car rolling again.

Knight nipped a cigarette from the open pack and asked, "Would either of you have a light?"

"I've got to blindfold you," the talkative member of the duo said, offering Knight a book of matches. "Boss don't want nobody knowing his hideout."

"Quite understandable," Knight agreed, lighting his smoke. That they were taking such a precaution bode well for his surviving this odd summons. Otherwise they wouldn't have cared what he saw en route.

They draped a silk bandana about his eyes and tied it snuggly behind his head. The man on his right gave the knot a tug and was content it was tight enough.

"Now just sit back and enjoy the ride, Mr. Knight. It ain't gonna take long."

True to the thug's words, the reminder of trip seemed short enough to the blindfolded Knight. The few sounds that reached his ears indicated empty streets and a less congested section of the city. The driver made several right and left turns, suggesting a route towards the northern heights district, away from the piers. Although a frequent visitor to Cape Noire, the debonair traveler was by no means an authority of its labyrinth of dark streets and narrow alleys. Were to scarf to be removed, he would have been totally lost as to his present whereabouts.

Still that did not bother him. The man had long ago learned to survive in the most adverse surroundings. He trusted his own special talents to see him through, regardless of where fate landed him.

At best guess, twenty minutes had expired, when the sedan stopped and the engine cut off. Knight was ushered out of the car. His hosts took hold of his shoulders and guided him up several cement steps.

"Watch the stoop," the disembodied voice to his right warned. "We're going inside."

Knight stepped up and felt a textured surface under his shoes. A few more steps, another door opening and closing and then hands were peeling the blindfold off his face.

The hallway light was dim and he only had to squint for a few seconds. Gingerly he rubbed at his eyes until they adjusted to seeing again. The vestibule he stood in was clearly the main entrance to an old Victorian house. A long winding staircase moved off to his right to a second story, another hall running beneath it to what he assumed would be the kitchen area. Directly to his front were twin doors of heavy oak, with ornate latticework and copper knobs. The place smelled of history and money.

Knight was smoothing the wrinkles from his sports coat, when the doors opened and two men appeared, each wielding Thompson submachine guns nonchalantly under their arms. At the sight of Knight and his two guides, they tipped their heads.

"Hey, Lefty," Bruno St. George greeted the wiseguy with the missing tooth.

"Bruno."

"Boss says to go right in."

"Thanks."

As the one called Bruno moved passed Knight, they eyed each other warily like junkyard dogs catching the scent of a possible antagonist for the first time. The sight of the machine gun had reminded the Brit he was entering the lion's den and he had to stay alert. As for the gun-toter, he clearly had the look of a dangerous man. Knight would make a point of remembering that face.

His escort pushed opened the fancy doors and Knight walked into Harry Beest's den. It was a posh, old world place combining the aspects of a library and private office. A huge fireplace commanded the far wall opposite the entrance, with bookshelves burying the remaining walls. To the right, upon entering, was a massive desk flanked by several cushioned chairs.

Harry Beest was standing in front of the desk, a sight Knight would never forget as long as he lived. Here was a brutish, hair-covered silverback gorilla standing upright in a three-piece herringbone suit with a white carnation adorning his lapel. Barefooted, his elongated feet were splayed out across the oriental carpet keeping his massive frame balanced.

If his body wasn't shock enough, the being's head was a frightening visage unto itself. A long, sloping brow extended over two small, almost invisible eyes and a protruding jaw with fat pink lips clung to a thick, foul smelling cigar.

"Here is he," Lefty said, indicating Knight.

Beest pulled the stogie out of his mouth with a knarled, gigantic hand. "Good work. Now leave us alone."

The voice was guttural, clearly having a difficult time shaping words. It hadn't been made to do anything but screech and grunt. It was bone chilling to the ears.

"Have a seat, Mr. Knight."

The beast in human guise, moved around the desk, allowing his guest access to one of the straight back chairs. As Knight sat, he saw that the chair behind the desk was a custom made piece designed of heavy timber to accommodate the owner's size and weight. Beest sat with a deep sigh, his back and spine released momentarily from the hellish punishment of gravity.

"Thank you for coming, Mr. Knight."

"Your welcome. Although I doubt I had any real choice in the matter."

The gorilla man laughed. It sounded like a small dog barking. "That's true enough. I appreciate a good sense of humor, Mr. Knight."

"I'm so glad."

"Okay, so enough of the small talk. You know who I am, right?"

"I doubt there could be another Harry Beest."

The small, black eyes glinted from the glare of the desk lamp. Knight, normally blasé about most things, now found himself cautious. It would be wise to choose his words carefully with this ..person.

"My sources tell me you are the best second-story man around. Is that true?"

"Yes. It is. Why?"

"I want you to steal something for me."

"I see."

"I'll pay you twenty-thousand dollars."

"That's a lot of money. What is it you wish me steal?"

"A garter belt."

"Oh. As in a lady's unmentionables?"

"Yah, you got it. The frilly belt thing that holds up her stockings. A garter belt."

"I see," Knight scratched his eyebrow. Could this possibly get any more bizarre?

"You know who Alexis Wyld is?" Beest asked, taking in a long drag on his odorous cigar.

"Wyld? Isn't that the name of your old..ah, patron?"

"Yah. Boss Topper Wyld. That's who I use to work for long ago. He brought me up through the ranks. Then he screwed me over because I fell for Alexis, his daughter."

Knight had heard the stories. He had never given them any credence until now.

"An interesting choice of words."

"Huh? What do yah mean?"

"Screwing. Seems there are many different variations of the term."

"Whatever." The wit of Knight's repartee beyond his intellectual grasp, Beest rambled on. "Bastard gave me over to that wacko professor, Bugosi. Ever heard of him?"

"I'm afraid I can't say I have."

"Well, lucky you. This Bugosi character had orders from Boss Wyld to make me suffer. So he goes and cuts my brains out and puts them into this monkey suit."

"Amazing!"

"What is fuck'n amazing is that when I broke out of his freako animal cage, I let the bastard going on breathing."

The British cat-burglar folded his arms over his lap, as his mind collated all the facts Beest divulged. The solution to the posed conundrum was obvious and Knight understood Beest's dilemma perfectly. "He's the only one capable of reversing the process."

Beest slammed his powerful hand onto his desktop. A pencil holder fell over, its contents rolling across the green felt writing cover. "The lousy bastard said, if I killed him, I'd stay this way forever."

"Then there is a chance he can put things alright again?"

"No," the gorilla-man's voice softened. "You see, my own body was chopped up after he took out my brain. On Wyld's orders. That way, I can never be me again. Not like before. The best I can hope for is a new body."

Knight felt his skin crawling. What kind of tortured soul was he dealing with here? Better to return the conversation to less horrific subjects.

"So you would like me to bring you one of Miss Wyld's garter belts."

"Yah. Right. Look, Knight, I ain't seen Alexis in ten years, but that doesn't mean I stopped loving her."

"Does she know that?"

"No. Oh, I'm sure she knows what I've become. Her father never kept that a secret. She made a few attempts to find me, way back when it all happened. But I stayed away for her good, as well as my own."

Beest crushed out his finished cigar in a pewter ashtray and grabbed a bottle of bourbon to its right. He splashed a generous amount in a tumbler, pointed to a second glass and asked, "Want a drink?"

"No, thank you. I'm fine."

"Suit yourself." Beest swallowed his drink in one gulp and then poured a second.

"Ain't no woman is ever going to love a freak like me again, Knight. Those are the facts of life. I've come to accept them. Still..a man gets lonely."

Beest looked into the amber liquid sloshing around in his glass, and then drained it. He smacked his wide, rubber-like lips and put the empty glass down. "I want you to get into her place, snatch one of her lacy garter belts and bring it back to me. That's the job. What do you say?"

"Alright, Mr. Beest. But I want the money in cash and payment on delivery."

"Fair enough. How will I know when you've got it?"

"It is now Tuesday. Have your men pick me up in front of the Gray Owl Club at midnight, Thursday. I should have the item by then."

Beest rose to his feet and reached a hairy paw across the desk.

"We have a deal, then."

Knight rose and shook the big mitt. "Agreed."

"My men will take you back to your hotel."

"Good night, Mr. Beest."

"I'll see yah Thursday."

With the end of his audience, Knight exited the creature's lair and rejoined to the waiting gunmen in the hall. Once again the scarf was wrapped around his head and sightless, he was taken away.

The City Morgue, located under the Municipal Center on Poe St., smelled of ammonia and bleach. It permeated the cold walls, with their heavy cubicles, and the slick linoleum floors. Bright florescent lights gave off an antiseptic glow that was functionary rather than comforting.

Detective Sgt. Dennis Sutter, opened the heavy steel door and led the way for the mother and daughter who had come to give a name to a dead boy. Sutter was a balloon like slob who'd eaten too many donuts in his twenty years on the beat. He had a three-day old growth of dark stubble on his two chins and for a forty-two year old, he looked and moved as if he was sixty. His gray fedora looked like someone used it to mop the floors. He hated the morgue and very much wanted this to go quick.

For Molly Kingman, the smells were familiar, having spent the majority of her life employed as a housemaid at the St. Ambrose Hotel. These were the scents of daily life and now, as she walked through the silent subterranean rooms, she was bolstered by their presence. Ammonia and bleach equated cleanliness to her tired and confused mind.

Cleanliness meant order, things in their right place. Attention to detail. Chaos kept at bay, if only for a short while.

At thirty, her clothes rumpled and worn, she held on to the arm of her oldest child, Nora, for emotional support. It was Sutter, in all his ineptitude, who had informed them that young Jacob Kingman had been shot to death in what the papers were already calling the Handy-Dandy Wipeout.

Nora Kingman was thirteen and a freshman in high school. Tall, with wavy brown hair and a pretty face, she resembled her mother before life beat her down.

"He's right over here," the smock wearing lab assistant, known to Sutter as Al, said as he pointed to a cloth-draped body on a steel table. It was a small figure, by its contours under the sheet.

Mother and daughter, hands held tightly, stood next to the table and waited. Al took hold of the sheet's corners, like a Maitre D at a fancy restaurant, and peeled it from the still form. Molly looked at the blue tinged face of her son and tried to understand how he could have come to this place. Less than twenty-four hours ago, he had been bouncing around their tiny kitchen, stuffing a cheese sandwich into his mouth, while attempting to tell her that he would be home early.

"Stay away for the bookie joints," she had warned for the millionth time, knowing fully well he would not listen.The easy money was too much of a temptation to a young boy trying to help his fatherless family stay afloat.

Now here he was, cold, lifeless and gone. The spark that had been Jacob Kingman was lost to her forever.

"Yes," she breathed at last. "That ..was my son, Jacob."

"Okay," Sgt. Sutter responded, looking at Al with a satisfied smug. The attendant nodded and started to replace the sheet but Mrs. Kingman raised her hand.

"Please, can we have a little more time with him?"

"Of course," he apologized, dropping the white shroud."Take as long you'd like. I'll be at the front desk with some papers for you sign when you are through."

He left them in their grief.

"We'll get the rats who did this," the fat cop said, awkward in the ensuing silence. When Molly didn't respond, he scratched his jowls. "I'll be outside if you need me."

Watching him walk away, Molly tried to understand a universe that allowed such a gross, obscene thing like this slovenly pig to live and took away her precious child. Alone with Jacob, she and Nora at last began to cry. The pain was so awful in its cruelty.

Temple Knight slept past noon. After taking a hot shower, he called room service and ordered breakfast. One of the benefits of staying at the Chandler Arm's was the five-star service afforded the clientele. No matter what the request, the staff always did their best to accommodate the patron's needs.

When the bellhop, a fellow named Artie Leeds, arrived with the wheeled cart twenty-five minutes later, Knight was seated in his terry-cloth robe reading the morning paper. Artie rolled the cart to where he was sitting and removed to the oval lid to reveal a plate of bacon and eggs, sunny-side up, wheat toast with orange marmalade and a pitcher of Indian tea.

Knight folded the Tribune, dropped it to the floor and handed the uniformed lad a crisp, twenty-dollar bill.

"Will there be anything else, Mr. Knight?"

"Yes, Artie, there is." Knight poured himself some tea. "There are two more of those twenties for you, if you can tell me where Alexis Wyld resides."

Artie Leeds' face lit up like the beam of a seacoast lighthouse. "Then that'll be the easiest forty bucks I've ever made." The young man pointed up to the ceiling and informed the gentlemen thief that the answer to his question was only a floor above them.

Leeds explained that Miss Wyld did reside at her family estate out in the suburbs. But at the same time, she maintained a penthouse suite right here at the Chandler Arms, which she used whenever business brought her into the city. That suite, the most lavish and expensive in the hotel, was the one directly overhead.

Knight could not believe his good fortune. Sometimes the fates were just too kind. Delighted that his job for Beest would not necessitate any extensive scouting and outdoor activities, he added another ten to the bellhop's payout. Added to his service tip, the fellow had just earned seventy dollars for very little effort. He left Knight whistling a happy tune.

The Brit looked up at the ceiling, imagining its layout would adhere to the building's overall style. Which meant it would not be all that different from his own rooms. He would be working in a familiar setting. All he had to do was discover if Alexis Wyld was in resident at the present time or not, then choose the proper time to make his entry. He could have plied that information from Leeds, but that might have made the man overly curious. Better to learn those details in other ways.

Setting down his half empty tea cup, Knight bit into the marmalade smeared toast and finished the remainder of his American breakfast with a ravenous appetite.

In a room forever in perpetual darkness, Brother Bones stirred. The ghost of a young woman began to take shape before him and he recognized the familiar harbinger. She was the spirit shade of a deceased prostitute who guided him on his endless missions of vengeance. Whenever innocents suffered, she appeared.

Now she was showing him the face of a handsome, young boy. Bones sat up in his chair and picked up the bone white skull mask that rested beside his pistols. He put on the porcelain death's head as the spectral images melted away into the gloom.

"I understand," the zombie avenger spoke. "He will be avenged."

Harry Beest stuffed the green bananas into his mouth, skins and all. As he ambled through the carpeted hall of his Victorian mansion, he tucked the heavy bunch of South American fruit under his left arm. His diet consisted of twenty pounds of bananas a day.

Once, when he was human, he had been a meat and potatoes man. His favorite meal had been a big, thick sirloin, medium rare with the blood juicing out between his lips when he tore into it. Then, becoming a gorilla changed all that. Suddenly any kind of meat, from pork chops

to hamburger made him vomit. He couldn't keep it down. That was how he learned that gorillas, at the least the variety he had become, were vegetarian. Now, his brutish, gigantic metabolism craved nuts and fruits. From bags of shelled, unsalted peanuts, which he kept stocked in the cellar to the cases of tropical produce he filled the huge kitchen freezer.

The chef he employed prepared only vegetarian meals.

Beest finished the last of the bananas and threw the empty vine branch away. It was after sundown and all of his domestic staff had gone home. Beest was dressed in a blue cotton bathrobe he had custom made, like all his clothes. He refused to succumb completely to his beastliness. Once, he had been a fine dresser, always fashion conscious in both work and leisure.

Banging open the kitchen door, he was blinded by the florescent lights overhead. Bruno St. Martin and Don Mackoy, in shirtsleeves, were seated at the small, square table eating thick pastrami sandwiches smothered in mustard. They were washing down the tasty eats with cold beers.

"Hey, Boss," Don raised his half empty brown bottle. "Me and Bruno were just having some dinner."

"Yeah, I can see that," Beest grumbled. "I ain't blind."

"Er, right boss," Mackoy swallowed hard. "You want a beer?"

"Yeah, I want a beer. I want lots of beer." Mackoy wiped his mouth on his sleeve and jumped out of his chair instantly. "And get me a couple bags of peanuts."

"Coming right up," Mackoy disappeared into the walk-in freezer and reemerged with a case of beer in his hands. Kicking the door shut with his leg, he set the beer on the table in front of Beest.

"It's a quiet night," St Martin offered, draining the last of his own bottle. He set it on the open newspaper he'd been leafing through when Beest walked in. There was a picture of young Jacob Kingman on the page.

Beest grabbed a bottle of beer, brought it to his teeth and bit off the cap. He swallowed the entire bottle in one long draught and then set the empty on the paper. Thank God he hadn't had to give up booze.

Mackoy, fishing in the food closet, came back to the table with three paper bags of nuts. He put them next to the case of beer. "Here you are, Boss."

Beest picked up a second bottle and as he started to bring the neck to his fat lips, he pointed it at St. Martin.

"Shooting that kid was sloppy, Bruno."

"It was an accident, Boss. Really." St. Martin punched Mackoy in the arm. "Tell him. We didn't know the damn kid was there when we opened up."

"Bruno's telling it straight, Boss. We just went in blasting away like you told us. It was just a bad break the runt was there. That's all."

Beest stuffed a dozen shelled peanuts into his mouth and chewed them hungrily. Then he drained his second beer.He belched loudly and slapped the beer down so that it knocked over the first he'd drained.

"Yeah, well it was still sloppy. It brings us all kinds of trouble when we shoot up kids. I don't like it one little bit."

"What do you want us to do?" St. Martin asked, wiping his mouth with a cloth napkin. "It's was just an honest mistake, is all. Sides, who gives a shit about some snotty nosed brat?"

Beest's tiny, black eyes bore into his most loyal associate. St. Martin had been with him a long time. Maybe he was worrying over spilled milk.

"Maybe. But if this causes me grief, I'm not going to forget who brought it to me."

With that, the man-monster put the bags of peanuts on the case of alcohol, picked it up and exited through the swinging door. He wanted to be alone: to eat, to drink and to think. The two men in the kitchen went back to their pastrami repast. Neither of them was worried about Harry Beest's comments. They had shot innocent bystanders before. It was no big shakes.

The gorilla gangster took his snack to his upstairs bedroom. There he stripped out of his robe, dropped it by the bathroom door, then sat down on the hardwood floor and resumed his munching. He preferred sitting on the floor. It suited the curvature of his spine better than chairs.

As the beer and peanuts vanished into his five hundred pound frame, Beest's thoughts traveled backward in time. Images of himself as Boss Wyld's first lieutenant flashed across the movieola of his mind. And, like the cutting room editor, his thoughts selected specific scenes to replay. The foremost of these were his early encounters with the Boss's daughter, Alexis.

At the time she had been sixteen and a student at very exclusive private school. Initially Harry would only catch brief glimpses of the raven-haired princess when she came home late in the afternoon. Always fearful for her safety, Wyld had two of his men detailed to escort her every day, to and from the ritzy academy. At the start, Beest hadn't given her a second look. She was just a teen-age girl in a typical school outfit of a blue blazer, white blouse and plaid skirt. She always had a stack of heavy books with her, but these the bodyguards carried. Alexis liked to be treated as if she were royalty.

Beest never knew how or why she became attracted to him, but it happened. The most vivid recollection came just prior to her seventeenth birthday. He had been coming out of the basement pool room with several of the boys. At the same time Alexis was coming through the front door. They made eye contact and he nodded politely. A thin smile of recognition glimmered across her dark eyes as she passed him and started up the winding staircase to her room.

Halfway up the steps, the girl stopped, twisted around and bent over at the waist. Beest, still watching her, felt his throat go dry when her delicate hands pulled the pleated skirt up over her shapely thighs to reveal her stocking tops and the garter belt that held them up.

"Damn it, I've got another run!" she cursed, running her fingers over her shapely leg where the tiny rip was evident.

Beest was sweating. Nylons and garter belts? Since when did teenage girls wear women's undies? Then Alexis's eyes fell on him and caught him staring. He turned away, mumbling, "Excuse me."

"Why? Don't you like the view?"

Beest turned in time to see her race up the stairs, her soft voice ringing with laughter. So, she was a tease, he thought. Now there was a dangerous temptation. Everyone knew how much Boss Wyld treasured his only child. What he would to do anyone crazy enough to touch her would chill the marrow of any sane man. Beest was smart enough to watch his back. Messing with the black haired vixen was not a part of his future plans in the organization.

The apeman swallowed his eight beer and burped. The memories were as bitter as always. No one likes to remember how stupid they were. He rubbed his rough knuckles on his legs and picked up another bag of peanuts.

He hadn't been wise after all. Sure, his brain knew the pitfalls of seducing the boss's daughter, but his libido was not so controllable. For the next several weeks it seemed everywhere he went in the mansion, he was always bumping into the girl. He began to comprehend that none of these were chance encounters. She was purposely putting herself where he would be.

Her beauty began to worm into his every day consciousness until the inevitable occurred one afternoon when her father was out of the house. He had been doing a security check on the mansion's upper floors to include the massive attic that was used for storage.

Creaking floorboards alerted him to someone coming up from the stairwell and he turned to see Alexis. She had on the school outfit, without the jacket. Images of the nylon tops and garter snaps flared through his thoughts and he knew the volcano that was his lust was about to erupt.

It was weird looking back after all these years, that the one thing he clearly remembered was her silence. She never said a single word as he took her in his arms and began to kiss her. Not one single syllable as his hands moved over her ripe, young body, exploring brutally. Then when he was taking her on the dusty, hard floor, she began to moan and scream as she locked her legs around his middle.

She'd been a virgin.

Beest swallowed peanuts, shells and all and felt his penis hardening. Now there was a joke. In his time he'd loved lots of woman and been a pretty competent lover. Then he screwed the boss's daughter. Put the old boots to her and made the chump mistake of falling in love. And the reward for that sorry attack of romance was to have the brains ripped out of his body and transplanted into this hairy carcass.

Now, as a jungle primate, he possessed the biggest pecker this side of King Kong and it was as much use to him as a third eye. It would have been so darkly ironic if it wasn't so pathetic.

Beest got to his feet, using the wall for leverage. He was drunk as he made his way into the gigantic, porcelain shower stall and tub. There he turned on the cold water and sat himself beneath it, again in the same leg over leg squatting position. Soon the fine spray was plastering his long, coarse hair over his entire body like a wet fur piece. His stiff sexual organ began to shrivel under the steady cascade. For some reason his inebriated consciousness thought that was the funniest thing in the world.

So funny, in fact, that he laughed until he cried.

Knight stepped out of the elevator just after midnight. The corridor was empty just as he had expected it to be. Dressed in his evening dinner jacket and black slacks, he appeared like a bon vivant returning from a night of revelry on the town. Exactly the image he wished to convey should he encounter others on his way to the south side corner penthouse. By the floor's layout, this would be the apartment directly over his.

The room number was 8-B. Knight gave the door a timid knock and held his breath. His sources in the hotel had informed that Alexis Wyld was not in resident at the present time. But then again, they had cautioned, that was always subject to change. She had the habit of showing up unannounced often. Which was why she maintained the suite in the first place.

When no one answered the door after two minutes, the sophisticated burglar went to work. From his jacket he took a small lock pick and opened the mechanism with two easy twist of his wrist. He swapped the pick for a pencil light and slipped into the room, closing the door gently behind him.

Again, the familiarity of his own digs, made his first surveillance easy. The small flashlight produced a wide beacon allowing him to move about the darkened rooms without difficulty. The living room was centerpiece of the floor plan, with a kitchen off to the right and the major bedroom directly across from the main entrance. Everything from the curtains to the thick carpet reeked of wealth and as he made he was through the room, his fingers itched to tackle the wall safe he knew to be hidden behind the portrait painting of Topper Wyld. Apparently the deceased crime-boss still held a prominent place in his daughter's life.

The major bedroom was huge, nearly twice the size of his own, with a bathroom and second bedroom along the far wall. Red satin sheets, pulled down and made, adorned the

four poster bed to his left. To his right was a walk-in closet and next to it was a massive vanity table with a round, theater like mirror over which were arrayed six naked bulbs. The other side of this table was a white stained bureau and most likely where the lovely lady kept her unmentionables.

Knight put the small torch in his mouth as he began to open the top drawer of the bureau. Neatly folded slips and pajamas were revealed under the harsh yellow beam.

He slid the drawer shut and started to take hold of the next one beneath.

There was a rattling sound of keys and he heard the front door opening. He let go of the drawer knobs just as light from the living area flooded through the open bedroom door. He killed the pencil light and tiptoed to the closet in two silent steps. He slid the door wide and disappeared behind the dresses and gowns hung on an overhead rod. There he put his back to the wall. He'd left the door opened a crack so that he could peer out without being seen.

"I'll be fine, boys," a female voice rang out. "You get a good night sleep and have somebody wake me at seven."

"Yes, Miss Wyld," came the masculine reply.

Good, thought Knight, she's alone and not with some amorous date. Still, he cursed his luck all the same. He'd played the odds and lost. Something, most likely business, had brought her back into city and it was his bad luck she arrived before he could finish the job.

Still, it might have been worse. She could have had a lover in tow and thus doubled the chances of his discovery. As it were, if he kept his composure, he would simply remain hidden and wait for her to fall asleep. Then he would complete his assignment and the get the hell out of there.

The bedroom light came on and Alexis Wyld walked in. She was gorgeous. A tall brunette, with a full, ripe figure, she moved on long, dancer's legs. She was dressed in a practical blue skirt with matching high heels. She wore a tan colored blouse and was taking off a silver buttoned jacket when she passed Knight's line of sight.Was she coming to the closet?

The jacket went flying across the room and landed over the stiff backed chair of the vanity desk. She kicked off her shoes at the same time she tugged at her earrings. These she deposited on the tabletop and then began undoing the buttons on her blouse. With each item of clothing she removed, the lady exposed more of her creamy, tanned skin.

Soon the skirt was crumbled in a heap on the floor and all she had on were her black lace panties and bra. She was truly a goddess and Knight understood why she had so infected the soul of poor Harry Beest. Her face was chiseled perfection, from its high cheek-bones, sculptured finely around full lips, a haughty roman nose and piercing blue eyes under delicate brows that bent like angel's wings. Then there was the immense sweep of her thick, lustrous black hair that draped sensually over her naked shoulders. Knight had seen few women with this kind of magnificent, breath taking beauty.

Then she was gone and for a second, he wondered if she had sensed his presence. A few minutes later there were sounds from the kitchen. When Alexis returned she was holding a small glass of ice water. She took a few swallows, set it down on the nightstand to the left of the bed and climbed in, pulling the sheets down. As mesmerized as he was by her looks, Knight was alert enough to realize her lack of stockings meant his targeted item would still have to be sought after in the bureau.

He was in a tight spot, but it wasn't the first time. The woman reached out, pulled the chord on the table lamp and the room went dark again. There was a small window in the bathroom and this now produced a gray shaft from the glow of the streetlamps below. The beam shot slid through the open door and onto the middle of the bed.

From his hiding place, the thief could see her still form under the sheets. He breathed slowly, stepped back and rested against the wall. There was nothing to do but wait and hope sleep came quickly to the mistress of the night.

Working the night shift at the morgue fit perfectly into Rob Davis's college lifestyle. A senior at Wagner City College, the job of night clerk allowed him ample time to work on his studies while earning a paycheck. Davis, a stocky Midwesterner with rust colored hair and a round, cheery face, was an English Lit major with aspirations of becoming a pulp writer.

To date the six stories he had sent Weird Tales had all been rejected, but that did not dampen his enthusiasm one iota. Davis was familiar with stories of how all the big name wordsmiths had learned their craft via the hard knocks of rejection slips.

Gulping down the last of the cold java in his paper cup, he put his feet up on the desk, crossed at his ankles, and took up the latest copy of Weird Tales he'd purchased on this way in to work that evening. Of all the pulps, Weird Tales was by far his favorite. At the moment he was halfway through a brand new Doctor Satan thriller by Paul Ernst.

Off course Davis's friends and associates thought it decidedly odd that he would while away his time in a morgue reading horror yarns. He didn't give it much thought, safe in his own ability to differentiate between what was real and what was make believe. Sure writers like Howard P. Lovecraft and Clark Ashton Smith could give one's nerves

a decent jolt to the old imagination. But that was the fun of it. It was like the adrenalin high of going through the haunted house at a carnival.

Besides, the dead were a quiet lot.

Davis smiled at his own, dark humor.

"Where is the dead boy?" A shadow fell over the student clerk.

Startled, he bolted upright nearly falling out of the swivel chair. Standing in front of him was a frightening specter in black. Davis came to his feet, dropping the magazine as he instinctively brought his hands up in fear.He felt his kidneys tightening and thought he would wet himself for sure.

The thing before him, manlike in appearance was tall, attired in a tattered black cloak and wearing a huge fedora whose brim concealed most of its face. But there was no face! Only a dazzling white skull shaped mask with two slits for the eyes. Davis thought of the bleached skulls he'd seen used in so many horror movies.Only this one was no prop.

"Huh." was all that came out of his restricted throat.

"Where is the dead boy?" The wraith's voice was deep and menacing. It was devoid of any warmth.

"In there," Davis managed to mumble, pointing to the main viewing area beyond the swinging doors. "All the bodies are in there."

"Show me!"

"Please don't hurt me. Please!"

Brother Bones leaned over the desk and brought his head closer to the trembling clerk. "No harm will come to you. I am here to see the body of Jake Kingman. Now show it to me!"

The scared young man ran to the doors, pushed through them and led the dead avenger to the cold wall of corpses. Quickly scanning the I.D. tags, he found the right container and pulled on the handle. The shelf rolled out revealing the cloth covered body of the Kingman boy.

Brother Bones lifted the cloth and gazed down at the rigid body now purplish in hue. He studied the half dozen bullet-holes that stitched the torso and decided his next course of action.

"Where are the slugs they took out of his body?"

"Wha..huh?"

"The bullet slugs. The coroner dug them out of the body. I want them."

Davis backed away as Bones came around the shelf. "I think there over here, in the evidence cabinet."

"Get them."

The college lad tore open the top drawer of the gray steel cabinet and began rummaging through its contents. He found a small manila envelope marked Kingman and quickly passed it over to the frightening masked intruder.

"Here. There were six in all, but the notation there says the M.E. gave two over to the police lab for their analyzing."

A gloved hand folded over the small packet and then was hidden within the folds of his shroud-like cloak.

"Go back to your reading, Mr. Davis." Then the figure exited the room like an ominous tide leaving only an eerie chill in its wake.

After which, Rob Davis, lover of scary tales and would-be pulpsmith, fell to the floor in a dead feint.

"Freeze right where you are!" Alexis Wyld commanded from her bed. "Make any kind of quick move and I'll put a bullet between your shoulder blades."

Temple Knight silently obeyed her directive, at the same time mentally admonishing himself for getting caught. He was badly out of practice.

There was a click and light filled the room from behind him. He was standing at the bureau, his hands buried in the second drawer where they had just found the sought after prize.

"Alright. Turn around slowly and put your hands up in the air where I can see them."

Knight pulled his hands free and pivoted about gracefully. The woman was sitting up against two big, fluffy pillows holding a snub-nose .38 caliber revolver. She was eyeing him as if he were a bug under glass.

"My, my, but you are a smartly dressed thief. I'll say that for you."

"Thank you. You're most kind."

Then she saw the lace garter belt clutched in his left hand and a puzzled look crossed her face.

"You came to steal my underwear? Intriguing. You certainly do not look like a pervert."

"Cough..I assure you, madam, I am not."

"Then why are you standing, uninvited, in the middle of bedroom with my garter belt in your hand?"

"Merely fulfilling an assignment I was commissioned to undertake."

"Really?" She was becoming more curious with each passing second. "Who the hell are you, my handsome thief and who hired you so steal my clothes?"

"May I put my hands down? It is awkward talking this way."

"You are lucky I didn't shoot first and ask questions later."

"For which I am most grateful, I assure you, madam. But I am, as you so acutely surmised, a thief. Nothing more or less. You've really have nothing to fear from me."

The piercing dark eyes drank in his words and he could almost see the thoughts racing through her mind. She indicated with the gun. "Okay, you can drop them. But, for your continued well being, I'd advise against any sudden moves."

"Thank you." He lowered his arms and flexed them over his chest. The garter belt flapped around. "That's much better."

"You haven't answered my questions."

"Right. I am Temple Knight, formerly of Birmingham, England."

"I've heard of you. They say you are one of the best cat-burglars in the game."

"Thank you."

"I was being facetious. If this is the kind of work you do, I am not overly impressed."

"Anyone can have a bad night. Besides, it is obvious to me now that you are a very light sleeper."

"Yes, I am. Been like that since I was a kid. So, who hired you, Knight?"

"Ah, yes, my employer. This is rather difficult for me, you know. Very unprofessional and all that sort of stuff."

Alexis twisted about and swung her bare feet off the bed so that she was now seated facing him directly, her soles touching the rug.

"Look, mister, so you're reputation will take a little tarnishing. It's a whole lot better than being shot."

"I see your point. It was Mr. Harry Beest."

She blinked and he knew the name had struck home. For whatever their past together, Beest had once meant something to this woman. Still, she recovered nicely. No Hollywood actress could have done better.

"I see. The gorilla man himself hired you to snatch some of my underwear."

"Yes."

"Why does it want it?"

"I'm afraid you'll have to ask him that, madam. I was not made privy to the gentlemen's purpose with the requested item."

"Not even a guess?" She threw off the satin sheet and stood. "Surely you must have some thought on the matter. Or do you just do the job and not worry about such things?"

She was ravishingly beautiful standing there in her bra and panties. Knight thought about the gun and its threat made her all the more exciting.

"I believe he still loves you."

Waving the .38 casually about, she approached him. "I see. Well, that certainly makes sense, doesn't it? That poor, pathetic man. If you can even call him that anymore."

She stopped in front of him. "How much is he paying you?"

"Ten thousand dollars."

"That's a lot of money for such a small thing."

"Yes, it is."

She pressed the barrel of the gun into his chest and held out her free hand, palm up. He handed her the suspenders. Her lips were signaling trouble. A trouble Temple Knight was all too familiar with.

"Well, Knight, if they are worth so much, then I would think you should have to earn them."

"And how am I to do that?"

Keeping the barrel pressed firmly against his breast, she stepped in closer and tilted her head up. "You're a big boy. Figure it out for yourself."

He grabbed her soft, naked shoulders and pulled her mouth up to his.

Their kiss was hot and greedy, each trying to outdo the other with the sexual want that blazed between them.

It was the first of many and Knight soon forgot all about the gun and the garter belt. He lost himself in the arms of Alexis Wyld.

The following night, Blackjack Bobby Crandall gripped the steering wheel of his DeSoto roadster as he wove his way through the fog-blanketed streets of Cape Noire. A gray blanket of mist had descended on the city shortly before dusk and now it seemed the entire world was lost in its embrace.

Bobby would have preferred being at the Gray Owl dealing cards and watching the suckers lose at 21. Unfortunately the macabre rider in the passenger seat next to him had other plans for evening.

Years ago, upon his arrival in the seaport, the freckled faced redhead had been kidnapped while driving for the Swede Jorgenson gang. He'd been taken to an abandoned warehouse to be tortured and killed. What had derailed that fate and saved his naïve neck, was the timely intervention of an angry ghost.

Now, all these years later, Crandall still had trouble believing what he had witnessed that night. The specter had invaded the body of his captor and replaced it. The result of that transference had killed Jack Bonello and then reanimated him as the lifeless entity men would come to know as Brother Bones.

"Turn right at the next set of lights," Bones directed, pointing with his clenched fist. In his gloved hand he held the lead slugs he'd obtained from the morgue the previous night. Without understanding how, Bobby knew those twisted pieced of metal were guiding their route.

"If I can see it," he retorted angrily. Crandall had stopped being afraid of his zombie associate after assisting him on several of his creepy missions. Still, he would always recognize the moral obligation he had to Bones for saving his life and so remained his aid. But that did not mean having to kowtow to the black-garbed death-dealer. Crandall had learned to speak his mind and although he never said it aloud, being a thing of few words, he sensed that Bones respected him for it.

"We are close, Bobby Crandall. I sense the end of our search is near."

They had been driving for almost twenty minutes, after leaving

Crandall's apartment. Now they were lost somewhere in the wealthier part of town. Despite the lack of visibility, Bobby was familiar with the area and the old moneyed homes erected there.

Bones' hand shook and tugged towards the end of the street. "There!" he spoke. "Stop the car!"

Bobby rolled to a stop against the curb opposite a massive, richly adorned three-story Victorian palace. In the fog it looked foreboding. Situated on the corner, its façade was illuminated by a single streetlamp.

"Look, somebody's going in," Bobby pointed as he silenced the roadster's engine. Under the streetlamp, a long, sleek sedan had stopped and delivered up three men.

As they started up the front steps, Crandall saw that two were big dudes, most likely gang members. They were on either side of a smaller fellow. As the front door opened, light from the inside parlor lit their faces.

"Hey, I know that guy?"

"Who?"

"The smart dresser those goons just took up the stairs. His name is Knight. He's a gambler from England. Comes into the club all the time."

"That is no concern of mine." Bones began to open his door.

"Hold on," Bobby interjected. "Whatever he's doing here, Mr. Knight isn't a bad egg, Bones. I'm sure of it."

The unreadable eyes studied him through the mask's slits. "Then he is in the wrong place at the wrong time."

Brother Bones exited the car and headed for the elegant house. In his hands were twin .45 Colt Automatics. Crandall watched him go and said a silent prayer for the poor bastards who were about to meet justice head on.

"There it is," Knight said, tossing the lace garter belt onto Harry Beest's desk. "One garter belt from Miss Alexis Wyld as requested."

Beest, swinging lazily on his gigantic chair, folded his powerful arms over his stomach. He was dressed in a natty tweed suit of brown with a white carnation in his button-hole matching his silk cravat. Knight was envious. He wished his own Hong Kong clothier were as talented as the tailor who dressed Beest.

"Although I am curious as to how one could distinguish it from any other such apparel?" Knight was standing in front of the desk, lighting a Regent cigarette as he spoke. "I mean, how do you know I just didn't purchase this one at the local five and dime?"

Beest chuckled his monkey laugh. He reached out with his right hand and using a single finger, scooped up the belt. "Mr. Knight, aside from the obvious handicaps this body curses me with, it also has some remarkable advantages."

Knight blew out a puff of smoke. "Such as?"

"An unbelievable sense of smell." Beest brought the garter belt up to his pinkish-brown nose and sniffed. "You would be amazed at the odors that exist in this world. Scents we humans never recognize."

His squat nose wrinkled a second time and his ape face smiled. "My memory is very much intact and the smell of her is all over this thing. The sweet, intoxicating smell of the only woman I ever loved."

"Then if you are satisfied, I'll take my money now."

Beest put down his new memento and pulled a thick envelope out from under his desk blotter. He tossed it to Knight. "You can count it if you want. Ten thousand dollars."

The Brit picked up the enveloped, peeled aside the flap and looked at a thick wad of greenbacks. He crushed out the half finished cigarette in the ebony ashtray as he relegated the packet to his inside jacket pocket.

"I'm sure that won't be necessary."

"Tell me something, Knight."

"If I can?"

"What did she look like? Did you get a good look at her?"

The irony of those words bore into the thief. The apeman was crossing over into dangerous territory.

"Only as she was sleeping," he lied wondering if Beest's other senses were as acute as his nose.

"But you saw her?"

"Yes." Part of the truth was better than nothing. "I saw her. She was...is a terribly beautiful woman."

There was loud crash from the front foyer that sounded like the door being shattered. Knight turned to look as Beest sprang to his naked feet.

Next there were voices screaming followed by multiple gunshots.

"What the hell?" Beest growled.

More shots and then the door flew open and two of his men came flying into the room as if shot from a cannon. Both men hit the fireplace and crumbled to the rug, their clothes blood smeared from bullet wounds.

The back door to the kitchen was flung wide and four of Beest's men, led by Bruno St. Martin raced into the parlor armed to the teeth.

St. Martin waved his Tommy-gun at the two dead men and looked to his boss. "What's going on?"

"Retribution," Brother Bones answered, boldly walking in opposite the gunmen, his two .45s smoking from his recent barrage. Behind him, in the hall, were two other dead men.

"BROTHER BONES!" St. Martin gasped. "I thought you were a fairy tale!"

"Bwahahaha," came the unholy mirth from the cold white mask.

"He's no fairy tale," Harry Beest supplied, coming around the desk to stand beside a very shaken Temple Knight. The thief was just starting to get use to a gorilla man. Now here was this frightening wraith borne of a thousand nightmares. Maybe this place was truly the home of the living damned after all.

"Hello Beest, it's been a few years."

"Yeah, Bonello, it has. Tell me, I can never get the stories straight. Are you Jack or Tommy?"

"Does it matter?"

"Naw, I guess not. So what I are you doing here shooting up my boys like this? I ain't got no beef with you?"

"Two nights ago one of your men murdered a young boy named Jacob Kingman. I have come to mete out justice to that killer."

"Oh. And how do you plan to do that, Mr. Spook? You got some kind of crystal ball or something to tell which one did the shooting?"

"No," Bones explained. "But these will do."

He opened his left fist and the four slugs snuggled between his palm and gun butt dropped to the floor.

"These were torn from the boy's body. Now they will show me which weapon they were fired from."

All eyes in the room were glued to the misshapen slugs on the rug. Then, as if imbued with supernatural life, the slugs began rolling. In unison, like a tiny train, they moved in tandem and came to a halt at the feet of Bruno St. Martin.

The killer was frozen, his gaze on the lead pellets at his feet. Then he looked at the white-masked reaper and swore.

"Aw shit!" He brought up his machine gun and let loose a volley. The room erupted with the deafening cacophony of gunfire.

"NO!" Beest screamed, but his voice was drowned out by the booming fuselage.

Red jets of flame spit from Brother Bones' twin pistols, as he began decimating his opponents. All the while his own body was slammed repeatedly by hot lead; he kept his feet and continued his assault. After all, he was already dead.

In his first volley, one of Bones' shots took St. Martin between the eyes. It came out the back of his head along with a gory chunk of brain matter and gristle. He dropped back through the open door from which he'd emerged minutes earlier. Then Don MacKoy went down with holes in his chest and groin, all the while still shooting his Thompson. The helter-skelter projectiles tore up the carpet and floorboards beneath. Acrid smoke cloyed the air.

For his part, as the second the gun battle had erupted, Knight had jumped over the massive desk and sought safety behind it. Head down, he prayed its bulk would protect him from catching a stray bullet.

Within seconds, two of Beest's men were dead and the remaining three were wounded and out of action. As the last shots faded into silence, Bones approached the dead figure of St. Martin keeping his .45's leveled at the body.

"Justice has been served."

"Oh, yeah?" Beest roared taking hold of his desk. "Then try this on for size!"

One second Knight was crouched behind the heavy wooden furniture and the next it was rising up off the floor. He looked up to see Harry Beest lifting the massive desk and swinging it like a baseball bat into the macabre Bones.

The desk smashed the night stalker into the wall with bone crushing force. It broke apart at the same time driving Bones partly through the wall. Beest released his grip and the shattered pieces fell everywhere. Brother Bones was buried under the biggest chunk of the debris.

Standing over the pile, Beest breathed heavily and slapped his hairy mitts together. "There. That'll teach yah to come busting up my joint. Shithead boogey-man!"

Beest turned and surveyed the damage done to his headquarters. Knight was slowly standing upright where the desk had once rested. The gorilla crime-boss saw the thief's eyes suddenly sharpen.

"Look out!"

Too late, Beest started to move as two shots rang out from behind. It was impossible, he thought, just as the two rounds tore into his back and drove him headfirst into the brick fireplace mantle. Dazed, his forehead cut and bleeding, Beest wavered on his feet.

Brother Bones, hatless, was rising up out of the scattered wreckage, his automatics trained on Beest.

Anger flooded Beest's mind and he bellowed with rage, momentarily forgetting his pain. He lunged. Bones, at point blank range fired two more shots. One hit the monster-man in the left shoulder and the second tore into his right thigh. Unable to stand, Beest went down like a tree, face first to the floor.

Brother Bones jumped onto the apeman's back and jammed the barrel of his guns against the back of the creature's skull.

"It ends here, Beest!"

"NO!" Knight cried out, rushing forward. Bones swung his nearest gun arm towards the thief. "Don't shoot him!"

"Stay out of this. It is not your concern."

"You claim to be an agent of justice."

"I am the avenging scythe that brings balance for the violence that men do."

"And what about Beest? Who will bring him justice?"

"He is not a victim."

"Oh, no? Are you blind as well as dead?" Knight pointed down to the barely breathing Beest. "Do you think this is anything less than perpetual torture? Look at him!

He's trapped in a monkey's body, for heaven's sake! Forever!"

Bones kept his guns steady as Knight took in a deep breath. It was all or nothing now.

"Hasn't he suffered enough?"

Beest, semiconscious, moved under Bones. "Shut..up..limey.."

"See, he wants you to kill him. He wants to die!"

Brother Bones stood and holstered his guns. He found his hat, pulled it over his head and then addressed the groaning Beest.

"Do not cross my path again, Harry Beest. You have been warned."

Bones pointed to the sweating Knight. "That goes for you as well."

Before the cat-burglar could think of a comeback, the undead avenger was gone.

Knight knelt beside Beest who was trying to lift himself up. Blood was visible all over his body, the expensive suit now a torn mess.

"Thanks for nothing." Beest grumbled, his face falling back onto the floor.

"You're welcome. Now stay still while I call for an ambulance."

"No."

"You need a doctor!"

The beady little eyes under the hard knotted ridge looked up at Knight. "No, idiot. I need a veterinarian."

"Oh. Right."

The morning mist that greeted the new day's sun was evaporating quickly by the time the funeral party arrived at the Forest Haven cemetery. Standing with her daughter at the newly dug pit, Molly Kingman gazed on the flower covered coffin and wondered who their unknown benefactor was.

The day prior, she had been prepared to call the people at the morgue and tell them her beloved Jacob would have to be laid to rest in the pauper's graveyard. She had no means to pay for even the least expensive burial. That was when Mr. Abraham Brody knocked her door.

Mr. Brody, a distinguished old man, was employed by the Forest Haven mortuary. He informed her that all the arrangements for her son's final resting place had been seen to by a person wishing to remain anonymous. As if that wasn't enough, Brody handed her a envelope with her name on it.

She later learned the funeral cost at the private chapel and the ensuing internment on this fine piece of land had billed out at one thousand dollars. The mysterious benefactor had paid it all. The envelope, now hidden away in her purse, had contained an additional four thousand dollars in one hundreds. She had nearly swooned at the sight of it.

Now, in the new clothes she had purchased for herself and Nora, she listened as the minister began to say prayers for her boy's immortal soul. Overhead shafts of brilliant sunlight cut across the sky and birds took flight.

Molly Kingman cried and prayed for her unknown angel.

Temple Knight arrived at the Northside Train station shortly after noon. He took his valise from the cabbie and gave the fellow a generous tip. The sky was becoming a vibrant blue in the cloudless sky.

Skipping up the steps to the main platform, he kept his free hand against his breast pocket to ensure that the remainder of his ten grand was secure. He still had half of it. Not a bad payday, considering all the grief and madness he had experienced in the past few days.

As he began to enter the station's interior, he took one last look at the Cape Noire skyline. Images twirled around in his mind like a mental carousel. The strange and sad gorilla man, Harry Beest. The exotic and cold hearted Alexis Wyld. And the most remarkable of them all, the ghoulish Brother Bones.

All of them caught up in this one place. Here where dreams were as cheap as a five-cent cigar and lasted just as long. Three days ago he had been happy to be back. Now, shrugging, he wanted to get on the next train bound for anywhere else.

Knight went to buy a one-way ticket to anywhere and left the city of dark dreams behind.

THE END

THE GHOST TRAIN

The black and green iron monster raced down its mountain tracks with the Herculean drive of its mighty pistons. It was coming on to midnight and a late winter storm was whipping through the lower foothills making visibility almost impossible. The single lamp atop the front of the Great Northern Flier barely made it twenty yards before being gobbled up by the ravishing swirl of white.

In the claustrophobic swelter of the vestibule cab, Engineer Chuck Grady wiped a dirty bandanna over his balding dome and cranked open the window to his right. Instantly cold air flooded the small compartment of gears and switches. Holding his gabardine cap in his left hand, with the red bandanna, Grady stuck his head out, letting the cold air slap his face with coolness.

"Geezus, Mary, Joseph!" Fireman Dan Newton cried out, from his seat across the cab. "Will you close that blasted window! It's freezing out there!"

Grady pulled his now red face back inside and grinned. Grady had a friendly face, round, beefy with a thick nose and a pepper-gray brush mustache. He was chewing on a wad of tobacco and spit out a huge gob into the converted coffee tin bolted on the floor by his feet. "Relax, Danny boy," he smiled. "I was trying to gage how far this blow is going to follow us down the mountain."

"Most likely all the way into Cape Noire," Newton offered. He was the younger of two, being thirty-three. Grady was sixty-one and about to retire in two more days. In fact this was to be his last run on Engine Number 699. When they rode back into the Brickyard at Station Central, he would be ending a forty-five year career as a railman.

"I think you're right. I hate these freak storms. I mean, two days ago it was bone dry all way to Pinkahm's Pass. Hell, it's almost March. We should be seeing signs of spring, not snow and ice."

"Geezus, Grady, never heard you to complain so much before. You're getting cranky in your old age."

The engineer narrowed his bushy eyebrows at the thought. "You might be right. All of a sudden I'm going to be staying home every day, instead of riding the rails. Am starting to get worried the boredom will drive me kooky."

"Thought you and Martha would spend more time with the kids. And what about all that deep-sea fishing you keep wanting to get back to."

"Oh, I know, you're right." Grady grabbed a silver thermos with a red plastic cover from his lunch kit and began unscrewing the top. "It's just change, I guess. I'm an old train yard dog and comfortable with my life. Can't believe forty-five years just came and went like that."

He started to pour coffee into the plastic cap and his own words echoed in his thoughts as the engine rattled back and forth doing a very easy seventy miles an hour.

"It's just life," Newton said philosophically. "That's all. It runs away with all of us eventually."

Grady sipped the hot joe and nodded. He used his free hand to pull the chained stopwatch out of his overall pocket and flipped open the cover holding it up to his eyes. It was midnight. They should reach the Eagle Pass Bridge in another twenty minutes and then it was just ten miles into the city proper and the end of the line. It would be good to get home and into a warm bed. His bones just did not like the cold anymore.

Thankfully the coffee settled easily into his stomach and he felt good again.

Engine 699 carried a radial stay boiler. It was constructed for a design and operating pressure of 225 psi. The boiler had a firebox measuring 138 inches long by 102 inches wide and burned oil. The Flier came with a Vanderbuilt type tender, which provided a capacity of 17,000 gallons of water and 5,800 gallons of oil. This water-bottom tender had a Commonwealth cast-steel frame and rode on two 6-wheel trucks.

On this night she pulled three passenger cars and four box-cars filled with assorted freight. In those first three cars were forty-eight men, women and children. Most were fast asleep in their padded seats. Several were reading under tiny overhead lights, while at the back of the last of these Pullmans, train Conductor Owen Lassiter was making out his log. They would be in Cape Noire within the next hour or so and he wanted to get a head start on his paperwork. Although the engineer was in charge of the engine and its mechanical well-being, it was the conductor who ran the train. He was the captain. Lassiter, like Grady was an experienced railman and the two of them had been a team on the 699 for almost seven years. He hated the thought that after tonight, the train would have a new steam jockey in the cab.

Wet snow plastered the windows outside and Lassiter looked at his own time-piece. They were nearing Eagle Pass, a savage cut in the mountain side that fell four hundred feet to a small, fast running creek. A black steel girded bridge stretched across the two hundred yards of empty space. Lassiter detested all such bridges. Most of them were ancient and he didn't believe for a second that any of them were structurally sound. The 699 crossed four of them in its regular run up through the foothills. Eagle Pass was the last going home and he would breathe a sigh of relief when it was behind them.

Damn, but I'm turning into an old lady, he thought, fighting down his own inbred fears. You'd think it was me being put out to pasture instead of Grady. Lassiter dug a five cent cigar out of his vest pocket and using a wooden match, puffed until a good smoke was wafting around his head. The cigar helped calm his nerves while outdoors, the wail of the storm continued to assault the fast moving train.

Had Owen Lassiter known what was transpiring at that very moment at Eagle Pass, he would have not have stowed away his anxieties, but acted upon them. But he was only a simple, good man, and he could not possibly guess that he had only a few short minutes left to live.

Barry Bottles hung tightly to the wet, cold girder as he wrapped the eight sticks of dynamite to it with heavy masking tape. He had on gloves to ward off the cold of the wind and falling snow that constantly fogged his glasses. Above him, stringing wire over the trestles of the huge bridge was his pal, Scratch Walker. Both of them, being city boys, were miserable having to work in the elements like this. Even though they had on appropriate winter clothing, from padded mackinaw jackets to woolen caps and scarves, boots and gloves, the mountain air at twenty-two degrees Fahrenheit was an ever present knife in their tortured lungs. The wind-chill brought the temperatures way below zero and both men cursed up a blue streak as they hurried about their mission of sabotaging the bridge before the midnight flier arrived.

Bottles had worked with TNT ever since his days in France with the U.S. Army during the Big War. Upon being discharged back into civilian life, the mousy little man with the wheat colored hair and poor eyesight discovered that his newly acquired skills were valuable in the underworld community of Cape Noire. He soon acquired a reputation as the best powder man in the city.

Now suspended over the Eagle Pass gorge, he was shivering, his nose was running and he was starting to lose the feeling in his finger tips. A hard tug on the sticky tape and the explosives for set. As set as they were ever going to be, Bottles figured, making sure the connecting wires were firmly connected. It was time to get off the slanted beam and climb back to the tracks.

Carefully positioning himself, the gangster got to his feet on the slick girder and shimmied his way back to where the support strut was cemented into the rock wall of the cliff. From there he made his way over snow covered rocks, climbing carefully back to the main tracks. Once atop the bridge, he started moving over the long expanse, seeing Walker's foot holes in the bed of snow that hid the giant wooden struts. Here, in the middle of the bridge, the wind had a natural funnel and it tore at his body, trying hard to propel him backward. Swearing for all he was worth, Bottles pulled his woolen cap further down over his ears and pushed through the blinding gale until he could make out his partner crouched back against the bridge where it connected with the opposite terrain.

Walker had a flashlight on the ground that ineffectively splayed out its small light over the bottom of the wooden charge box. Bottles joined him, knelt in the snow and picked up the flashlight. He held it over the top of the square box so that his pal could see the mounting nipples clearly.

"WOOOOOOO!"

A loud whistle split through the howling storm from behind them and Bottles recognized it for what it was. The Flier was fast approaching from the north.

"That's the train," he said loudly, so as to be heard over the freezing wind. His breath plumed forth like an ethereal spirit escaping his mouth. "Hurry it up, she's almost here!"

"I'm trying," Walker said, fumbling with the bare wire tip for the third time. "I can't feel my freaking fingers in this cold."

"WOOOOO...WOOOO!"

The train whistle sounded again and Bottles shoved the electric torch into Walker's hand and shoved him aside. "Here, let me do it!"

Without any arguments, the other man, a tall, gaunt fellow, twisted the beam and allowed the experienced Bottles to take over. Nipping his glove with his teeth, the veteran powder man tore off the leather garment and went to work with his bare right hand. No time to think of the cold now. Bottles grabbed the wooden handle and yanked it up to its full foot extension. The twin steel nipples were slick with snow, but he managed to twist the copper wire ends around both and wound them tightly. In the few minutes it took, his hand was almost numb and rosy pink in color.

With both connectors wired, all that remained to close the switch was to depress the plunger.

Now the train was almost on them and they could feel the twin tracks to their right start to vibrate with its approach. Bottles extended his neck and tried to peer through the curtain of snow at the inky blackness beyond the track funnel cut through the solid rock of the mountain. He saw the Flier's cyclopean yellow light as it bore down on the old bridge. Now the very air was vibrating with its lonely blaring call.

"WOOOOOOOO!"

"Fire it!" Walker begged, realizing the fast coming locomotive was almost on top of them.

Bottles gripped the plunger with both hands and shoved it down as hard as he could. The wires made contact and the single hot charge rippled along its path to the TNT bundle strapped to the support brace. There was a loud booming and then the top part of the bridge where it met the path buckled upwards. A huge chuck of track was torn away and the entire bridge seemed to slant sideways off kilter. The brace beam beneath was no longer whole but twin segments shorn in half offering no weight to the girders above them.

Then the 699 barreled onto the bridge and hit the empty slot where the tracks were missing. The entire engine, all 420,000 pounds of it slammed down onto the ruined section and fell off to its left side. In the cab, Grady and Newton were thrown over as the world they lived in suddenly tilted over. The cowcatcher tore up logs and plowed through the steel railing as if it were kindling and then dove over the side pulling the rest of the engine with it. A second before Chuck Grady's head hit the boiler plate and snapped his neck he knew he was never going deep-sea fishing again.

The massive train fell like an ungainly diver for the rocky creek below, its tender coming down with it as well as the Pullman cars and a huge portion of the crumbled bridge. Inside, those unlucky to be awake screamed for all they were worth but no avail. There was no one to hear their death cries. To know their final agonizing moments of gut-wrenching fear that flooded their very souls. When the massive boiler smashed into the earth below, it caved into itself like an accordion and then the steam, the oil and the heat all combined to explode. The fireball shook the very mountain's sides and lit up the night like a bonfire provided by the devil. Then the remaining heavy freight units cascaded down atop the unholy pile and added fuel to the blazing inferno that had once been the Great Northern Flier # 699.

Atop the plateau by the remaining half of the Eagle Pass Bridge two men stood gazing down at their handiwork and felt the blast of hot air assail them. Eyes wide, Scratch Walker gulped and breathed, "Holy shit! Holy freaking shit!"

When the 699 failed to arrive in the rail yards, the night manager of the station notified his superiors. The snow was still coming down hard as the night wore itself into pre-dawn and it seemed like all of Cape Noire was layered in white like heavy frosting on a cake.

With dawn, the weather abated but thick clouds covered the heavens and a gunmetal sky lent a depressing atmosphere to the new day. A farmer snow-shoeing in the area discovered the smoldering wreckage and hurriedly raced home to put in a call to the local authorities. The time was ten-twenty-five A.M. By eleven, the area was swarming with fire crews from the city and surrounding suburbs, along with the state police and representatives of the Transportation Dept.

An army of some two hundred surrounded the charred metal monstrosity that had once been a working iron-horse. Now, it rose from the creek bed, a massive pile of smoking, hot debris twisted every which way under ashen skies, its black pall rising ever upward in an endless stream. Firemen continued to dowse the death sculpture, while others with pry-bars attempted to dig into the wreckage wherever possible in hopes of finding life.

State Trooper Commander David Anders didn't expect his people would be salvaging anything but the dead. In his twenty-two years on the force, he had never seen anything like this mess. Standing on the slippery rocks just below the ruptured carcass of the mighty engine itself, he felt like an ant surveying the remains of a giant buffalo. And the analogy tickled his imagination in a morbid way. Yeah, it was the Indians who'd first called the great machines, Iron Horses. Now this one was broken beyond repair.

Anders tilted his head back and took hold of the binoculars he had draped around his neck. Bringing them up to his eyes, he squinted, adjusted the focus and pointed the lens to the twisted remains of the bridge high above the gorge. Slowly he let his eyes study every foot of the open section that had torn loose. He lowered the lenses and tried to peer under the actual trestle where the main support girders had set. They were gone now.

So what had caused a supposedly sound bridge to buckle like that? Anders logical mind began ticking off possibilities. All of which were criminal in nature. He was getting a hunch, an ugly one. Like a mental itch he would have to scratch to satisfy. But to that he would need to help of Cape Noire's finest. He went back to his radio car and started to make his calls. As he opened the sedan door, he spotted three black birds circling the smoky column with unnatural interest. Crows. Again the Native American imagery. The people knew the black birds as representatives of Chaos.

Anders shrugged his disdain at the omen. It was going to be a very long, long day.

Two o'clock that afternoon in the headquarters of the Great Northern Railroad Company, General Manager and owner, Cyrus Swan prepared himself to meet the press. They had started gathering in the reception area of his office on the sixth floor of the Brownwell Building shortly after noon, when the word of the bridge calamity swept throughout the city's fourth estate.

Swan, a portly man in his early fifties, was a dapper dresser always wearing only the latest in fashion trends. Now, seated behind his massive oak desk, in his ornate office filled with train pictures and maps, he took a quick gulp of whiskey from the bottle he kept in the top drawer. Even in his three hundred dollars custom tailored suit, he looked frazzled.

"You think that's a good idea?" Frank Andretti asked, as he watched his boss down the alcohol. Andretti was the Chief of Operations for the railroad and Swan's second-in-command. He was average height, with curly black hair and a thin mustache. Unlike Swan, who had a background in business, Andretti was a true railman who'd worked himself up through the ranks.

They were a Mutt and Jeff pair who, although from different worlds, had a strong working relation that allowed Swan to maintain his posh lifestyle while the real day to day responsibilities of the railroad were left to Andretti's capable handling.

"Look, you want to deal with the ladies and gentlemen of the press, be my guest," Swan said waving his empty glass towards the frosted glass window of his office. Vague shadowy forms were milling about out there, waiting for the okay to come charging in.

"No, thanks," the C.O. returned. "But there gonna want blood, Swan. This is the biggest train disaster since the collision back in '28. And then we only lost a few people."

"What's the number up to?" Swan's fat features had a pasty look to them.

"With the crew..." Andretti's voice caught in mid-sentence, as he thought of the men who had been his friends, his peers. Gray, Newton and Lassiter. Their faces were so vivid in his mind's eye, it hurt to think of them gone. "Fifty-five. Six of those were children."

"Oh, hell. But it was an accident, right? They can't hold us responsible, right? I mean, the snowstorm, the icy tracks and that old bridge up there. That had to be what caused it, right?"

"I don't know, Cyrus. Look, the transportation office has there best people on site, working with our guys. They'll figure it out eventually. The always do."

"I suppose so, but for now it all falls on me to deal with those press people." Again, Swan pointed to the door.

"It's what you do best, Cyrus. You have the knack."

Swan made a face and slipped the empty glass back in drawer beside the half-empty bottle.

"Right, I do. Very well, you may tell Gladys to let them in. I'm as ready as I'll ever be."

Andretti nodded and started for the door. For a second he wished he were any place else in the entire world. Cracking the door, he said, "You can all come in now."

And they did, pencils and notebooks in hand, photographers rushing in to start popping flashes. Cyrus Swan put both hands palm down on his desk and smiled. It was a weak smile.

As the day wore on, the good citizens of Cape Noire became aware of the Eagle Pass disaster either by the bold headlines on the three daily rags or the airwaves of WXYZ, the radio voice of the city. By late afternoon most of the public had digested the awful facts and, unless they had a personal connection to the fifty-five victims, went on with the routine business of living.

Note so for one tormented soul who spent all his time, when not fulfilling his unholy crusade, sequestered in one of two bedrooms of a small, back alley flat. He never opened the windows except at night, disdaining the light of day. Long ago he had ceased to be a living, breathing man. Now he was a creature trapped between the gates of this world and the next; an undead spirit forced to exist in his rotting, mortal flesh until the powers of beyond released him from his karma.

He was Brother Bones, the zombie avenger and now he was seated in the darkness of his room contemplating the emptiness around him. On the bureau behind his chair was a bone-white mask carved in the shape of a skull and twin, silver-plated .45s. The icons of his endless war against evil and savagery.

It was coming on dusk and through the small slit at the bottom of his window shade, the sliver of gray daylight was dissolving. With it the gloom of his sanctum began to deepen like quicksand.

A familiar voice whispered from that pit of blackness. It was the girl's voice, the one who had haunted him from the beginning of his current incarnation. She was a spirit guide responsible for bringing him the ghosts of those innocents cruelly robbed of their lives. Bones had endured countless such confrontations with the spectral remnants of the lost from every walk of life, young and old, male and female. What he had never experienced until now was a gathering so large as the one that suddenly invaded his private domain.

They filled the room, ethereal figures all frozen in ghoulish horror by the last moments of fear that had ushered them into death. Bones came to his feet, his hands involuntarily rising up in a defensive gesture to ward them off. So many ghosts, all crowding around him, pressing in on his fragile grasp of sanity. All that was left of it.

"Who?" he stammered with his cold voice. "Who are you?"

One specter, a man in a conductor's attire moved forward and the voice of the girl, the long-ago prostitute he had murdered, said simply, "These are the passengers of Train # 699."

Then, as one, the spirits mouthed the silent words...AVENGE US! AVENGE US! AVENGE US!

Bones blinked and they were gone, but not their silent cries of anguish and damnation. They would be trapped in the in-between worlds until he, and he alone, found the fiend behind the heinous sabotage and delivered onto that person, or persons, final justice.

Brother Bones picked up his skull-head mask and adjusted it over his twisted features. He picked up the automatics and slid them into the leather shoulder rigs tied about his torso. Once he donned his torn, ebony duster and oversized fedora, he was ready to face the world once more.

A half hour later, Blackjack Bobby Crandall, the young card dealer who owned the apartment and acted as Bones' aide, came stomping into the living area slapping his gloved hands together.

"Damn, but its bloody cold out there!" His cheeks were cherry red. Then he looked up and saw Bones standing in front of the bedroom door fully clothed.

"Aw, hell."

"We are going out," the black apparition declared.

"Damn it, Bones, it's near freezing out there."

"Would you prefer the fires of hell, Bobby Crandall?"

The freckled-faced Crandall tightened his jaw. It was useless. You couldn't argue with a dead man.

"Where are we going?"

"Into the mountains. Come, we've no time to waste."

Crandall turned, pulled open the front door and held it wide for the creepy gunman. It was going to be a long and miserable night. He just knew it.

Under the glare of the harsh incandescent spotlights, the construction crew worked throughout the long, frigid night. Their directive was to dismantle the wreckage of # 699 until all human remains had been located and removed for proper identification and then transported to the city morgue.

It was a grueling job and the thirty men working the graveyard shift were all bundled like Eskimos against the bitter wind chill that swept down the mountain. From a distance, on a little traveled back road, Brother Bones watched the bulldozers and other pieces of heavy equipment meticulously picking apart what had once been a magnificent machine of steam and speed.

He and Crandall were parked in a small roadster a half-mile below the demolished Eagle Pass Bridge. Although the engine was running, they had killed the headlamps to avoid being seen by the workers at the site. A light snow had started falling, as if to add to Crandall's misery. The front heater of the outdated automobile provided little warmth.

"Stay here," Bones ordered. He opened his door and climbed out. "And keep out of sight. You must not be seen."

"Hey, no problem," Crandall huddled closer to the dash board where the warm air barely made it through the floor vents. "Just hurry it up, okay?"

When he got no reply, Crandall looked up and Bones was a fading outline walking off into the trees.

At the bridge, the state police had strewn wooden sawhorses and connected them with yellow police tape to warn off intruders. Tied to several of these impromptu barricades were several oil lanterns on either end of the bridge. They provided just enough illumination for the wreck crews to keep a watchful eye on the weakened span. There was always the slim chance more pieces might break apart and crumble thus endangering the folks below.

Since the bridge itself was out of commission, all train runs had either been cancelled or rerouted on to other lines. Still, Commander Anders was concerned that reporters or other curiosity freaks would try to enter the area and hurt themselves or corrupt what was still an active crime scene.

Anders had spoken to the Captain of the Cape Noire Police Bomb Squad and come morning, one of their specialized teams would comb the bridge looking for any evidence of foul play. Till then, the area was off-limits.

Brother Bones plodded through the thick carpet of snow, his heavy, black overcoat tugged at by a fierce gust of wind. He moved easily around the sawhorse cordon and started across the tracks where they crossed onto the bridge. The limited glow of the lanterns cast the structure in a crazy quilt pattern of moving shadows. Aware of the workers below, Bones seem to glide over the span, always keeping inside the gray zone, hidden. Half way across the mighty brace, the bridge slanted radically where Engine 699 had plowed through its railings and collapsed its support frame.

There was a thirty yard gap which stopped the avenger's progress. He studied it, his gaze seeking anything that would provide him with the clues he required. As it happened, the oddity he was seeking lay at his very feet, atop a wide expanse of unblemished snow. A small red plastic cap. The color jumped out at him like a drop of blood on white satin sheets. Bones crouched and picked up the small object no more than an half inch in circumference. He held it up to the slits in his skull mask and his cruel eyes burned with recognition.

He was holding the cap from what had been a red-colored stick of dynamite. Brother Bones closed his gloved hand over the small cap and then brought the fist to his ceramic forehead. Images began to coalesce in his consciousness, images of a diminutive man with thick glasses and thinning yellow hair. And with the image came a name, Barry Bottles.

Brother Bones rose, carefully put the dynamite cap in his coat pocket. He walked away from the bridge retracing his steps. Somewhere in the sleeping city below was his prey. As he moved, the undead hunter envisioned the look on Barry Bottles' face when justice came calling. It would not be a pretty picture. Horror never was.

Leo Scratch Walker had never been comfortable around woman. He was a shy man who had been raised by a domineering mother and three older sisters. Meaning, for most of his adolescence, he'd been a slave to all their capricious, selfish whims. By the time he ran away from home, he had developed a hardened wariness of the opposite sex.

Even after joining the mobs and getting his cherry popped by a gangland moll, Scratch still preferred the company of men. He always felt awkward around dames. Thus, when Barry Bottles had called him earlier in the evening, suggesting they hire a few party girls and celebrate their new found wealth, the tall, scrawny looking Walker had begged off.

Bottles all but begged him over the phone, claimed he was going to get some really high class birds, not the fifty cent cheapies who crowded the sidewalks of Old Town after dark.

But Scratch had stayed firm in his resolve. He promised Bottles he would come over if he later changed his mind. After dinner at a local diner, he spent the better part of the evening at a bar near his apartment. Seated at the far end of the bar, away from the entrance, he had wiled away most of the night drinking beer and chewing the fat with Pops Carter, the black bartender who also owned the joint.

As the night wore on and the alcohol began to work its way through his system, Scratch starting noticing some of the working girls coming and going around him. The cabinet radio behind the bar had alerted them to the bitter cold outdoors and so most of the girls had elected to do the majority of their hustling indoors this fine Cape Noire night.

Seeing them romancing their respective clients at the tables against the back wall, Scratch began to get an old familiar tingle. The thought of his pal partying with lots of free booze and a couple of sweet young ladies seemed more and more inviting with each new sudser he consumed.

"Don't you have any place better to be?" Pop actually asked him just prior to midnight. It was as if the old guy had read his very thoughts.

"Hell, right I do," Walker said, careful not to slur his words. He knew he was drunk, but that was no reason to act like a lush. The one thing his mother and sisters had instilled in him was a code of proper behavior when out in public.

He shoved a twenty across the bar with his latest empty soldier and jumped off the stool. He gave the old man a wave and headed out the door.

The night air was a rude awakening and for a split second, Walker nearly turned around and headed back into the bar. But what the hell, Bottles only lived two blocks up the road. He could make that in minutes. And after his ordeal up on the mountain last night, that was a piece of cake. He pulled the collar of his coat up, tugged down on his woolen cap and started down the sidewalk at a fast clip.

Traffic was extremely light at this late hour. Several checker cabs crawled by, their back seats empty and one black and white police radio car. Having nothing to hide, Walker waved to the coppers in his most friendly manner, watching them roll by. The cold and new falling snow had given them an easy patrol for sure.

Barry Bottles lived in the middle of a worn tenement block where all the houses looked alike. Big ugly affairs rising ten stories high and divided into twenty apartments each. Most of them hadn't seen any maintenance since Noah climbed out of the ark.

As Walker started up the cement stairs, he looked up the building's front to see if he could make out Bottles window on the sixth floor. It was too dark and he couldn't tell if the light was on or not. He did not notice the small sedan parked in the alley to the right nor the young, freckled face man behind the wheel. His mind was on getting out of the cold and up those long six flights of stairs.

A single, naked bulb at the middle of each hall landing was the only illumination provided the inebriated Walker as he made his way up the first set of stairs. Litter of every variety covered the stairs and landings. The wallpaper had faded years ago and there were chunks torn off wherever he looked. Clutching the wobbly railings, Walker plodded along like a weary climber scaling Mt. Everest. He fervently hoped Bottles had some good stuff waiting for him. He was going to need it when he reached his door.

Five minutes later he was reaching the fifth floor landing. Suddenly there was a loud crashing noise like that of splintering wood; the all too familiar sound of a door being kicked in. Then the scariest voice he had ever heard called out from somewhere above him. "Barry Bottles, justice has come for you!"

BLAM! BLAM! Gunshots rang out. They echoed through the thin paper walls around him and he froze. The commotion was coming from the sixth floor just ahead one more flight. Female screams erupted next, several of them, then footsteps rushing frantically into the hallway.

Walker kept moving and was almost bowled over the two, half-dressed women racing down the stairs. Their eyes were wide with unbridled terror and they paid him no mind, forcefully shoving past him. Walker fell back against the wall and grabbed the second bimbo's wrist stopping her hard. She nearly fell on her derriere at the tug of his grip.

"Let me go, mister! Please!" she blurted, gasping for air. "He's some kind of monster! You gotta let me go!" She was young, maybe eighteen, wearing way too much make up. It was smeared across what might have been a pretty face before she started turning tricks. Now, lipstick rouge smeared on her trembling lips, eyes the size of quarters at what she had just witnessed. He had never seen such fear before. Walker released his hold and she was gone, charging down the steps two at a time to catch up to her friend.

What the hell was going down? It sure wasn't cops. But what had the girl meant when she said monster? His alcoholic stupor was evaporating quickly. He reached under the backside of his jacket and pulled out his gun, a snub-nosed .38 caliber Smith and Wesson. Holding it up and out, he started around the fifth banister pole onto the final set of stairs to Bottles' apartment.

From there, he could see the broken door to his friend's apartment. Something had smashed it in and now it was suspended on its hinges in two parts. Gunshots rang out again, louder this time as he was closer to their source. There was a cry of pain and Barry Bottles came flying out of the demolished doorway, his body splattered with blood from half a dozen bullet holes. He landed on his back with a hard thump and didn't move.

Walker dropped to the stairs to hide as someone emerged from the apartment, smoking pistols in hand. Crouching down as much as he could, Walker felt his heart racing. Above him soft footsteps moved to where his Bottles lay. Stifling the fear in his throat, the two-bit hood raised his head to look over the top step. There an eerie apparition in coal black was looming over the body of Barry Bottles. From this angle all Walker could see of Bottles were his shoe-less feet in tan colored socks.

When the silent shooter moved, his white mask under the brim of the big hat came into view and Walker nearly wet his pants. Son of bitch, it was Brother Bones! He'd heard enough stories over the past few years, to know this could be no one else. The undead avenger had come calling on his friend and shot him dead. And he'd certainly be next if he didn't do something fast.

His first instinct was to inch himself down the stairs, staying out of site, until he could get to his feet and run for it. But what if that fiend heard him moving and spotted him before he could make his break? From his lofty position, the creepy assassin could easily blow him away. No, he had to wrestle his urge to bolt and stay put to see what Brother Bones would do next.

For the answer to that question, Walker didn't have long to wait. The dark, wraith like figure put away his twin automatics and dropped to one knee beside the bloody remains of his victim. Bottles had met his end wearing socks, boxer shorts and a gray, sleeveless tee-shirt. Bones took hold of Bottles' head with both hands and raised it up, putting his own masked visage close.

"Death is no sanctuary from my justice, Barry Bottles. I will not release you until you name the one who hired you!"

Sheeeit! Walker's face started to sweat and he gripped his pistol tight. He's talking to a corpse! What the hell? Did that ghoul honestly expect to get an answer?

"Tell me, who hired you? WHO HIRED YOU?"

Walker could not tear his eyes away from the macabre scene. It was like living a nightmare. All of sudden Bottles entire body shook and his head started to shake in Bones' hands. The dead man's mouth popped open and from deep within his lifeless shell two words spilled free. "Cyrussss... Swannnnn..."

It was the final straw for Scratch Walker's tenuous grasp on sanity. He jumped up and rushed over the last few steps screaming all the while, "Get away from him, you fucking ghoul!"

He started shooting as Brother Bones spun around, releasing the dead man. Walker's first two shots hit Bones dead center and arms wheeling out, he fell backwards onto the dirty floor. Walker kept shooting, the fear that gripped him propelling him on until he'd emptied his entire clip.

Brother Bones, hat askew, lay prone at the crook's feet, unmoving. When the sounds of the hammer hitting empty chambers finally penetrated his consciousness, Walker stopped pulling the trigger and starting gulping air. He felt bile rising in his throat and willed it down. Losing his lunch wouldn't help now. As if anything could.

His pal was dead. His pal who had somehow spoken from beyond the grave, at the demands of the spooky, black clad enforcer. And now he had killed Brother Bones. He had killed Bones! Mama Walker's one and only boy, Leo. Absolutely freaking amazing. As jumbled thoughts spun through his mind like a runaway Ferris-wheel, he realized the gunshots might have awakened others in the building. Although most people in this part of town tended to mind their own affairs, a running gun battle in halls was enough provocation to invariably compel someone to call the cops.

Walker knew he had to run. Looking down at Brother Bones, he was intrigued by the skull-shaped porcelain mask. More importantly what was hidden behind it. Wiping his mouth with the back of his hand and looking around at the closed apartment doors, his curiosity grew. It would only take a second to lift it up and see what no one else in Cape Noire had ever beheld. Imagine the tales he could tell. The man who not only finished Brother Bones, but also unmasked the bastard. It was too good an opportunity to pass up.

Walker went to one knee and using his free hand, took hold of the ivory white mask. Odd, there were no strings affixed to it. Strange. How did it stay on? He pulled it off and looked down at the face of Bones. The overhead bulb gave off just enough light for the true horror to be seen. A horror beyond comprehension, a rotting effigy locked forever in a process of eternal corruption. Walker's mind began to unravel, unable to deal with the abomination that was Bones.

"NOOOO..." he screamed. Then Brother Bones opened his eyes and Walker's mind crumbled completely.

In his car, parked in the alley, Bobby Crandall stomped his right foot on the floor boards between the clutch and gas pedals to keep the circulation moving in his body. By his wristwatch, Brother Bones had been inside the apartment building just over a half hour. Crandall was always anxious when chauffeuring his benefactor on his clandestine missions.

Long ago, Brother Bones had saved Crandall from being murdered simply because he'd been in the wrong place at the wrong time. It was a terrible life debt that obligated the young gambler to the macabre agent of spectral justice. Crandall was really a decent guy and he understood, at a spiritual level, that what Bones did somehow adjusted the scales of good and evil. Without the undead avenger, the forces of darkness would roam the city streets unchecked. That could not be allowed. Thus Crandall saw Bones' role as that of a cosmic exterminator and in his own soul, he was okay with being a part of that ongoing crusade.

The front door to the building opened and the tall man he had spied a few minutes earlier came stumbling out. He was screaming at the top of his lungs as he went down the stairs and into the street, his feet slipping on the snowy layer. From his vantage point, Crandall could see the man was raving as if he'd lost all his marbles. As if he'd seen a ghost.

The side door yawned and Brother Bones got in.

"Drive. We've two more stops before this night is over."

Crandall sat up straight, shifted the sedan into first gear and began to move out onto the road. As he turned the wheel right-ward, the crazy man ran off in the opposite direction.

"That your work?" Crandall asked.

"He saw what no man may see." Bones unconsciously reached up and touched his mask.

"Where to?" Better to drop the subject, the kid thought. He really didn't want to know what that poor devil had seen. Not ever.

"Miller Heights," the reaper said. "We are going to pay a visit on Mr. Cyrus Swan."

When the first pioneer settlers discovered the deep water basin that ran up and down the rocky coast of Larimar County, they were quick to realize the benefits of such a harbor settlement. Cape Noire would eventually establish its economic foundation on its ability to move commerce via the giant sailing ships that crossed the world's oceans. But prior to building those hundreds of docks and warehouses, immigrant laborers found work in the cavernous rock quarries located to the north.

Canadian settler Paul Douseau saw the market for building supplies and bought a huge parcel of land on which he built a brick making factory. With the crushed gravel coming in from the quarries by horse drawn wagons, Douseau's facility worked twenty-four hours a day producing millions of red clay bricks that would ultimately find themselves into every major edifice of the rapidly mushrooming metropolis.

At end of the Civil War, the railroads came west and soon Douseau was transporting his bricks all over the country. He shrewdly made a deal with the Great Northern Railroad to establish its first station on an unused portion of his property. With easy access to the freight tracks, it became routine to move tons of bricks on a daily basis. Those booms days lasted until the end of the century. The Douseaus made their fortune as Cape Noire matured into a thriving, bustling port with an ever growing population.

But alas, all good things do come to and end. As cheaper building materials were invented, the demand for bricks dwindled. At the same time rail commerce was increasing and Great Northern was quick to take advantage of this shift in fortunes. In 1895 Douseau's heirs sold the last of the original property, abandoned buildings and all to the railroad. Soon the land was cleared and more tracks laid until a vast maze of railroad lines criss-crossed the two mile area creating a bustling, active depot. Dozens of mile long trains came and went with precision regularity like the lifeblood of the city, keeping its mighty heart pumping.

Still the old timers who worked the mighty locomotives continued calling the place the Brickyard, even though those who knew why were long since gone to their eternal reward.

It was shortly after 1 A.M. when the snow stopped falling. It was a little while later that Bobby Crandall's gray sedan wound its way through the tight corridors of the Brickyard, its headlamps scouting ahead through the dark for the secluded spur situated far beyond the view of the main station house.

After the car came to a stop, an ominous figure emerged from the back seat dragging something bulky out of the vehicle. That something was Mr. Cyrus Swan, his hands and feet bound by thick, horsehair rope. Dressed in flannel pajamas, the portly prisoner was speaking at a machine gun clip trying to plead with his captors.

Brother Bones, pulling Swan's tied hands, dropped him on the hard ground and signaled for Crandall to depart. As the car rolled away to disappear behind a row of empty box cars, the silent avenger dragged the fat man over the wet ground to a set of railroad tracks that ran off into the distance beyond the borders of the depot.

"Why are you doing this?" Swan cried for the hundredth time since he'd been awaken from his bed and brutally manhandled by the frightful man in black. "Who are you?"

"I am your justice, Cyrus Swan," Brother Bones spoke for the first time since abducting the railroad tycoon.

Roughly he pulled the big man onto the tracks and positioned him so that he was perpendicular to the two steel lines. The calves of his legs lay over one track while his beefy neck rested on its cold mate. Swan was not stupid. Understanding his predicament, he tried to shift his body but his captor had come prepared.

From his coat pocket Brother Bones took two more coils of rope. The first he wound around Swan's thick neck and the rail track itself, making it tight so that the man coughed.

"Stop this...please! I can pay you. Anything you want. Tell me!"

"Money means nothing to me," Bones said as he used the second piece of rope to secure Swan's legs to the second track.

In his hurt and fear, Cyrus Swan saw the abject ridiculous imagery of it all. He was being trussed up like some movie serial queen in those cliffhangers they played in Saturday afternoon matinees at the Bijou Theater.

Finished with his task, Brother Bones stepped back away from tracks and stood at Swan's feet, looking down at him through the slits in his vacuous looking mask.

"Cyrus Swan, you are responsible for the deaths of fifty-five innocent souls. Now the time has come for you to pay for your crimes."

"What?" Spittle flew from Swan's trembling lips. "You're nuts! I had nothing to do with that wreck!"

"You're lies fall on deaf ears. I know the truth, Cyrus Swan. Now you will meet the fate you deserve."

As if on cue a long, shrill train whistle sounded off in the gloomy distance. Although the snow had ceased falling, thick storm clouds hid the skies. The whistle sounded again, long and loud. It was approaching the yards.

Swan couldn't even move his head, but he knew instantly he was tied to the track of that oncoming train.

"No, listen, you got it all wrong," he pleaded, his eyes trying to peer off to the side to where the tracks vanished into the maze of parked trains.

"I'm innocent!"

"Ha..ha..ha..ha," Brother Bones' laughter was without mirth, a harsh, barking thing that set Swan's nerves on edge.

WOOOOOOO! The train was getting closer. Swan thought he could make out some kind of glow just over the horizon beyond the boxcars. It would be on them in mere minutes.

"Alright, alright," he cried. "I did it."

"I know," Brother Bones said matter-of-factly.

"The company was busted, going bankrupt," Swan ranted, trying to get it all before his doom arrived. "There was nowhere I could turn. I did it for the insurance money."

Brother Bones stood unmoving before him.

"That's everything. Alright! I tell the police, I'll confess."

WOOOOOOOO!

"Just let me go!"

The tracks beneath him began to vibrate.

The masked specter did not budge.

"Let me go, I told you what you wanted to hear!" Swan tried to move, to squirm, but the restraints were too strong. The rope around his neck cut into his soft flesh and he started to gag.

"Please," he managed weakly, tears running down his cheeks.

"Your confession changes nothing. Your words are empty, Cyrus Swan. Brother Bones metes out justice. There is no mercy here."

"What?" Swan's eyes were bulging in his head. The tracks were vibrating stronger.

Suddenly a yellow light appeared and the whistle blared like the peal of a thousand angry demons. The train was roaring around the curve and coming on at a powerful, piston-driving speed.

Swan eyes darted from the big yellow light to the now hazy figure of Bones, who seemed to be backing away from him.

"NOOOO..I don't want to die!"

The train was on him and Cyrus Swan screamed, his pathetic cry lost beneath the trembling roar of the massive steam engine. What the dying tycoon could not see was the three silver numbers stamped just beneath the unforgiving light, 699.

Chief of Detective Dan Rains kept his hands in the pockets of his tanned trench coat as he walked along the tracks with Levi Hoffman, the Brickyard's Yard Master. Hoffman was a man in his early fifties, with a hard body used to the most severe manual labor. Decked out in heavy work boots, jeans and a lined jacket, the friendly railman was shaking his head and pointing towards the tree-line beyond the tracks.

"I don't get it," he said to the taller Rains. "This is an isolated spur. It doesn't connect with any of the working lines. It just stops two hundred yards on both ends. We only use it to park old cars due for demolition."

The two men were moving back to the crime scene where the medical examiner was studying the body of the late Cyrus Swan.

"And you say you found the body tied up like that around seven o'clock this morning?"

Hoffman nodded, he had a two day old beard over his long face. "Yup. About seven. I punch in at six every morning. Have a cup of coffee with the night crew before they go home, then I come out here and make my first round."

As they neared the center of activity, a police photographer was leaning over the body snapping pictures.

"And there he was, Captain," Hoffman continued. "Tied up there like some stuffed turkey on a Thanksgiving table. I called you boys right away."

Rains extended his hand and shook Hoffman's. "Well, thank you for you help, Mr. Hoffman. You can go now."

As the man walked off, Rains joined his investigative group. Sgt. Patrick O'Malley was the senior blue. He was a bullish fellow with orange colored hair and a pug nose.

"Anything worth looking at?" Rains asked the veteran copper.

"If by that you mean evidence, Lieutenant, we're plum out of luck on this one." O'Malley pointed to the ground at their feet. "Snow and all turned any kind of footprints to slush. We found some tire tracks but they're of no use to us either."

"Okay, Pat. Just clean it up the best you can and see what's keeping that ambulance."

The cop tapped his hat in salute and headed for one of the two parked patrol cars nearby.

Rains stepped over to the tracks to where Jeff Durham, the medical examiner was still kneeling by the dead man.

"Weird, isn't Rains?" he puzzled, adjusting the horn-rimmed glasses over his round face. "Somebody being tied up like this on a track that's not used."

"Tell me about it." He looked down at the corpse, the eyes were opened and the mouth grotesquely wide. "There's not a mark on him, is there?"

"No. I can't swear to it but right now my guess is he died of a massive coronary. Probably about five to six hours ago."

"Heart attack, huh. But his face?"

Durham stood and slapped the snow and mud off his pants. "Exactly. It's fear, Rains. He was frightened to death."

THE END

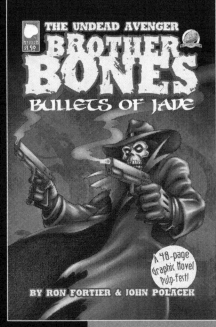

Situated in the rural back country of Edwardian England is an old, mysterious house whose unique owner earns his living as a Spirit-Breaker, a hunter of ghosts. A former military veteran, Sgt. Roman Janus has devoted his life to aid those haunted, both emotionally and physically by obsessive wraiths whose spirits are still anchored to our world.

Airship 27 Productions is thrilled to present *Sgt.Janus – Spirit Breaker* by Jim Beard. Part detective, part occultist, Janus is himself a man of mystery whose own past is shrouded and the motivations behind his calling kept hidden. Within this volume you will find eight tales as narrated by his clients, each with his or her own perspective on this uncanny hero and his amazing career. Filled with suspense, terror and agonizing pathos, each a solid mesmerizing journey into the unknown world beyond.

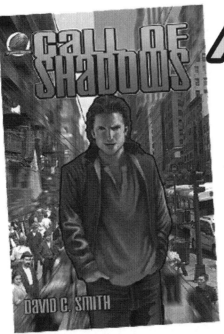

A MAN OUT OF TIME

Restaurant owner Steve Beaudine is killed in a car accident and his beautiful wife, Ava is severely injured. After months of physical recuperation, she returns to AVA'S with the desire to keep the business going. But Tony Jasco, her husband's partner, has plans to sell the eatery and split the profits. Ava adamantly refuses to terminate what had been Steve's dream. She is determined to make it work no matter Jasco's opposition.

Then the mysterious David Ehlert enters her life with a fantastic story, one straight out of a fairy tale. He claims to be a wizard and that Jasco is trying to have her killed to gain his own ends. Ava simply can't believe such a fanciful claim...until they are attacked by magical dark forces. Suddenly she finds herself the target of a twisted, dark magician and her only salvation is Ehlert, a man claiming to have been born in 1886 but still looking young and fit.

Writer David C. Smith spins a colorful, fast paced thriller that introduces a fascinating new hero in the vein of the classic golden age pulps but with a decidedly modern day twist. It is the story of a haunted man out of time seeking redemption for past sins in a world of arcane mysteries and magiks. CALL OF SHADOWS is a masterful thriller by a veteran writer that will keep you on the edge of your chair from start to finish.

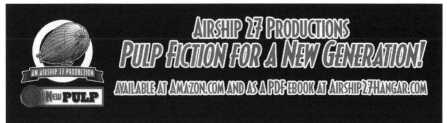

Made in the USA
Middletown, DE
22 July 2015